MUSIC BOX

JOHN C. HOUSER

Dreamspinner Press

Published by
Dreamspinner Press
5032 Capital Circle SW
Suite 2, PMB# 279
Tallahassee, FL 32305-7886
USA
http://www.dreamspinnerpress.com/

Music Box
© 2014 John C. Houser.

Cover Art
© 2014 Reese Dante.
http://www.reesedante.com
Cover content is for illustrative purposes only and any person depicted on the cover is a model.

ISBN: 978-1-62798-425-6
Digital ISBN: 978-1-62798-424-9

Printed in the United States of America
First Edition
January 2014

For the It Gets Better Project and all who feel its message.

CHAPTER 1

JONAH GRIPPED the heavy case and urged his legs to move faster. If only he hadn't stopped to chat after sixth period, he might have avoided the bastards. He'd almost made it out of the parking lot and out of sight, when Antony and his sidekick Justin banged out of the front entrance. Even from three rows away, he'd caught the flash of Antony's grin.

"Fuck." He stumbled over a crack in the concrete, and the case bashed him in the knee. Why couldn't he have picked a smaller instrument to play in Jazz Ensemble? He'd wanted to please Mr. Gaston was why. Mr. G had turned his fucking blue eyes at Jonah and asked him to fill in because he needed a baritone saxophone player. Jonah had been so surprised to be noticed, let alone asked to help, that he'd said yes without stopping to think. It hadn't occurred to him what it would be like to drag the oversized instrument all over creation. It didn't help that he was short for his age and skinny. If his parents would just let him get a car, things would be different, but cars were not toys for irresponsible teenagers, so there would be no car for him. Never mind that he was probably the most responsible teenager in the entire fucking town. You couldn't tell his dad that.

Jonah glanced over his shoulder to see Antony and Justin jogging lazily in his direction. Antony waved merrily without picking up his pace. It wouldn't look cool to appear in too much of a rush. He said something to Justin and batted him in the arm. Justin laughed and shook his head, leering at Jonah. Neither boy carried a heavy pack or an instrument case like Jonah's. They didn't need to work to catch him.

Jonah tried to pick up speed, panting with the effort. Another block and he would make it to the city bus stop on Main Street, where he could catch the number 12 home. It had been weeks since he'd taken the yellow school bus parked on 5th Street. It wasn't worth the hassle. If he was lucky, the city bus might come along before the creeps caught up with him.

No city bus ground its way up Main when Jonah reached the stop. Trying to escape was futile now. They would catch him. Maybe they would only tease him this time and leave his shit alone. Yeah, and maybe an alligator would climb out of the sewer and bite Antony in the ass. Jonah put the saxophone case down and sat on it. He might as well catch his breath.

"What's your rush, Whale Bait, got a gig or something?" said Antony, sauntering up.

Jonah just looked at him and waited for what would come next.

Antony pressed the toe of an expensive Nike trainer to the side of the saxophone case and shoved it over, forcing Jonah to scramble to his feet. Justin circled behind Jonah and tugged the handle of Jonah's pack, pulling him off-balance.

"Quit it, asswipe."

"Who you calling asswipe, Whale Bait?" said Antony.

"Who do you think, fucker?"

"The pretty boy's got a mouth on him, doesn't he?" said Justin. He yanked on Jonah's pack, forcing Jonah to stumble backward. "I think he needs his mouth washed out."

"He's got a dirty mouth all right. Been sucking something nasty, have you, Whale Bait?" said Antony.

Jonah was too busy trying to keep his feet as Justin pulled his pack from side to side to answer.

"Faggots like sucking cock, don't they?" Antony grabbed the crotch of his low-slung jeans. "You'd like a taste of this, wouldn't you?"

"Fuck you!"

Antony palmed Jonah's head like a basketball and pushed it to his crotch. "Yeah, you'd like a taste of that, wouldn't you?"

"Mr. Winfield? Perhaps you'll stop playing with your friends and come inside now. It's time for your lesson."

Antony let go of Jonah's head, his mouth dropping open in surprise at the sound of the man's voice. Justin must have let go of Jonah's pack, because the side-to-side motion stopped. "Who the hell are you?" said Antony.

"You're standing in front of my shop. Come inside now, Mr. Winfield. Don't forget your instrument."

Jonah gripped the handle of his saxophone case and lurched into motion. He hadn't registered that Antony and Justin had caught up with him in front of Avakian Music, but it was sort of ironic now that he thought of it. The music store was where his father had rented the saxophone after Jonah had begged to be allowed to join Jazz Ensemble. "You are a pianist. What do you want with a saxophone?" his father had asked. "I'll pick it up," Jonah insisted, and he had too, even though he'd never signed up for lessons.

The man who'd spoken, Mr. Avakian, Jonah supposed, held the door to the shop open and gestured impatiently as though Jonah were late. "Now, unless you boys want a lesson as well, why don't you stop blocking the door to my shop?"

"Fuck you, old man," said Antony, but he was backing away as he said it.

Jonah watched them leave, the tension in his body draining, leaving an irritating tremor in its wake. "Thanks, Mister."

Avakian smiled as though they knew each other. He reminded Jonah of a praying mantis—improbably long limbs and angles draped in a pale-green shirt, and an oddly formal way of holding himself. "You're welcome," he said.

"How did you know my name? I've never been here before."

"I rented one baritone saxophone this year. The man who rented it said he was a fool to do it, but it was not worth arguing about, because his son would only hound him until he got what he wanted."

Jonah's face warmed. "Right."

"He said you wanted to play in a jazz group. Do you like it?"

"It's all right, I guess."

"He said you didn't play the saxophone."

"I don't, I mean I didn't."

"But you do now? Are you taking lessons somewhere?"

"I'm not taking any lessons. Mr. Gaston said I should try."

Avakian's smile faltered. "That would be Mr. Gaston from the high school?"

"Yeah, the band director. He conducts the band and orchestra too, but I don't play with them."

"I see. So Mr. Gaston thought you should try the baritone saxophone."

"I know it sounds funny, but he knew I play the piano and we got to talking, and I told him I'd taught myself to play the guitar, so when he couldn't find anyone to play the bari sax, he asked me to try it."

"So you're a prodigy."

"I don't think so. I just pick things up fast."

"Have it your way." The man's smile was back. It was broad and white and contrasted nicely with the olive tone of his skin. His eyes were good too, big, almost black—not as striking as Mr. G's blue, maybe, but with a good-humored gleam. Avakian cocked his head sideways. "Perhaps you'd like to try our new Steinway? I'd value your opinion of it."

Nobody outside of school had ever before asked Jonah's opinion about much of anything, so the question took him a moment to process. "I guess that would be okay. Actually, it'd be kinda cool, but I don't really know anything about pianos other than ours. It's a Baldwin, not a Steinway. Well, and my Aunt has a Yamaha, but I've only played that once, so I don't know that it would be fair to compare it...." He was babbling, so he closed his mouth.

"Follow me." Avakian straightened up, and it struck Jonah again how tall the man was. He had to be more than six feet, compared with Jonah's midget-like five foot two. Jonah followed him through the display area, past a glass case filled with cornets, clarinets, and flutes. Another case displayed violins and violas. He continued past a double row of filing cabinets with labels like "Quartet, string" and "Guitar, solo," through a curtained archway, and into a large back room. Guitars, mandolins, and other stringed instruments hung from pegboard walls. A row of narrow doors lined one wall. Jonah peered through an open one and saw a music stand and walls lined with acoustic insulation. The faint squeak of a clarinet drifted from behind another. A gleaming black Steinway grand mounted on heavy-duty rollers took up the center of the room.

"Wow, that's a concert grand, isn't it? What does *that* cost?"

Avakian chuckled. "A lifetime of practice."

"I'm not sure I should—"

"Don't be silly. Here, let me raise the bench for you."

The bench adjusted, Jonah sat down and rested his fingers on the keys. "What should I play?"

"Whatever you like."

Jonah closed his eyes and recalled a piece he'd heard on the radio. He'd been trying to work out the notes for the last week or so and thought he had most of them right. After running through it in his head, he opened his eyes and started to play. He was tentative at first, but Avakian stepped from his line of sight and said nothing, so after a minute he relaxed and focused on the music. It wasn't quite what he heard in his head, but it was pretty close. When he finished, he sat for a moment and let the faint sounds from the street filter back into his consciousness. The clarinet had fallen silent.

"Scarlatti," murmured Avakian from behind him. "My mother is very fond of that one."

"Scarlatti? Is that who wrote it?" said Jonah.

"You didn't know? Where did you get the music?"

"I don't have any music. It's just something I heard."

Avakian came around to peer into Jonah's face, as though he were looking for clues to a mystery. "You played it from memory? How many times have you heard it?"

"Just the once, on the radio. I've a pretty good memory for stuff I hear. Sometimes it takes me a while to figure out how to play it." He wiggled his digits. "Which fingers to use."

Avakian blinked. "I see. What do you think of the piano?"

"I like it. I mean, it's a little stiffer than our Baldwin, but...." Jonah played a scale. "It's more predictable." He tapped a key. "This one doesn't sound right."

"One of the strings is flat," said Avakian. "I haven't had it tuned yet."

"I guess."

"Have you a piano teacher, Mr. Winfield?"

"Can you call me Jonah? Mr. Winfield sounds like I'm in gym class or something."

"Jonah." Avakian nodded. "You may call me Davoud if you wish."

"Davoud? That's like French or something, isn't it?"

"Something like that."

"Cool."

"Forgive me, Jonah, but I'm really very curious to know whether you have a piano teacher."

"Not really. Mrs. Olivetti used to give me lessons back in Chicago, but we moved, and Dad said he couldn't afford to hire someone anymore."

"I'm sorry to hear that."

"It's okay. I mean, I know I could learn faster if I had a teacher, but I like to work things out on my own."

Avakian grinned suddenly. "Yes, I do too."

PAUL KNEW it was coming. It buzzed in his head when he was conducting and made him ask the orchestra to repeat sections because he'd forgotten to listen for the critical phrasing. He bore it as a tension in his shoulders that didn't loosen after an hour of running. Charlie Wong, the principal, had told him at the end of the last budget cycle that the budget cuts would mean another music class cut or moved to an after-school activity. Paul knew the required course load, and that he was the youngest history teacher in the high school, but he'd managed to keep those facts cocooned in separate parts of his psyche like components of an unstable explosive. In Charlie's office, that careful ignorance ended with the words "You can't teach another section of history, Paul. You'll have to teach something else."

He'd never taught anything but music and history. He didn't want to teach anything else. Music and history were his twin lodestones. His interest in them gave him the energy to endure… everything.

Paul dropped into the chair behind his desk and stared at the mementos on his wall: an aerial view of the place in East Sussex where the Battle of Hastings was fought, a stage shot of Angelo Debarre at the Montreal Jazz Festival.

"Mr. G? The band's ready…. Do you want me to start them on something?" It was Virginia Ruff, his drum major, her eyes widening as she peered around the door of his office. He really had to pull it together.

"Thanks, Ginny. Why don't you get them started on 'Africa.' I'll be along in a moment."

"Okay, Mr. G." She hesitated for a second.

"Go, please. God knows what they'll get up to if you don't give them something to do."

Charlie's suggestion was that Paul should teach AP English. Paul had been good at it in school. He'd certified in both English and history when he started teaching, and could probably muster some enthusiasm for the topic. But did he have the patience to read student writing? The acid that flooded his gut as he imagined himself trying to pry coherent sentences from the likes of Billy Preston didn't bode well. Maybe it really was time for the change. Maybe he should pursue the music career he'd abandoned for the safety of education. Even as he thought it, he knew he'd never take the risk. He didn't have what it took. He'd known that as a teenager. While he might be good enough, he just didn't have the personality. He needed the stability of a regular salary. And he needed Jazz Ensemble to keep him from coming apart during the school day.

PAUL DROPPED into the hardwood chair he kept beside his desk for visiting students and leaned it back on two legs. "Gaston speaking."

"Paul, it's Davoud Avakian. I was hoping to speak to you about a student of yours. Jonah Winfield?"

He brought the chair forward with a crash, possessed by a sudden desire to hang up the phone. Jonah was *his*. Special. Not someone to share with the peculiar owner of Avakian Music. Even though he didn't get Avakian's students until long after they'd been through the ceremony of instrument selection—the annual event when Avakian "helped" elementary students pick instruments like some kind of human sorting hat—he was still skeptical about the whole business. No one had ever complained to him about the instrument they'd chosen in Avakian's shop, but it still made Paul uncomfortable that the owner of the business that rented musical instruments to the children was also the man who told them what to play. Wasn't there a conflict of interest? What if Avakian had too many flutes to rent and not enough clarinets. Wouldn't he be tempted to steer impressionable kids to the instruments he had on hand?

A soft sound transmitted over the phone reminded him that Avakian was still waiting for a response.

"What about him?"

"He was in the other day."

Paul waited for the soft-spoken man to spit out his business.

"Some thugs were bothering him in the street in front of my shop."

"Is he okay? I don't have Jazz Ensemble until fifth period, so I haven't seen him today."

"He wasn't physically hurt. I can't speak to his state of mind."

"Is that why you're calling? There really isn't anything I can do unless I catch them on school grounds. I'll try to look out for him, but I can't follow him around all day. If they assaulted him, you should call the police." Paul's sense of guilt sharpened his tone.

"I didn't call to ask for your intervention, Paul."

"Then what do you want?"

"I asked him into the shop to get him away from the thugs, and he told me that he plays the piano, so I asked him his opinion of our new Steinway grand."

The man was too weird, Paul thought. Why would he do that? Did he ask everyone who said they played the piano to give him an opinion on his most expensive instrument? "Uh, okay."

Avakian continued in the same soft baritone, as if he didn't sense Paul's discomfort. "He is a talented pianist."

"Yes, he is."

"That's why I called. I've invited him to use the piano after school whenever he wishes."

As if that explained anything. Could the man not come to a point? "Listen, I have a class coming up…."

"I'm curious why you steered him to the baritone saxophone."

Stepped on your toes, did I? Now the call was beginning to make sense. "He asked to join Jazz Ensemble. What was I supposed to do? We don't use a piano, and he was eager to join."

"But the baritone saxophone? The bullies would never have caught him if he hadn't been dragging around that monster."

The guy would make a good Jewish mother. "I needed a bari sax. I suppose you've never steered someone to an instrument just because you had one to rent."

Paul knew he'd probably gone too far when, after a pause long enough for someone to count to ten, Avakian responded with an uncharacteristically sharp tone. "I have never done such a thing. Never."

"Believe it or not, he's really taken to the sax."

"I suspect he would do well with any instrument."

"So what's the problem?"

"He should develop his talent as a pianist. He has an amazing gift."

"Being in Jazz Ensemble is good for him. He feels he has something in common with them."

When Avakian finally answered, his mild tone was back. "I see. Perhaps you're right. Thank you for your time, Paul."

"DAVOUD? ARE you there, Davoud?"

Davoud spun idly on the stool behind Avakian Music's sole cash register. "Yes, Mother. Who else would answer my cell?"

"I don't know. Your voice sounds strange. Are you sick?"

"No, I'm fine, Mother."

"You don't sound fine."

Maybe he was a little out of sorts after the talk with Paul Gaston. The man never failed to irritate him—no less when he was right. Maybe being a member of the jazz group wouldn't hurt Jonah after all. The extraordinary boy would need friends and a sense of belonging. A sudden flood of memories from his childhood threatened to overwhelm Davoud's senses: the chlorine smell of the high school swimming pool where he took lessons three years running in order to escape the torture of gym class, the heat of his father's grip as he watched his mother get into a taxi to leave on one of her endless tours, the spatter of winter slush from the taxi's spinning tire as it pulled away.

"Davoud?"

"Did you need something, Mother, or did you just call to say hello?"

"There's no need to be rude about it."

Davoud sighed loudly enough to be heard over the telephone connection. "It's nearly quitting time, Mother. I have to close out the register."

"But I have news for you, my baby boy. Mother is coming home."

He loved his mother. He really did. Moreover, he respected her. She was an extraordinary singer and musician. But the prospect of her imminent retirement from the opera stage and return to the family home was terrifying. First, there was the problem of the Music Box, as they called the family-owned building that housed Avakian Music on the ground floor and family apartments converted from hotel rooms on the others. Proceeds from the music store, which had once paid upkeep on the Music Box, no longer covered the rising cost of maintaining the old building. The poor performance of the store embarrassed him. This year he'd been forced to get creative with the budget in order to pay for new windows and a replacement boiler. If his mother came to stay, she'd certainly find out what he'd done. Worse yet, the third-floor apartment where she'd raised her three sons needed more than new windows. There was a smell of dampness in the old place that suggested a leak in the plumbing or—God forbid—the roof. His own apartment on the second floor looked seedy. The laminated kitchen counters were peeling, and the old refrigerator barely kept a carton of milk cold enough to last the week.

He would have to ask her for rent.

Then there was his personal life. His mother knew he was gay. He'd announced that the day he returned from college, eighteen years ago. She'd cried. His father's slumped shoulders had spoken eloquently of resignation. Davoud had surprised no one then. What he dreaded now was for his mother to find out how small his social circle had become. It wasn't just that he had no lover. He had so few friends left—most of them having abandoned small-town life to pursue work in larger cities where jobs were easier to find and advancement was quicker. Davoud felt he'd been drifting along half asleep and hadn't woken until she announced her retirement.

She would try to set him up.

"Davoud! I swear it's like talking to a ghost. Did you hear me? I'm coming home."

"I heard you, Mother. So it's official, no more tours after this season? You've told Marty not to book you?"

"That's right. These old pipes have nearly sung their last."

"I hardly believe that. When do you expect to arrive?"

"In two months. In time for the holidays. I'll e-mail you the details. You'll have the apartment cleaned this time? Last Christmas, I thought I was going to choke to death on the dust."

"I'll see what I can do."

"Have you heard from your brothers?"

"No, it's early yet. I expect they'll let me know their plans eventually." Amir would pick vacation days to avoid Chicago Symphony performances and bring his wife and daughter. They'd stay in 1B. Rasul was touring somewhere with his string quartet and would undoubtedly call at the last second to announce his imminent arrival and requirement for a room, as if the Music Box were still a hotel. Davoud sometimes wondered if his brothers thought he had a staff to call upon for cleaning and room preparation. Even if Avakian Music employees would have stood for it, they had long since been reduced to

Marta, his full-time clerk, some part-time music teachers who watched the register for him during the busy times, and a part-time janitor. All the others in and out during the day were independent contractors, part-time music instructors who paid a commission for the use of a practice room and some help with marketing.

It had been easier to manage the shop when his father was alive. The heart attack that had claimed Farhad Avakian three years ago had left a hole in more than the schedule. His father's absence could still catch Davoud by surprise and leave him gasping.

"You'll enjoy seeing your brothers again, won't you? I know you miss them."

He did actually. Even if he sometimes wanted to strangle them.

"Yes, Mother, I do. I've got to go close out now. I'll look for your e-mail."

IN COLLEGE, someone once asked Paul what it felt like to play jazz. He'd struggled for words, unable to explain how improvising with a set of skilled musicians took on the dimensions of a whole world, unwilling to confess that the intimacy he experienced went beyond any he'd felt in his limited relationships. Part of the attraction was that his companions were competent enough to set aside technical concerns and simply express musical ideas as they played: harmonic concepts, melodies, rhythms, even jokes. He could, without the embarrassment of words, get to know a person with a degree of intimacy difficult through other means—even the rushed and awkward sex with boys he picked up at gay bars or the campus gay club. This was before everything had to be LGBT or—heaven save him from political correctness—LGBTQ. It was just the "gay club" in those days. Often, while improvising, Paul knew what his drumstick and horn-wielding friends would do before they did. Occasionally, one would surprise him with a sure-footed gentleness or quivering rage entirely foreign to his persona outside the practice room. He cherished those glimpses of his friends' inner lives all the more for their rarity.

The Martin Luther King High School Jazz Ensemble was not composed of musicians of the same caliber as his old college group. But there were moments when they got it right, and they transcended the chalk dust, grubby linoleum, and arthritic music stands of the band room. On those days, the nagging issues of student discipline and reduced funding for the arts fell away, and Paul played lead or rhythm guitar with the simple joy and abandon of his youth.

Jonah's arrival at the start of the fall term had both sharpened faded memories and inspired an overwhelming yearning for physical intimacy Paul hadn't experienced since his last relationship. He wasn't attracted to Jonah. The boy was cute, in a birdlike way, flash-headed and small-boned, but he was twenty-three years Paul's junior. Even if he'd had the balls to risk it, Paul was no chicken hawk. The feelings Jonah evoked were protective. Paul had also been an outcast in high school. Never having been a parent, he didn't feel particularly competent to help, but he wanted to anyway. No, it was not sexual attraction, but the intimacy of playing guitar with a revitalized jazz ensemble that had reawakened, through some odd transference, his sexual desire. Paul found himself thinking about visiting the town's only gay bar. Maybe he would give it a try after work one day.

This afternoon, he planned to have Jazz Ensemble sight-read newly acquired Count Basie tunes composed by Sammy Nestico. He listened for the fifth-period bell with the pent-up energy of a randy teenager waiting for his girl behind the bleachers. When it finally rang, Paul grabbed his guitar case and burst out of his office, nearly knocking down his hapless first trumpet in the process.

"Sorry, Billy."

"Hey, Mr. Gaston. What's up? Somebody spike your fruit punch?"

As usual, Paul didn't know whether Billy Preston's question contained a hidden barb, or whether it was merely intended to be funny. Was the mention of fruit a reference to his sexuality? He'd never actually told a student he was gay; in the sexually charged and increasingly politicized high-school atmosphere some things were perilous and best kept outside school grounds. But he'd always figured some of them knew.

"Sorry, just excited to try the new Sammy Nestico stuff."

"Who's Sammy Nestico?"

"I mentioned it last time? Count Basie's composer and arranger?"

"Oh yeah. Guess I wasn't paying attention."

Once again, Billy had him at a loss for words. Was he supposed to chastise the boy or just take his admission that he hadn't been listening as a joke? "So you were mesmerized by the soft sheen of Julie Patterson's hair? Intoxicated by Sandy Benson's perfume?"

Billy's quizzical look said his effort at humor was wasted. "You sure you're okay, Mr. G?"

"Come on, Billy. We've got some sight-reading to do."

"I hate sight-reading."

"Yeah, but it's good for you. Like spinach. It makes you a stronger musician."

"You know I'll probably never pick up the trumpet again after I graduate. My brother left his trombone behind when he went to college. It's still in his room, and he was better than I'll ever be."

"Don't say that, Billy! Hasn't anyone ever told you there are things the adults in your life don't need to know?"

Billy shrugged. "Yeah, but they weren't talking about music, Mr. G."

"WARM BREEZE," the title song from Basie's 1981 album of the same name, started off well enough, assisted by the confident buzz of Jonah's bari sax. Billy managed to get through the long Sonny Cohn solo, missing notes but sticking with it. But when they reached the tenor sax solo, Paul looked up from his guitar to see the lead tenor sax red-faced and shaking her head. Carol was a solid player, but she tended to shy away from solos unless she'd had time to practice them to death.

Paul waved the group to a halt.

"I can't, Mr. Gaston. I'm not good enough. I sound terrible."

"It's all right, Carol. This isn't a performance. The point is to do your best and stick with it. If you get behind, just keep counting and come in when you can."

"But...." Carol still sounded pretty shaky.

"Would it help to have someone take it with you?"

Carol shrugged. "Maybe."

"Anyone want to try it with Carol?" Paul looked around the room. Five saxophone players were suddenly intent on blowing spit out of their instruments or marking up their scores. Billy caught his look and glanced away quickly, probably relieved to have gotten through his own solo and not wanting to mess up a good thing. The scores came with the solos written out so no improvisation was required, but the Nestico pieces still pushed his students' technical limits. Paul glanced at the far end of the line. Jonah's eyes were glued to his saxophone. Paul knew Jonah would do it if asked, but he wouldn't volunteer. The boy didn't like to call attention to himself in class or show up anyone.

"Jonah, would you mind helping Carol out?"

Jonah looked up and caught Carol's eye. "If she doesn't mind."

Carol grimaced, red-faced but rallying. "Sure."

Paul tried for his most reassuring smile. "Let's try it again from the start. I'll take the Basie part."

"WHY DID Nestico call it 'C.B. Express,' Mr. G? I mean Count Basie only plays like four notes in the whole thing." Shelly's face revealed nothing but curiosity, but Paul still wondered if the question was intended seriously. Shelly was a junior, second trombone, technically proficient, but not the most sensitive kid.

"It moves along like an express train, doesn't it?" he said. Shelly frowned, apparently quite serious. It occurred to Paul she'd probably never been on a train in her life.

"Yeah, it's fast, Mr. G, but that's not what I meant."

Jonah shifted uncomfortably in his seat. "Basie was playing a lot, Shelly. Laying out the chords and rhythm," he said. "It's just that you only notice him when he fits his notes into the spaces between the other stuff."

Paul gave Jonah a thumbs-up. "Jonah's right, Shelly. Basie was playing the whole time. Nestico certainly expected that the Basie band would be playing his composition, but I don't know what was going on in Nestico's head when he named it."

"Whatever." Shelly snapped the buckles on her trombone case. "I just thought he might have been friends with Basie or something."

Was Shelly's question an idle one? Or had she read about the other great jazz collaborators, Duke Ellington and Billy Strayhorn? Some suggested their relationship might have extended to the physical. Strayhorn and Nestico were both from Pittsburgh, come to think of it, but nobody ever suggested they had shared the same sexual orientation.

"Mr. G, would you mind if I stuck around for a while and played the piano?"

Paul's hands paused at their task of wiping down his guitar. There was an urgency to Jonah's voice he didn't like. He thought immediately of what Davoud Avakian had said about thugs bullying Jonah. Was the kid trying to avoid another confrontation?

"I would have thought Avakian's Steinway would be better than our old clunker." Paul watched Jonah to see how he took the implication that he might want to head over to Avakian's. Something dark flashed over Jonah's face, but it was quickly replaced by a grin.

"Yeah, that's a nice ride, but it doesn't come with a rhythm guitar."

Paul laughed out loud. He knew something was going on with Jonah. He should probably question the boy about the bullying, but Jonah had him pegged. The temptation to jam won out. He could ask about Jonah's troubles later. "Okay, hotshot. What do you want to play?"

WHERE WAS Mr. G? He was never late for Jazz Ensemble. Jonah was pretty sure he hadn't been in his office when he went by, although he hadn't paid attention, because Mr. G was usually already in the band room and strumming though the day's chord changes when Jonah got there.

Billy must have been thinking the same thing. He stopped to comment as Jonah got out his sax. "Mr. G was late to band today. Ginny took us through 'Africa' twice before he showed. Ginny said he was just staring like he didn't know what day it was."

"He didn't say anything?"

"Nope, just picked up the baton and started in like he'd been there the whole time."

Billy shrugged and went up the shallow risers to blow some soft notes on his horn. Jonah fidgeted with his sax but held off warming up. He didn't like the idea of an unreliable or unhappy Mr. G. The music teacher's classes were damn near the only good part of high school. The idea that something could happen to Mr. G made Jonah feel a little sick. Who would conduct Jazz Ensemble if Mr. G left? Few substitute teachers could play Django Reinhardt riffs or fill in for Count Basie. But it was more than that. Mr. G made Jonah feel as though he mattered.

"Why are y'all sitting around like mannequins? It's not like you've got blisters yet." Mr. G pulled the door shut behind him. That was one of Mr. G's favorite phrases. Never mind that most players never got blisters. Everyone knew what he meant. You only had to shake hands with Mr. G to get it. The man had serious calluses.

Mr. G was okay. Jonah felt his chest loosen, and he blew a few quick runs on his sax.

"How about we try 'Warm Breeze' again today. Carol, are you ready to take the solo on your own?"

CHAPTER 2

THEY CAUGHT him off guard. Usually, when Jonah stayed after to play with Mr. G, Antony and Justin were long gone by the time he left the relative safety of the building. He was humming and kicking through fallen leaves in the parking lot on his way to the bus stop on Main, when he was slapped on the back of the head from behind. He spun around to face his attacker. Antony moonwalked behind him, grinning happily. Justin leaned against the side of an old sedan belonging to a teacher. Unfortunately, that teacher was nowhere to be found. A group of wrestlers from the varsity team was hanging around the door nearest the gym. That explained why Antony and Justin were still at school—Justin was on the wrestling team. He'd probably stayed for a practice. A couple of cars lined up along 5th Street with their engines running, but Jonah couldn't tell if their drivers were paying any attention.

"Hey, Whale Bait, how they hanging? Oh right, yours ain't dropped yet."

"What do you want, Antony?"

"What do I *want*?" Antony got in Jonah's face. "Hey, Justin, Whale Bait wants to know what I want. What do you think of that?"

"Pretty Boy knows his place. Fags who don't know their place get beat up, right?"

Antony pressed his groin against Jonah's abdomen. Jonah felt Antony's belt buckle through the thin cotton of his T-shirt and a softer bulge below that. "Got a boner yet, Whale Bait?"

Jonah's gut twisted in revulsion, and he backed away, his heels knocking his saxophone case. "Get off me, asswipe."

"You got a dirty mouth. You been sucking dirty things again?"

"I bet that's what he's been doing with that faggot music teacher after class. Pretty Boy's been sucking his teacher's dick."

Rage and shame flooded Jonah like a hurricane. He hit Antony in the face without considering the consequences.

Antony wiped his mouth and looked around to see if anyone had noticed him get punched. Jonah caught the eye of a guy in a letterman's jacket who was chatting up a couple of girls in tights and long sweaters a few cars away. The asshole saw him all right, but all he did was point and say something to the girls that made them look and giggle.

"Hold him." Antony apparently thought them no more likely to interfere than Jonah did.

Justin twisted Jonah's arms behind his back before Jonah could run. Antony took his time and put his whole body behind his swing. Jonah managed to turn his head so the punch glanced off the side of his mouth, but it still hurt like fuck. He tasted blood and tried to spit at Antony, but Antony danced back and the bloody gob fell short.

"Whoa, none of that, Whale Bait. Now I'm gonna have to teach you how to treat your betters."

Jonah tried to pull away from Justin, but the goon probably weighed twice as much as he did, so he had the pleasure of watching Antony wind up for a pile driver to the gut. It bent him over and left him gasping for air.

"Leave him alone!" Jonah was peripherally aware of a familiar voice yelling from some distance. Justin must have shoved him, because he fell backward over his saxophone case and slammed an elbow on the cement. He curled into a ball, holding his arm.

"Jonah, are you okay?"

"Does it look like I'm okay?" he gasped. He felt a touch on his arm and flinched. It was withdrawn.

"Jonah, look at me. I need to know if you're okay."

Jonah tasted bile, but he swallowed repeatedly until the burning in his throat abated. He rolled onto his back and squinted at his teacher. "Shitheads caught me off guard."

Paul knelt on the pavement and examined him. "Jesus, your mouth is bleeding. Who were they? Who did this? They ran off before I could get a look at them."

"Just some assholes."

"Jonah, they assaulted you. I have to report this. Tell me who they were."

"I can't. They'll make my life hell."

"Worse than this? Can you stand up?"

"I just have to catch my breath." Jonah staggered to his feet and tried to look as if he didn't feel like puking.

Paul took his good arm. "Come inside with me. We have to wait for the police."

"Please don't call the police. It was my fault. I let them get to me. I threw the first punch."

Paul frowned, but he didn't say anything as he led Jonah back into the school building. They went into the reception area. Paul pointed to a chair. "Sit." He went into the office and came out with the principal, Mr. Wong, in tow.

"There were two of them. I saw one hold Jonah's arms while the other hit him."

Wong peered at Jonah's mouth and frowned, the wrinkles around his eyes deepening. "Sit with him, Paul, while I call his parents."

"Please don't call my parents, Mr. Wong. It was just a stupid argument that got out of hand. I'm okay, really I am."

"I'm sorry, Jonah, but you've been hurt on school grounds. I really don't have any choice. Wait here with Mr. Gaston, please."

Jonah tongued the swollen place inside his cheek, which was bleeding. He had to stop this before they started asking questions he didn't want to think about, much less answer. He waited until Wong was back in his office. "Mr. G, do you think you could find some ice? I think my mouth is swelling."

Jonah felt bad at Paul's guilty look. "I'll check the lunch room. Be right back."

As soon as his teacher was gone, Jonah grabbed his saxophone case and lugged it toward the 4th Street exit. He picked it because it led to a narrow walkway between houses, and he knew he'd be able to get out of sight more quickly that way. He slowed only when he'd turned the corner a block down from the narrow passage. He had to get somewhere he could think for a second. He had to come up with an explanation for what had happened before he talked to his dad.

By the time Jonah got to Avakian Music, his mouth really hurt and his stomach felt like he'd belly flopped onto a submerged tree stump. The gray-haired woman at the counter smiled at him, but he didn't want to risk an interrogation, so he waved and headed through the curtain to the practice area as though he owned the place. There was a sign for restrooms beyond the last practice room. He dropped his saxophone case by the Steinway and went into the men's room, locking the door behind him.

DAVOUD WAS in the storage room when he heard the silver bell attached to the front door tinkle. A few seconds later, he heard a clatter as something heavy was dropped in the next room—probably some rebellious student who'd rather be playing Super Mario or out on the basketball court instead of practicing his instrument. Ten minutes later, having finished his inventory, he stepped out and was more than a little surprised to see a baritone saxophone case on its side under the Steinway grand. Only one student could have left that particular case, but it seemed out of character for Jonah to be so cavalier with his instrument. Where was the boy anyway? He stuck his head through the curtain into the front of the store.

"Marta, did you see the kid that came in here with the bari sax?"

Marta looked up from the novel she kept on the counter next to the register. "Blond kid, pointed chin, looks like he's twelve?"

"That's the one. Don't let him hear you describe him that way."

"No offense intended, boss. He went that way, hasn't come back. Somebody I should know?"

"He's Paul Gaston's student. I told him he could practice on the Steinway after school."

Marta's eyebrows went up. "The Steinway?"

"He's talented. I don't imagine he'll break it."

Davoud returned to the practice area. The saxophone case hadn't moved. The sound of a flautist running up and down scales drifted from one practice room, but he heard no raspberries from a bari sax. Only one place remained, unless the boy had gone straight out to the back alley. He knocked on the men's room door.

"Keep your pants on. Can't a guy take a shit without being harassed?"

"Jonah? Are you okay?"

There was a pause. "Sorry, Mr. Avakian."

"I apologize for bothering you. I'll wait until you've finished." Davoud heard water running and then the sound of the paper towel dispenser. He did not hear the toilet flush. He went to stand by the piano.

Jonah left the restroom with a hoodie shadowing his face. He leaned awkwardly against the arched entrance to the back corridor. "Hey, Mr. Avakian, mind if I play a little?"

"Not at all. I'm pleased to see you."

Jonah made no move to come into the room. Davoud channeled a horse whisperer: *Okay, my skittish friend, I won't push.* "I'll be in the front, if you need me."

"Thanks, Mr. Avakian."

He waited until Jonah was well into a late Count Basie tune before peeking. The boy hunched over the keyboard with his eyes closed. He'd pushed his hood back onto his shoulders, revealing soft spikes of blond hair. The natural pout of his lips was distorted by a swollen bruise on the right side of his face.

Again! Davoud marched angrily to his office and called the only person to whom he could think to complain.

A woman answered the phone. "Martin Luther King High School."

"May I speak to Paul Gaston, please."

"Mr. Gaston has gone for the day. To whom am I speaking, please?"

"Never mind." Davoud hung up. What could Paul do anyway? He should raise the matter with the principal. He picked up the phone and put it down again. Maybe he was overreacting. He ought to talk to Jonah before going overboard, but unless he misjudged the boy, he would need a little whispering.

Davoud breezed into the room and went straight to his double bass, deliberately avoiding the boy's questioning look. "I'm fond of Sammy Nestico. Would you mind if I sat in with you?" He unsnapped the catches on the case without waiting for an answer.

The notes from the Steinway slowed and then returned to tempo. "I didn't know you played, Mr. Avakian. I guess I was pretty stupid to think you wouldn't, I mean, you owning a music store and all."

"I could use the practice. You're supposed to be calling me Davoud, remember?" Davoud hoisted the heavy double bass and sneaked a glance at the boy. "You're sure you don't mind?"

Jonah's eyes were on the piano keys. "Suit yourself." He ended the piece he'd been playing and dived into a set of rapid chord changes. The boy might as well have slapped him in the face with a glove.

Davoud suppressed an impulse to smile. *Bring it on, kid. You're dealing with an Avakian.* He matched the changes, plucking a sparse line to compliment the boy's chords. He could sense Jonah looking at him, but he kept his head down and slid into a driving rhythm of his own. Jonah followed for a while and then grunted before transitioning into an old Django Reinhardt/Stéphane Grappelli arrangement. That had to be Paul's work. Davoud followed, no longer concealing his grin. He risked a glance at Jonah. The boy glowered and pushed the tempo until they sounded like an old 33 1/3 disc at the 78 setting. Sighing dramatically, Davoud leaned over as if to catch his breath. Delight and disappointment flashed across Jonah's face in rapid succession. Davoud laughed and snatched his bow from the case at his feet. Diving back in, he sawed through a complete Grappelli violin solo, albeit three octaves lower than Grappelli ever did it. Jonah stared, slack-mouthed. Davoud waggled his eyebrows until Jonah burst out laughing.

"I didn't know you could do that on a bass fiddle."

"Few would bother," a familiar voice commented dryly from the doorway.

"Hello, Paul. What brings you here?" Davoud asked.

"Oh shit," said Jonah, dropping his hands from the piano.

PAUL REELED, unsure if it was the music or the wrenching shift in his perception of Davoud Avakian. *Holy shit! The man plays like Edgar Meyer.* He'd lived in the same town with Avakian for most of his life. He knew, or thought he knew, all the musicians in town, but he'd had no idea about Davoud. Rubbing goose bumps on his arms, he tried to focus on the matter at hand. "'Oh shit' is right, Jonah. You are in a heap of trouble. What were you thinking, running out on me and the principal like that?"

Jonah winced and opened his mouth as if to speak, but Davoud got there first. "I presume this has something to do with the bruise on his face?"

"It does. I have to call Charlie Wong and tell him I've found our missing student. His father is raising holy hell." Paul tapped the call symbol on his phone and found the favorites entry for the school.

"Martin Luther King High School."

"Hi, Charlie, it's Paul. I've got him. He's fine."

"Thank goodness. Where are you? I've got to tell his father he's all right."

Paul watched Davoud put his bass away with deliberate care. The man wasn't just tall, he had fingers like a basketball player. The double bass suited him. "I'm over at Avakian Music. Listen, the kid's fine and it's late. Can we sort this out tomorrow? Tell his father I'll have him home in about twenty minutes."

"Fine, but I want to see the both of you in my office first thing tomorrow morning."

"You bet. Thanks, Charlie."

Paul disconnected and examined Jonah. "You've got some explaining to do." Jonah's joy of the minute before had faded to sullen distrust.

"Why is Jonah in trouble? It looks to me like he's been hit." Davoud peered at the bruise on the side of Jonah's mouth. "Will you tell us who did this to you?"

"Just some guys. Look, it's no big deal. I wish everyone would just leave me alone."

Paul met Davoud's concerned look. He followed the man's example and tried to soften his tone. "Jonah, I understand you'd like us to forget about this, but we can't. There are laws about things that happen in schools. Mr. Wong and I, we have to investigate this incident and report to your parents. We've no choice."

Jonah crossed his arms. "Fine. Investigate all you like. I've got nothing to say."

"All we want is to help you, Jonah. What's so terrible that you can't tell me?"

Jonah didn't answer. Nor would he meet Paul's gaze.

"Perhaps this isn't the best time to pursue your inquiry," Davoud said quietly. "You've promised to get the boy back to his family."

Paul sighed and looked at Davoud. When had the man gotten crow's feet? He tried again to soften his tone to match Davoud's. There was no point starting a pissing contest. "Okay, Jonah. We can talk about it in the morning. Get your things together and I'll give you a ride home. Davoud, may I speak to you for a moment?" Paul led Davoud into the sheet music section, which was empty of customers. He kept his voice low. "You told me you'd interrupted something the other day in front of your shop. Jonah was arguing with two boys, right?"

"Yes, there were two of them."

"Could you write out a description for me? I saw two boys fighting with Jonah this afternoon in the Martin Luther King parking lot. One held him while the other hit him. He won't tell us who they were or what they were fighting about, but I'm betting they were the same kids you saw."

Davoud grimaced. "I don't know how accurate it will be."

"Do you think you'd recognize the boys if you saw them again?"

"Possibly. I'll certainly be on the lookout for them."

"Good. I don't know why Jonah won't help. If they started it, all he has to do is identify them and they'll be suspended. We have a no-tolerance policy for violence."

"He may feel he's to blame, or he may be afraid of retaliation."

"It's possible… I don't know, but our Jonah is a bit of a ratter. I can't see him being that easily intimidated."

Davoud's crow's feet deepened as he smiled. "I can't either."

Paul found himself returning the smile. He was beginning to understand how Davoud charmed kids into choosing the right instrument. There was a directness and warmth in Davoud's regard that made Paul feel as though he'd just said something brilliant in class. He called in the direction of the back room, "Come on Jonah. It's time to go."

"DAD, IT was no big deal. It was just a stupid fight."

John Winfield raked his fingers through his thinning gray hair. "Jonah, physical violence is always a big deal. Mr. Wong said one of the boys held you while the other hit you. You could have been seriously hurt. Those boys must face the consequences of their actions."

Jonah was tired. He respected his dad's attitude toward violence. In his youth, his dad had been an advocate of nonviolent protest against apartheid in South Africa and for a nuclear test ban treaty. That was actually pretty rad. His favorite picture of his dad was of a striking young man leading a gaggle of besloganed protesters outside a bank building in Chicago. The snapshot had always held pride of place on their mantle. But there was no way Jonah was telling his dad what Antony and Justin had said about him and Mr. G.

"Dad! Please don't. Just don't. I'm asking you to leave it alone."

They sat at the kitchen table, the remains of the dinner his dad had insisted they eat before talking arrayed before them. His dad had strong opinions about nutrition and family togetherness. They always ate dinner as a family. It was like the eleventh commandment. His mother would have been with them, except she was in Washington preparing briefs for some big civil rights case. She was always preparing to argue some big case. After his dad had lost his job in Chicago and they'd moved back to his hometown, she'd traveled more and more. The way Jonah figured it, she'd won a trophy or something for debate when she was in high school and had apparently never thought of anything better to do with her life than argue.

John started removing dishes from the table. He raised his eyebrows at the uneaten veggie lasagna on Jonah's plate. "You're not going to eat that?"

"Not hungry."

John sighed and took the plate to the sink with the others. He turned on the faucet and began to rinse for the dishwasher. "Even if I were willing to let it go, Jonah, Mr. Wong wouldn't be. You were assaulted on school grounds."

"You don't understand. I can't say anything."

John came back to the table, sat down, and planted his elbows on the table. "Look at me, Jonah. Are they threatening you? Are you trying to protect somebody?"

"No! I told you, you don't understand."

"Then help me, son."

Jonah tapped out a rhythm on his knee. He hated lying to his dad, but telling the whole truth was impossible. He closed his eyes. "Dad, I threw the first punch. Just like you've always told me is wrong. They were just giving me an eye for an eye." At least the part about hitting Antony was true.

"I swear there is no more idiotic or damaging phrase in the Bible. Why did you hit the other boy? You know what we've always taught you about fighting."

"It was wrong, Dad, I know that. I was mad. I didn't think."

"I see. You'll have to suffer the consequences. But those boys were wrong too. I don't see why you insist on protecting them."

The rhythm Jonah tapped on his knee morphed into something Latin. "It's not them I...." *Shit.* He stopped tapping. Now his dad would never give up.

His dad's mouth twitched. "Okay, have it your way, son. You'll get no allowance this month, and we'll put off driving lessons for another six months. Persons with poor impulse control should not be driving cars."

"Dad! We talked about this. How am I supposed to get to the Jazz Ensemble gigs?"

"Mr. Gaston might give you a ride."

"I can't ask him! The other kids will... never mind. May I be excused?"

"I'll be up in an hour to check on your homework."

Jonah stomped away from the table. The whole world conspired to fuck up his life.

JOHN WINFIELD leaned forward and spoke without preliminaries. "I spoke to my son last night, Mr. Wong. He has admitted to me that he punched the other boy first. He is prepared to accept whatever consequences you deem appropriate."

Paul had just taken a seat at the principal's conference table along with Jonah and John Winfield. The back window of Charlie's office faced the courtyard at the center of Martin Luther King High School. The day was fine and sunlight streamed in through the uncurtained window, leaving the principal's face in shadow. Charlie came around his desk and took a seat across the conference table from Jonah, his phlegmatic features revealing mild surprise. Jonah's father rested a hand on the back of Jonah's neck. The boy seemed comfortable next to his father. His posture was relaxed, but his eyes were down, and he tapped a rhythm on the battered tabletop.

Paul caught Charlie's gaze. The principal motioned for Paul to start. "I'm pleased that Jonah is willing to take responsibility for his actions, Mr. Winfield, but I'm a little confused. What I saw in the parking lot looked rather one-sided to me. One boy holding Jonah and another boy punching him. Has Jonah told you who the other boys were?"

"No, he has not, Mr. Gaston, but the other boys' actions don't relieve him of responsibility for his own violence."

"I have to say I'm pretty surprised to hear there was any violence on Jonah's part," Paul responded. "It doesn't seem characteristic of him."

Jonah's father removed his hand from his son's neck and rested it on the boy's fingers to stop the tapping. "I was surprised too, but I suspect that Jonah is protecting someone. Nevertheless, he said that he hit another boy, and I don't believe him to be lying. There should always be consequences for violence, no matter what the circumstances. That's what my wife and I have always taught Jonah."

"Has Jonah told you why he hit the other boy?" Charlie said.

"I don't really see that as relevant. Hitting is always wrong, Mr. Wong."

"I don't disagree with you, Mr. Winfield," said Paul, "but words can be violent too. They tear down or bruise just as fists do."

"Right now, we're in an unusual situation," said Charlie. "I have a reliable witness of violence toward your son and no witness of any violence he may have committed. I'm uncomfortable passing judgment on him without understanding the circumstances. Frankly, I'd like to hear more from Jonah."

Jonah's hand escaped his father's and he began tapping again, but he neither looked up nor spoke.

"There's another factor to consider as well," said Paul. "Did Jonah mention that there has been at least one other incident with the same boys?" Jonah's head came up quickly. Paul continued before Jonah could deny it. "Davoud Avakian told me he stopped two boys from hassling Jonah in front of his shop the other day."

"Is that true, Jonah?" said Charlie.

"It was no big deal. They were just teasing me."

"Davoud told me that one of them grabbed your pack and the other was making crude gestures. He described them as thugs."

"Jonah, have you had trouble with these boys before?" said Charlie.

Jonah hesitated, his gaze shifting from Charlie to Paul. "No."

Paul had only to look at Jonah's father to know the boy was lying. The man's dismay was painful to see.

"Jonah...." Winfield's tone was low and urgent.

Jonah stood suddenly, knocking his chair over backward. "I told you I don't fucking want to talk about it." Jonah's voice rose. "Why won't you listen to me! You're making a big fucking deal about nothing!"

"That's enough," said Winfield. He tried to put a hand on Jonah's shoulder, but the boy shied away from him.

"Don't touch me!"

Paul saw shock in Winfield's eyes as he let his arm fall back to his side.

Charlie's expression was grave. "Mr. Winfield? Paul and I need to consult for a minute. Would you and your son mind waiting for us in the reception area?"

Winfield was still in shock, but he didn't resist when Jonah grabbed his arm and dragged him out. "Come on, Dad."

"Paul, why didn't you tell me there was a previous incident?"

"I'm sorry. I was going to, but I wanted to talk to Jonah first and try to find out what happened."

"I'm not happy about any of this. There's something going on with that boy, and he's not talking. That's a recipe for trouble. I pulled his records. He has no history of violence or disciplinary problems besides a couple of complaints about inappropriate language. His grades are stellar. What made him strike the other boy?"

Paul sighed. "I think the other boys may be bullying him."

"Do you have any evidence? Jonah might have instigated both incidents."

"Davoud Avakian's report suggests—"

"But Jonah won't confirm it."

"Come on, does he look like a bully?"

"He talks like a rooster. Do you know who his friends are? They'll know what's going on."

"I'm not sure. I've seen him talk to members of Jazz Ensemble… he's never mentioned anyone, or any problems to me."

"There's no point in kicking yourself, Paul. He's not at an age when boys talk about their feelings."

"Yeah, but he and I…." Paul stopped. They'd jammed together, not talked.

"I'm going to put the word out to his teachers to keep an eye on him. I want to know if anyone says so much as *boo* to him."

"I'll ask the kids in Jazz Ensemble."

"Be careful what you say. Jonah is obviously sensitive about this. Don't embarrass him in front of his peers."

"I'll be discreet."

"Go get Winfield, would you? I want to speak to him again."

Paul went to the reception area. Jonah and his father sat together, but Jonah was tapping again, and his father was looking as if he'd been abducted by aliens. It was easy to feel sympathetic.

"Mr. Winfield? Mr. Wong would like to speak to you again for a moment. Jonah, wait here, please."

When Paul ushered Winfield back into the office, Charlie spoke in reassuring tones. "Mr. Winfield, I know that you want what's best for your son. So do I. That's why I feel it's pretty important we not act impulsively, but wait until we're sure that we've got a clear picture of the situation."

"I've already canceled his allowance and postponed driving lessons. He didn't seem... I mean he accepted it without complaint. I took that to mean he understood the lesson."

"I think he understands the point about physical violence, Mr. Winfield. If I may, I would suggest that patience might be the best approach until we know more. I want to assure you that if any of our students—including Jonah—are involved in violence of any kind, we will take every appropriate action. We have a no-tolerance policy for violence."

CHARLIE WAS wrong. Paul was certain Jonah wasn't starting fights. How could he have missed it? His favorite student, a boy with whom he felt a special connection, was being bullied, and Paul had been so wrapped up in his own worries that he'd missed it. Some bigot in a bar had once explained to him that all fags were incapable of deep emotional attachments or long-term relationships. At the time he'd been too ashamed to admit he was gay or to confront the man. The incident had stayed with him into middle age, flaring back into life like a trick candle in moments of self-doubt. He knew he was overreacting, but he felt off-kilter.

Paul caught the tip of a running shoe on an exposed root and nearly stumbled into the bushes that lined the riverbank. *Idiot!* Catching his balance, he shortened his stride and concentrated on his breathing. He'd headed out for an early morning run in the park that followed the Onaka River through town. The gravel path along the bank was a favorite place for early morning runners, many of whom he knew by sight if not by name. The path's proximity to the school and his apartment had been a factor in his decision to stay in town. He sometimes ran to work, showering in the boys' locker room before school started. In the summer, the tall willows and other water-loving trees along the path kept the route shaded. This time of year, shorn of their leaves, they offered little shelter from the wind.

For years, Paul had counted on running to slow his racing mind and to gentle him with the release of serotonin, but today it wasn't enough to overcome the feeling that he'd failed Jonah. He would make it up to the boy. He would find redemption in helping Jonah fight his demons. He'd have to work to build the boy's trust. Direct questioning had not worked. The little ratter was too damned stubborn for that. Maybe the answer was in the shared experience that had brought them together in the first place: music. Playing together could build trust, but he'd have to quit living in his own personal bubble and talk to the kid too.

Taking the initiative with Jonah was risky. He'd heard Dan Savage talk about it in an address at an education conference. It was one thing for gay people to help one another in college or after, when they were considered adults. But God forbid any openly gay man or woman should try to help a troubled teen who showed interest in same-sex relationships. Such attempts, no matter how platonic and well meaning, left the adult vulnerable to hysterical charges of recruiting or molestation. Gay teens were hands-off for gay adults. Teachers who ignored that rule lost their careers or worse. Never mind the fact that suicide rates among gay teens significantly outpaced those of straight kids. Never mind that most gay kids knew they were different by age ten or so, even if they didn't label themselves as gay. Never mind the growing body of evidence that same-sex attraction was determined at an early age and was at least partially genetic in origin. Gay teens were hands-off during puberty, just when they most needed to talk to someone. Savage's response to a spate of teen suicides had been to help found the It Gets Better Project, a suicide prevention and antibullying initiative.

It occurred to Paul that he'd been assuming Jonah was gay or at least questioning. He wondered whether Charlie had made the same assumption. If so, the principal had said nothing before or after the Winfield interview. Maybe Jonah wasn't gay. His small size and baby face were probably enough to make him a target. It didn't matter, did it? Jonah needed the adults in his life to step up. Paul would be one of those adults, no matter what.

He would need allies. Paul's only protection was for everything he did to be open and above reproach. Charlie could help, as long as his feelings about homosexuality didn't get in the way. It was not an issue they'd ever discussed. Like most schools, Martin Luther King High School maintained a kind of "don't ask, don't tell" policy with gay staff. It was good that they'd already discussed Jonah, and that Charlie had encouraged Paul to help, but Paul had to wonder what Charlie's reaction would be if he told the principal he was gay. As with his students, he'd always assumed Charlie knew.

Who else could help? The thought echoed in his head as he reached the mile marker where he usually turned around. He'd hardly been aware of covering the ground. He turned back toward the apartment. It was nearly time to get ready for school.

To: davoud@avakianmusic.com
From: aida@avakianmusic.com
Subject: Travel Plans

Darling Davoud,

Marty has sent my itinerary for next month (attached), which ends with my arrival home on November 14. No need to meet me at the airport. I can take a cab to the Music Box.

How I'm looking forward to seeing you and resting for a while in our lovely apartment with all its memories!

I don't have the stamina for endless travel anymore. Airline service has gotten so appalling! On my flight to London, even though I arrived a <u>full five minutes</u> before departure time, they had the gall to put me in one of those awful little seats in the back. Apparently they were overbooked—how exactly was that my problem?—and had given away my seat in first class. I was compelled to go into Diva Mode, as you call it, just to get on the plane. By the time we arrived, I thought they were going to have to extract me from that tiny seat with a crane.

Have the boys called? I'm <u>so</u> eager to have an American-style Thanksgiving together with all my children and grandchildren. My Darling Son, don't you ever wish for children? You say you've no choice about being gay, but I fail to see why that means you can't have a family. The opera world is chockablock with gay people; they're practically hanging from the rafters. <u>They</u> don't spend their Saturday evenings at home. Are you seeing anyone? What happened to that nice librarian I met last year?

Oh dear, I see I'm going on about The Forbidden Topic again. I know I'm supposed to let you live your own life as you see fit, even if your choices are incomprehensible.

Love and Kisses,

Aida

To: aida@avakianmusic.com
From: davoud@avakianmusic.com
Subject: Re: Travel Plans

Mother,

There is no need take a cab from the airport. I'm happy to meet you at the baggage claim as usual. A cab would be far too expensive. The Music Box will not collapse in my absence.

I would have liked to have been a fly on the wall in the departure area. Did you clamp yourself to the ticket counter and threaten to sing your despair until they relented? I'm laughing out loud at the picture. Marta would be calling for help, except she already knows I'm mad.

No, I've not heard from my brothers. Why don't you ask them for their plans?

No, I'm not seeing anyone. Tom took a job in Chicago. I told you that last May, when he moved.

Something interesting did happen the other day. I saw a very small student with a very large baritone saxophone case being hassled by thugs on the street in front of the shop. I interrupted them and pretended the boy was late for his lesson. It turns out he's a talented pianist with an extraordinary ear: he played me a note-perfect Scarlatti sonata from memory, having heard the piece once on the radio. He's a bit of a rough-cut diamond though—swears like a sailor, when he's not being scrupulously polite to me. Turns out the high school music teacher, Paul Gaston—I don't think you've met— encouraged him to take up the saxophone so he could play in a jazz group at school. I know what you'll say about that, but I think Paul was only trying to help the kid fit in better at school. I could have used some of that kind of help when I was green.

Anyway, it's time for Marta's break, so I have to go.

Love,

Davoud

"What is that smell?" Aida sniffed and stopped a few feet into the apartment. "Davoud darling, have you been mixing chemicals in here?"

"It's just the floor cleaner, Mother."

"It did not smell like this the last time I was here."

"No, I had it professionally cleaned this time."

Aida sniffed again and wrinkled her nose. "We must open the windows."

"It's thirty-six degrees out. You'll catch pneumonia." *And my heating bill will go through the roof.*

Aida ignored Davoud, marched to one of the double sash windows that lit the living room, and yanked upward. She must have expected the stiff movement of old windows, because the window flew upward and hit its stops with a bang. Aida's arms flew upward too. She lost her grip and tumbled backward onto the Persian carpet in tangle of woolen overcoat, faux-fur wrap, and silk scarf.

Davoud ran to kneel beside his mother. "Are you all right?"

Aida looked up at him with her mouth open. "That one *always* sticks!"

"I'm so sorry, Mother, I should have warned you. I had the windows replaced this summer. The heating and cooling was so expensive...."

"You had windows replaced... oh dear," Aida giggled. Davoud sighed and offered a hand, but Aida ignored him. She burst out in a full-throated laugh, moving her arms and legs as though she were making a snow angel. "It's so good to be home!"

Davoud, as always, gave in to her charm and collapsed onto the floor with her.

THE RESPITE did not last.

"Davoud, I want you to come up here and tell me something isn't rotten in the state of Denmark." His mother's peremptory tone crackled over the telephone connection.

"Mother, I'm covering the register right now."

"Have one of the staff take over. You're the boss, dear, there's no need to behave as though you're some clerk off the street."

The staff? Was his mother delusional? She apparently thought he had some hidden army of minions to do his bidding. When was the last time she'd actually read one of the financial statements he sent to every shareholder in the family business? Marta was getting a turkey club at the café across the street. No one else was in the store, not even a customer, unfortunately. He really had to speak to her about Avakian Music's finances, but he'd hoped to put it off until after the holidays. "Marta is at lunch. She'll be back—"

"Well, get someone else. I really cannot deal with this smell one second longer."

The temptation to hang up on his mother buzzed through Davoud like an electric current. He concentrated on his breathing for a moment. She was old, accustomed to getting her way, and entering into a retirement that might not live up to her expectations. He really ought to be patient with her. "I'll come up when I can, Mother. Whoops, here's a customer. I have to go now."

Hanging up the phone, he surveyed the empty store. He really ought to inventory the sheet-music collection. Scores were always disappearing into the practice rooms or student backpacks. He was sure that most of it was forgetfulness rather than deliberate theft. Department stores put security tags on nearly everything these days, but putting them onto sheet music was too ridiculous to contemplate.

Davoud had to assume that Avakian Music would survive the lean times. Eventually the economy would improve. Schools would start funding the arts again.

CHAPTER 3

JONAH SKIDDED around the corner to his locker. The long corridor ahead was filled with students on their way to class, their greetings and horseplay echoing in the tiled space. The bell had just rung the end of fourth period. He was in a rush to get to Jazz Ensemble.

"Hey, Jonah. On your way to the band room?"

Jonah turned to find Billy Preston pacing him. Billy was disheveled in his ratty uniform of faded black jazz camp T-shirt and baggy jeans that threatened to slide off his hips. An earbud stuck out of one ear, the other dangled on his chest.

"Billy, hey. I… I've gotta drop off my pack."

Billy nodded and bounced along beside Jonah, listening to something loud and consisting mostly of bass on his iPod. Jonah was surprised and a little uncomfortable with the company, since Billy had never before done more than wave lackadaisically from his spot on the back risers in the band room. Jonah stopped at his locker and dialed the combination.

Billy flipped straight brown hair from his eyes. "You ever listen to house music?"

Conversation? Billy actually wanted to engage in conversation? "Uh, not really. My dad, he doesn't… I mean it's not the sort of thing you play on the piano." Jonah threw his pack in the locker and slammed it. At first he wasn't sure Billy had heard his answer. The blaring beat from the dangling earbud was pretty loud.

"Piano?" Billy looked at him quizzically. "Black box with old elephant teeth glued on the front? Makes funny noises when the cat walks on it?"

"Uh... they mostly don't use ivory anymore. Did you know elephant tusks are actually elongated incisors? Nowadays, the white piano keys are actually made of plastic. The black ones are wood, ebony usually, but...." *Shut up, shut up. He's gonna think you're a nerd.* He bit his lip to stop the verbal incontinence.

"Right. So ya play?" Billy popped the other earbud out and fixed him with an inquisitive look.

Billy's eyes weren't brown like Jonah'd thought, but a light amber, like caramel. Jonah looked away before Billy noticed him staring. "Since I was little."

Billy's head bounced. "Huh."

"Hey, Billy," said a passing girl with short blond hair and freckles. Billy smiled and waved. Billy was pretty popular, judging from the smiles and waves he got from some of the guys and a lot of the girls. It felt like accompanying a movie star.

Billy stopped at a locker and started to fiddle with the combination. Jonah wasn't sure if he was supposed to stop or if he should keep going, so he slowed and tried to look as if he were in no hurry to get to class.

"Hey, wait up, Whale Bait." It was weird how much more pleasant the nickname sounded when it came from Billy. Still, he wasn't completely sure he liked anyone calling him that. Billy must have noticed, because he pushed the hair out of his face and examined Jonah critically. "You're right. Whales are mostly vegetarians." He winked and turned to hoist his trumpet from his locker.

Jonah's body warmed as if he'd stepped into a sauna. What was happening today? He'd fallen through a wormhole into some alternate reality—that would explain it.

At the band room, Jonah swerved from the open door. "I have to get my sax." He crossed the hall to Mr. G's office. He kept the instrument there since the case was too big to fit into a locker. Mr. G was gone, but the case was propped against the side of the desk instead of behind the door. Jonah froze. Spray-painted in big white letters on the side of the case was the word *Faggot*.

PAUL JOGGED into his office looking for the notebook he used in Jazz Ensemble and skidded to a halt. Jonah knelt on the floor by the desk, frantically scrubbing the side of his saxophone case. Paul's tissue box sat beside him on the floor. "Jonah, what's going on?"

Jonah put his body between Paul and the saxophone case. "Nothing. I have to go home. I'm sick. You better get to the band room or you'll be late."

"Jonah, stop. Let me see that."

"No, it's none of your business."

Paul put a hand on Jonah's shoulder just as the door burst open behind him.

"Hey, Mr. G, have you seen Jonah? He was right—"

"Leave me alone." Jonah jerked away from Paul's touch.

"Whoa! What's going on?" Billy stepped around Paul to get a better look. "Oh shit!"

Jonah clearly didn't know who he wanted to see the case less. When he tried to block Billy's view, Paul knelt to see what Jonah'd been trying to clean off the case. The edges of the letters were smeared, but the word was still plain. He sighed and straightened to close the door.

"Jonah! Leave it. It's not going to come off that way."

"That's just mean." Billy prodded the case with his toe. "Whoever did this, Jonah, they're just assholes."

"You're going to tell everyone, aren't you?" Jonah's tone was flat, but there was a tremor in his limbs as he stood.

"No way," Billy said. "It's none of their business."

Paul wished fervently that the issue was as simple as Billy made it sound. "Jonah, it will be okay. Mr. Wong will have to know because this is hate speech, but I'm sure he—"

"He'll tell my dad." Jonah's eyes glittered.

Paul fell silent. Jonah was right. If he told Charlie, the principal would almost certainly tell Mr. Winfield. If Jonah were gay and not ready to come out to his father, it could put the boy into a difficult situation.

"Come on, Mr. G, doesn't Jonah have a right to privacy?" Billy asked.

Before Paul could answer, somebody started knocking on the door. "Mr. G, are you there?" It was one of his students from Jazz Ensemble.

"Crap." Paul caught Billy's eye. "Could you do me a favor and go start them on something?"

"Sure, Mr. G." Billy reached out as though to touch Jonah's shoulder. "You going to be okay, Jonah?"

Jonah blinked at Billy. "Yeah, I guess. Motherfuckers. They're just motherfuckers, right?"

"Right." Billy opened the door just enough to slip out. Before the door clicked shut, they heard him explaining. "Hey, Tony, Mr. G's got to take care of something. You want to help me get us started on 'Satin Doll'?"

Paul put his back to the door. "Okay, Jonah. Here's the deal. I'll hold off telling Mr. Wong on one condition. You have to inform me if this stuff keeps happening." He hesitated. "And we've got to tell Mr. Avakian, because I think you're going to need a new saxophone case."

Jonah looked away. "Why can't everyone leave me alone?"

"It's nothing to be ashamed of."

"Yeah, right."

Paul put the saxophone case on his desk and ran his finger over the hard outer shell. "Do you know what one of these costs?"

Jonah's shoulders dropped. "Fuck."

"We can look it up online. I guess about three hundred."

"Maybe we can paint over it."

"It's possible, but you still have to tell Mr. Avakian about the damage, since it's his. Why don't we go over together this afternoon and discuss it with him?"

"I don't want him to stop letting me play the Steinway."

"He's not the type to hold this against you." It wasn't until Paul voiced the thought that he actually considered Davoud's reaction, but he was sure he was right. Davoud was a kind man—certainly not a homophobe. "Come on, Jonah, you feel like some Duke Ellington?"

"What about…?"

"Just bring the sax and leave the case here. We'll smuggle it out later. Nobody will see."

Paul was relieved to see Jonah reach for the horn. Music would do them both good.

"YOU'RE NOT mad?" Jonah and Paul faced Davoud in a tableau like a father-and-son portrait: Jonah in front, Paul with a reassuring hand on the boy's shoulder. The case was on the counter. Davoud considered Jonah's question.

"I am angry, but not at you, Jonah, not for this."

"You won't tell my dad?"

Davoud glanced at Paul in surprise. He would have thought the teacher would have already done that. Secrets could backfire. Had Paul considered the risk?

"Mr. G said he wouldn't tell so long as I tell him if this shit keeps happening."

"I see."

"Do you think we could paint over it?"

Davoud scraped the white paint with a fingernail. "It depends on what kind of paint they used. I have some cleaners, paint thinner, I'd like to try first."

Paul smiled. "See, what did I tell you?"

Jonah relaxed for the first time since they'd come into the shop. "Mr. G said you wouldn't hold it against me."

You did, did you? Davoud caught Paul's eye and nodded. "He judged correctly."

"Hey, I have an idea," said Jonah. "We've been working on some Duke Ellington in Jazz Ensemble, but we could use a good bass player to practice with. You want to join us? We're working on 'Satin Doll' with the ensemble, but I want to try some of his other stuff. You've played Ellington, right? Or you could pick it up? I know you could, because you were really good when—"

Paul laughed. "Give him a chance to answer, kid."

Davoud strove for gravitas. "If you're sure you want me...."

"You've got some sheet music we could borrow, right?"

Davoud couldn't quite suppress a faint sigh, but he covered with a smile. "I imagine we do."

"DAVOUD! SINCE when is Avakian Music a place for this nonsense?"

Paul, lost in the moment, hadn't even noticed the woman come into the room. The interruption made her comment particularly grating.

Davoud dropped his bow immediately, his face red, looking more like he'd been caught wanking than playing the music of one of America's renowned composers and performers.

Jonah stopped too, indignant. "Hey, we were just getting good."

"If you wish to get good, young man, I suggest you practice something more appropriate."

"Mother, it's not for us to say what's appropriate for our customers."

This is Davoud's mother? thought Paul. Jonah's mouth dropped open.

"I'm just saying—"

"I really wish you wouldn't," said Davoud sharply. "Mother, may I present Paul Gaston." Paul reluctantly put down his guitar and rose. "He's our local high school music teacher. And this is Jonah, one of his students." Jonah managed to close his mouth. "This is my mother, Aida."

"I'm pleased to meet you, Mrs. Avakian," said Paul.

"I generally go by Kazmi."

Davoud rolled his eyes. Aida Kazmi... something clicked in Paul's mind. "Jonah, do you have a notebook in your pack?"

"What? Sure, I guess."

Davoud closed his eyes and sighed dramatically.

"You might want to get it out—and a pen. You've just been introduced to one of this century's great altos. If you actually greet her, she might consent to give you her autograph."

Aida preened, obviously delighted to be recognized.

"Alto? You mean like an opera singer?" said Jonah.

"Diva is the word you're looking for," Davoud said dryly.

Paul laughed. "How about star? As in, shining down from the firmament upon the lucky few able to hear her."

Davoud groaned. "Please stop, Paul, her head will explode and I'll have a huge mess to mop up. What are you doing here anyway, Mother?"

"I came down to see if you would join me for dinner, but I see you're busy corrupting youth with your monstrous taste in music." Aida beamed at Paul. "You, sir, were obviously already corrupted."

Paul made calming motions at Jonah, who had jumped to his feet and was obviously preparing to defend them both—and Ellington too.

"Jonah is the student I told you about," said Davoud.

"I gathered. Perhaps it's not too late to save him," said Aida, turning to Jonah. "I understand you're fond of Scarlatti."

Jonah looked at Davoud in confusion. "You told her about me?"

"Nothing too damaging, I don't think. I mentioned that you played a Scarlatti piece for me."

"It was just something I heard—"

"On the radio," Aida interrupted. "So he said. What else have you heard on the radio, Jonah?"

"Umm, there was something by Schumann I thought was pretty good. I don't remember the name."

"Oh good. Do give it a go for us."

Jonah shrugged and returned to the piano. He sat quietly for a moment, and then started to play. He'd hit only a few notes before it was obvious he'd chosen well. Aida's expression softened and her eyes grew damp. Davoud grinned. Jonah was too busy to notice. When he finished, Aida was silent.

"You didn't like it?"

"Oh no, Jonah," said Aida, clearing her throat. "I liked it very much. Would you like to know what it's called?"

Jonah nodded. "Sure."

"That was Schumann's *Kinderscenen*, Scenes from Childhood, Opus 15, Number 1, *Von fremden Ländern und Menschen,* Of Foreign Lands and Peoples."

"Wow, I don't know if I'll remember all that."

Paul caught Davoud's grin and answered with one of his own. Jonah might not remember the name, but he'd remembered every note.

"Well, I think it's high time for some nourishment," said Aida. "Do you think Jonah's family would mind very much if we fed him?"

"My dad won't mind," said Jonah. "We hardly ever eat together anyway." He pulled a phone from his pocket. "I'll call him. I gotta go to the men's room. Be right back." He trotted in the direction of the back hall.

Paul started to put his guitar away. "That's very kind of you, Ms. Kazmi, but I better be heading home now. I have papers to grade."

"Oh no, Mr. Gaston. You must come as well. And you must call me Aida. Ms. Kazmi sounds like a *young* woman, and I am very old. So very very old." She waited until Paul had finished with the guitar and took his arm, whispering, "I think Davoud likes you. Do you like him?"

BRIGHT SUNLIGHT on his comforter made Davoud squint and blink. He'd overslept. He groaned and rolled over in bed, rehashing the previous night's outing. *It's happening. She's trying to set me up with Paul.* Thank goodness Jonah had gone to the men's room, so there was no one else present to witness his humiliation when she'd stage-whispered her question for Paul at a volume to reach the back rows. Fortunately or unfortunately, Davoud didn't quite know which, Paul's answer had been too soft to hear. Whatever he'd said, it had not deterred his mother. For heaven's sake, he'd not even been sure Paul was gay. He still wasn't, but it was apparent Paul was no bigot.

His mother had been her most charming throughout dinner, telling Paul and Jonah raunchy and appalling stories about the behavior of seemingly every opera star and conductor of the past fifty years. The stories were funny, but Davoud had heard them before, and he wasn't really in the mood to listen. Between his worries about the roof and the prospect of her continued interference in his private life, he was distracted and out of sorts. The only good thing about the evening had been the obvious pleasure she'd brought to Paul and Jonah.

Watching Paul laugh out loud, the lines in his face relaxed, his blue eyes wide open and shining, was a revelation. His interactions with Davoud prior to Jonah's arrival had been so stilted and sour, Davoud had not thought of Paul as having a sense of fun, but his easy laughter and outrageous flirting with Davoud's mother displayed another side of the man.

If Davoud didn't get up soon, he'd be late opening the shop. Rubbing the grit out of his eyes, he slid out of bed and padded to the bathroom, his bare feet chilly on the hardwood floor and colder still on the bathroom tile. It was nearly Thanksgiving, and the weather had finally turned. With the cold would come winter heating bills. His conversation with his mother about the roof had brought no relief to his financial worries. She was oblivious to his hints that Avakian Music had no resources to pay for the repair. Cranking the faucet, he stepped into the shower without waiting for the water to heat, shuddering at the touch of the cool water. He washed quickly as the shower came up to temperature, and then rinsed, reveling in the feel of the hot water on the back of his neck.

Reluctantly climbing out, Davoud stopped to look at himself in the full-length mirror that backed the bathroom door. There was something undignified about a six-foot-five-inch forty-year-old man with a thirty-inch waist. In school he'd been called "Davy, the human toothpick" and treated to suggestions that he join the circus to earn a living in the freak show.

Even his father, trying desperately to help him find something that fit for a school concert, had once muttered something about shopping for a toothpick. (In his father's defense, it was virtually impossible to find dress shirts with a fourteen-and-a-half inch neck and thirty-seven sleeve without visiting a specialty shop.) His father had been mortified to look up from the clothing rack to see tears in his son's eyes. Davy had no way of telling him that it wasn't the toothpick comment that had set him off, so much as his recent discovery of the ancient meaning of faggot—a bundle of sticks—and the realization that the contemporary meaning applied to him as well. Somehow faggot and toothpick were linked in Davoud's adolescent mind. Farhad Avakian had apologized profusely while Davy stood mute, unable to explain or comfort his father.

He'd been fifteen at the time, a full year into the three-year growth spurt during which he had seemingly been exposed to some kind of magnetic field that only allowed growth in a single direction. It started with his feet, which stretched to a toe-stubbing size twelve, and continued with his hands. It wasn't long before he received the first of annual invitations to try out for the basketball team—nonstarters all. There was no way Davoud was going to expose himself in the locker room more than required for gym class. The teasing about his build was bad enough; the thought of what would happen if the sight of showering boys loosed a stick from his bundle was mortifying.

Where was the filling out that was supposed to happen as you matured? Perhaps it was a form of self-flagellation, but Davoud still used the same belt his father had given him for Christmas on his sixteenth birthday. Regular applications of shoe black and brass polish kept the belt looking new enough. Since that year, he'd moved the prong of his belt buckle exactly two holes. He had, in fact, gained twenty pounds since his seventeenth birthday. He attributed that to additional muscle on his arms and thighs, and a slight broadening of his shoulders, but his torso still looked like he'd been caught in a taffy machine. He lifted a leg to dry himself and caught sight of his scrotum. His balls couldn't actually be shrinking, could they? Did that happen when you aged? It had to be the chilly temperature since he'd turned down the heat in his apartment. Thankfully, his home phone rang before he foundered in an investigation of this new indignity. He scrambled to dry himself and answer.

"Mr. Avakian? It's John Winfield, Jonah's father. Is this a bad time? I want to speak to you about my son."

Davoud squeezed the handset between his neck and shoulder, freeing a hand to secure his towel around his hips. The device slid off his shoulder and he grabbed for it with both hands. The towel slid to the floor, leaving him stark naked in the chilly kitchen. "No problem, Mr. Winfield. What can I do for you?"

"It was kind of your mother to invite Jonah to dinner. Please express my gratitude to Ms. Kazmi when you see her next. He could speak of nothing else when he got home. I had no idea that Ms. Kazmi was your mother. I've enjoyed her recordings for years."

Davoud shivered as he felt a rivulet of cold water make its way from the back of his neck down his spine. "Thank you. I'll tell her you called." John Winfield fancied opera? Perhaps it was not entirely a fluke that his son was a talented musician. He didn't understand how his mother managed, without fail, to be gracious to her fans. He was certain celebrity would exhaust him. "Was there something else, Mr. Winfield?"

"My son didn't bring his saxophone home last night. He was evasive when I asked him about it. He said he'd left it at the music store. I don't know what's going on with Jonah. He's been so moody. I just wanted to make sure everything's okay. He didn't damage the instrument, did he?"

This was exactly the sort of question Davoud had feared when he'd heard that Paul had agreed to keep the vandalism of Jonah's saxophone case a secret. On the other hand, it was Jonah's right to tell his father when he felt ready. "Oh, no. The saxophone is fine." It was a lie by omission, but what choice did he have? He could only pray that Jonah and his father would talk soon.

Winfield's sigh was audible over the phone. "I see. Maybe I'm imagining things. It's been hard on Jonah with his mother gone so much lately...."

"Jonah is a fine young man, Mr. Winfield. He's at a difficult age, but I'm sure he'll navigate it with grace." Davoud was now shuddering uncontrollably from the cold.

"You've been very kind to allow my son to practice on your Steinway, Mr. Avakian. I didn't want to forget to thank you."

Davoud was going to have to get a wireless phone, one that would reach into the bedroom—if he didn't die of pneumonia first. "It's a pleasure to hear him play. He's remarkably talented. Have you considered arranging lessons for him?"

Winfield was silent long enough for Davoud to wonder if he'd offended the man. He was shivering so much, he was afraid he'd drop the phone before Winfield answered. When the man finally responded, his voice was tight. "I'm afraid our finances don't allow for many luxuries."

"I didn't mean to pry, Mr. Winfield. I'm sure Jonah doesn't feel the loss."

When Winfield finally hung up the phone, Davoud fairly leapt for his room and the clothes laid out on the bed.

PAUL PEERED from his bedroom window at marbled gray skies and slanting rain. Retreating to bed, he considered skipping his morning run. Long habit won out after a couple of drowsy minutes of internal debate, and he dragged himself out of bed and into his running gear. Outfitted in full-length tights and a breathable shell, he squished down the damp gravel path by the river, thinking about the previous day's events.

Jonah hadn't acknowledged it, but his tormentors clearly thought he was gay. Although Jonah was small and delicately featured, his sexual preference didn't seem obvious to Paul. Aida's stories about the opera world had given the boy an opportunity to say something if he'd wanted to out himself, but he hadn't. Nevertheless, it seemed like progress to know something about why Jonah was being attacked. Maybe time and tolerance from the adults around him would help the kid open up.

What a kick it had been to meet Ms. Kazmi—Aida. She was a delight; her combustible moods—a single story might encompass many—were an entertainment designed for the pleasure of her companions. Davoud was a surprise too. He'd obviously not relished Aida's interference in his private life, but there was something attractive about his efforts to include Jonah in the conversation and help him feel at ease. The man was genuinely kind. Not bad-looking either, with big dark eyes, crow's feet, and long bones. What would it be like to kiss him? Damned if he wasn't getting hard at the thought. He laughed out loud and shook his head, sending a shower of droplets flying around him. Good thing there weren't many runners out in the foul weather or he'd be making a spectacle of himself.

Aida couldn't possibly think Davoud was interested. Paul knew his behavior toward Davoud, until recently, wouldn't have impressed a man with such an old-fashioned sense of courtesy. He could fantasize, though, couldn't he? Maybe their mutual interest in Jonah would bring them together again, and he could try to redeem himself. He hoped so.

AFTER HIS morning history class, Paul retrieved his lunch from the desk drawer and leaned back in his office chair. Stretching his legs, he put his feet on the scarred surface of his desk—the same crudely made oak piece that had been in the office when he started at Martin Luther King High School. He shifted until his buttocks fit into the shallow depressions scooped from the hard seat. How many predecessors had thinned their trousers on its unforgiving surface? While the current school had been built in the '70s, he was fairly certain the furniture dated from the previous building. His lighthearted mood lasted until the noon bell, which was followed by a more modern chime from his smartphone.

"Gaston speaking."

"Hi, Paul, it's Davoud."

"Hey, Davoud, it's good to hear from you. Please convey my thanks to your mother for dinner last night. I can't tell you how much I enjoyed meeting her."

"I'm certain the feeling was mutual."

Did Paul detect a note of irony? If so, it seemed uncharacteristic of the man. "Are you calling about the case? Were you able to make any progress on the paint this morning?"

"No, I was not."

Did Davoud mean he hadn't made any progress or he hadn't called about the case? Paul waited for the man to signal his intent. When the silence on the other end grew long, he hastened to add, "I didn't mean to hurry you. Jonah can play keyboards in Jazz Ensemble for a few days. It'll be good for the group."

"I'm sure his flexibility is an asset."

Again, Paul waited for the man to get to the point.

Davoud sighed, and Paul heard a muffled sound like Davoud had shifted the phone from one hand to the other. "Are you sure it's a good idea to keep the nature of Jonah's trouble from his father? He called this morning to ask about Jonah's saxophone. I didn't mention the case, but I was uncomfortable dissembling. Do you plan to talk to Jonah about it?"

"I kind of hoped he'd come... to one of us. That he'd feel comfortable enough to talk to someone."

"That would be best, but I worry that it might make matters worse for Jonah if Mr. Winfield finds out we've not been straight with him."

Paul dropped his feet to the floor with a thump. This dancing around was stupid. Was Davoud's pun meant as a joke? It was so difficult to read the man. "Davoud, I'm trying to do right by Jonah. What do you suggest?"

"Perhaps I'm making too much of this. You've had more contact with Winfield. Do you think him likely to blame Jonah for his troubles?"

Paul's impatience got the better of him. "You mean for being gay."

"That, or for being less... manly than he would like, regardless of his sexuality."

The conversation had rapidly turned irritating. It was one thing to question your own decisions. It was quite another to have them questioned by someone else, especially someone who had such difficulty expressing himself directly. "Honestly, I don't know. He seemed pretty rigid about punishing Jonah for hitting the other boy, but I don't know what to make of that."

"I see. Well, thank you for your time."

"You're welcome." Paul disconnected, wishing he hadn't answered in the first place. Davoud was right in thinking they walked a balance beam, but the only thing to do was to question Jonah again. Jonah wouldn't welcome that. He tossed his lunch back into the drawer. A walk would do him more good at this point than a hummus and bean sprout sandwich.

CHARLIE WONG stuck his head into Paul's history class at the end of fourth period to ask for a consult after school. After Charlie left, Paul gathered his papers and headed for the band room, his mood spiraling downward. He could think of two things Charlie might want to discuss: next year's class schedule or Jonah. Paul's thoughts on teaching another subject besides music or history had been paralyzed before Jonah's problem surfaced. Since then, he'd managed to ignore the issue entirely. Charlie's suggestion that he teach AP English hadn't grown more appealing over time. He knew other Martin Luther King High teachers, most of whom already taught a full course load of academic subjects, wouldn't sympathize, but he hated the idea of another stack of papers to grade every night. He wasn't a lazy teacher. He knew he'd spend the summer boning up on his new subject and the fall dutifully grading papers. No, the real issue was that his most satisfying interactions with students were in his music classes. He had something special to offer there, and his students felt it too.

A discussion of Jonah's problem was even less welcome. If he didn't mention the saxophone case, Charlie could accuse him of both dishonesty and insubordination, since he'd asked to be notified of further incidents. If he told Charlie, Jonah would feel betrayed. Reaching the band room, he tossed his briefcase onto the desk and ran a hand through his hair. It was past time for a haircut—or a new job.

"Hey, Mr. G. How're they hanging?" Billy Preston bopped into the office like he was auditioning for a reality show.

"Hi, Billy."

"You going to be on time today? I wouldn't want to have to write you up for tardiness."

"I haven't been that bad lately."

Billy raised an imperious eyebrow, looking uncannily like Margaret Thatcher addressing an auditorium of Labour MPs.

Paul rolled his eyes. "I'll be over in a minute. Is Jonah there yet? I have to speak to him."

"I'll send him over. This gonna take long? Should I get 'em started on something?"

"Thanks, Billy. That'd be a help."

Billy trotted out. A minute later, Jonah poked his head into the room cautiously. "What's up, Mr. G?"

"Have a seat."

Jonah sat gingerly on the edge of the chair beside Paul's desk.

"I have to apologize to you, Jonah. I did something stupid the other day, and now I've got to fix it."

Jonah looked at him warily. "What do you mean?"

"I told you I wouldn't mention the saxophone case to anyone. I shouldn't have said that. Mr. Wong has asked to speak to me, and I can't afford to lie to him. He asked me to inform him of any further incidents involving you and your, uh, friends."

Jonah tapped an angry rhythm on his knee. "I thought I could trust you."

"I'm really sorry, Jonah, but I could lose my job if I lie to Mr. Wong."

"My dad is gonna fucking think I'm gay."

Paul wanted to ask whether Winfield would be right.

"Would it help if I let you go early? Your father works at home, right? You could talk with him before I meet with Mr. Wong." He was pretty sure Winfield was currently unemployed, but homemaking was work, right?

"He'll be mad I didn't tell him yesterday."

"For what it's worth, I'm in trouble with Davoud too. Your father called him this morning to ask about your saxophone."

Jonah seemed to shrink into himself. "Fuckity fuck fuck fuck." He matched his profanity to the beat of his tapping. "I suppose he already told my dad."

"As a matter of fact, he didn't. But I think he was pissed that he had to lie by omission."

"He's not gonna let me play the Steinway anymore, is he?"

"He's not mad at you, Jonah. If anything, he's disappointed in me."

Jonah looked up, the movement of his hand slowing. "It's my fault, isn't it? I should never have asked you to keep quiet."

"Don't give yourself a hard time. I'm the one who screwed up, not you. I should have known better."

"What's Wong gonna do? Maybe I could talk to him. Tell him it wasn't your idea."

"It's solid of you to offer, Jonah, but I think I've got to deal with this on my own."

CHARLIE ALIGNED the pens on his desk, his expression glum. "I can't say I'm not disappointed, Paul."

Paul combed a hand though his hair, and then made himself drop it to his lap. It wouldn't help for him to go around with a wannabe mohawk. "You're not the only one. I can't excuse it. It's just that Jonah was so upset, I didn't want to make it worse. I agreed not to say anything without thinking it through."

"Does Jonah's father know about the case?"

"I sent Jonah home to speak with him. I thought it only fair he have the chance before you call."

"I see." Charlie stared out the window of his office into the center courtyard. Paul followed his gaze. The single ancient hickory that shaded the courtyard in summer was bare of leaves, the shadows formed by its branches stark in the late autumn sun. "I'm not inclined to think this lapse warrants a reprimand. You've taken corrective action on your own. But I am disappointed at your lack of judgment. I'm going to have to call Mr. Winfield and apologize for not informing him of the incident yesterday." He turned back to examine Paul. "I don't know that I can protect you, if he chooses to complain to the district."

"Maybe it's just as well."

Charlie narrowed his eyes. "Paul, you're not thinking of quitting over this? It was a mistake, but nothing to end a career over."

"It's not just this business with Jonah. It's the budget cuts in the music program, having to teach something new. I don't know that I have it in me."

"Paul, you get some of the best teacher evaluations in the school, and not just in your music classes. Why would you throw that away?"

"The music classes are where I can make a difference." Paul took a breath. "It's more than that. I need the music. It keeps me sane."

"Have you thought about my suggestion? You might find AP English more satisfying than you think."

"I'm not sure I have the patience to read student compositions."

"You already read their history papers." Charlie frowned. "What else would you do?"

"I got gigs as a studio musician when I lived in Chicago."

"Enough to live on? Wouldn't you miss the teaching?"

"I'd miss Jonah."

Charlie's normally plastic face lost expression until his skin seemed draped on a mannequin's head. "We don't have a bigger problem here, do we?"

Paul was shocked that Charlie could even think such a thing. He stared, unable to respond to the insinuation. "Jonah is my *student.* I would never... I don't even... what must you think of me to...."

Charlie shook his head and blinked. "I'm sorry, Paul. I have no cause to suggest any impropriety on your part."

Charlie's apology came quickly, but Paul was still shaken. So much for the question whether Charlie knew he was gay. He left the principal's office more unsettled about his future than ever.

THE BUS pulled to a stop where a man and two women stood frozen, their faces obscured by scarves and hats, apparently too wrapped up in their thoughts to step back or signal the bus driver to go on. When no one boarded, the driver closed the doors and drove on, muttering. The middle-aged black man had given Jonah a dirty look when he got on, as if to ask what he was doing out of school in the middle of the afternoon. Why the fuck couldn't everyone just leave him alone? Why did they have to get up in his business? He'd just wanted a little more time to be his father's boy before they had The Talk—the talk he'd known was coming for months, the talk that smelled of ozone before a storm. Was it selfish to want to delay until he could put a name to his condition without his gut clenching? Everything would change. Whatever his reaction, his dad would never see him the same way again. His easy friendship with Mr. G—his first with an adult where he felt himself on something close to an equal footing—that would change too. No matter how tolerant his father and his music teacher might be, they would see him differently, as someone he didn't yet know how to be.

How had Antony known what he himself had only barely begun to understand? He noticed boys and not girls, but it wasn't like he'd ever done something stupid like trying to kiss a guy. Had they caught him staring at some guy's crotch? He seldom let himself look at anyone for long, girl or boy, for fear they'd notice. Did other people see him as Antony and Justin did? The thought made him want to hurl.

Jonah yanked the cable to signal for a stop. The cable sprang back into place with a loud snap. He looked down the aisle and saw the bus driver's eyes in the mirror. He went to the back door and waited until the bus ground to a halt and the door opened before giving the man the finger, knowing even as he did it that he'd be embarrassed next time he saw the guy. He might as well get used to the feeling.

Reaching the house, he unlocked the door and shoved it open, knowing his father would hear and want to know what he was doing home early. "Hi, Dad, it's me."

His dad met him in the foyer while Jonah was hanging up his coat. He looked like he'd just woken from a nap, his button-down shirt rumpled, his feet bare. "Jonah, what's going on? Why aren't you at school?"

"I have to tell you something. Mr. G sent me home to talk to you."

"What happened? Did something happen at school?"

"Nothing happened. Well, nothing happened today. I just need to…." He stopped talking, his throat dry.

His dad blinked and his sleepy, irritated look changed to concern. "What's wrong, Jonah? Why did Mr. Gaston send you home?" When Jonah didn't answer, he put an arm over Jonah's shoulders and steered him toward the kitchen. Jonah sagged into his dad's embrace, wanting to believe it wasn't the last time he'd be able to do so. "You feel cold. Would you like some hot chocolate?"

"Thanks, Dad." His stomach felt sour and wobbly, but he welcomed the reprieve.

His dad sat him down at the table and got a tin of cocoa powder out of the cabinet. He never bought hot chocolate mix, but made his own hot chocolate out of cocoa power, sugar, and whole milk. When Jonah was little, it had been a special treat on Sunday mornings, before they went to Mass. Jonah still associated the taste of chocolate with the musty smells of wet wool and old hymnals.

When his father finished, he set mugs at Jonah's and his own place and sat down. "Watch out, it's very hot."

Jonah lifted the mug and blew on the surface of the liquid, concentric rings spreading from the center. His father sipped, watching Jonah. Jonah put the chocolate down, unable to taste it.

"You know how I left my saxophone at Avakian Music yesterday?"

"Yes, I called Mr. Avakian to ask about it."

"He told you it was fine, right?"

"Yes, he did."

"It's not his fault. I asked him not to say anything."

"Say anything about what?"

Jonah took a shaky breath. "Somebody painted something on the case while it was in Mr. G's office. I tried to get it off, but Mr. G said I was just smearing it around and I should take it to Mr. Avakian to see if he could get it off. If it won't come off, we'll probably have to pay for the case, and they're really expensive, like three hundred dollars or something. I'm sorry, Dad, I know we can't afford to buy—"

"Why did you ask Mr. Avakian not to tell me about the case?" The vertical lines between his dad's eyebrows got deeper. "If somebody did it while the case was in Mr. Gaston's office, it wasn't your fault."

"No, it wasn't my fault. I just tried to get the paint off, but it was already dry and I—"

"Hold up, Jonah. I'm trying to understand. Why did you tell Mr. Avakian not to say anything? Because of the expense? We're not so bad off that we can't manage somehow, even if we have to put aside a little every month until we can replace the case. You'll be using it for another couple of years, right?"

"But I can't... I can't use it anymore."

"Why not? What's a little paint? What did they put on—"

"*Faggot*, Dad. They put 'Faggot' right on the side of the case, in big letters." Jonah watched his father's face, hardly able to breathe. His dad wasn't stupid. Whatever else he was, John Winfield was not stupid. Jonah watched his father's expression change from concerned to something different. Not mad, not hurt, but defeated. He looked defeated, like the day he'd come home and told them he'd lost his job. Jonah feared that look more than any other.

"I'm sorry, Dad. I'm sorry."

"It's not your fault." Jonah watched tears form in his dad's eyes. "It's not your fault."

CHAPTER 4

DAVOUD WAS updating the accounting software in his office when he heard the front door jingle. *Let it be a new customer wanting a French horn or a piano, something new-roof expensive.*

"Davoud, it's Paul," yelled Marta from her spot behind the register. "Should I send him in?"

A shiver traveled Davoud's spine, whether out of association with the morning's chilly call or from something else, he wasn't sure. He shoved his keyboard out of the way and tried to look more relaxed than he felt. "Send him in."

"Hi, Davoud." Paul opened the door tentatively. "I'm not interrupting?"

"Just bookkeeping. I should thank you for the break. Are you and Jonah looking for another jam session?"

"No, Jonah's not here." Paul looked around the small space curiously, his gaze skittering off the bookshelves and file cabinets without resting. "I came to apologize for screwing up and putting you in an awkward position with John Winfield this morning." His trim frame slumped against the door, and he thrust a hand through his short, strawberry blond hair, leaving it sticking up in tufts. "I had to tell Wong about Jonah's saxophone case today. I'm afraid neither of them are happy with me right now."

Davoud couldn't help feeling sympathetic. "I was afraid that wouldn't end well."

"I'm sorry I got you caught up in it."

Davoud tried to smile reassuringly. "Don't concern yourself. I don't imagine Winfield will take his business elsewhere. I hope Jonah isn't having too hard a time of it."

"I sent him home to talk to his father."

Paul looked so distraught, Davoud found himself wanting to comfort the man. "I hope you won't think me too forward, but would you consider joining me for dinner tonight?" When Paul didn't answer right away, he continued. "I was just going to grill a chicken breast and toss it into a salad. I can add another."

After a frozen moment, Paul came to life like a marionette whose strings had been plucked. "Thanks, but I should probably be getting home. Papers to grade...."

Davoud hoped his keen disappointment wasn't too obvious. "It's no trouble, really. I'd enjoy the company."

"I can't believe you're so forgiving."

"You were trying to save Jonah some heartache. I should blame you for that?"

"You keep surprising me. I don't know what to think."

"How so?"

"You're kind."

Davoud snorted. "You don't expect kindness? Never mind what that says about you. Do I look mean-tempered? I assure you, I feel that way sometimes. Ask Marta."

"A surly bear, our Davoud," Marta commented dryly from the other room.

"Marta, don't you have work to do?"

"Listening to the two of you is way more fun."

Paul's face pinked to match his hair.

Davoud affected bearish irritation. "You have embarrassed my guest. I must fire you now."

"Yeah, and who's going to sit out here all day while you dally with the handsome customers?"

Davoud shrugged. "She's right, Paul, I can't do without her. Come upstairs and have a glass of wine at least. You look like you could use a drink."

Davoud was relieved to see Paul smile. "Okay."

PAUL TRIED to compose himself, but Davoud's invitation, just when he thought he'd completely blown it with the man, had him flustered. *Exeunt the villain*, enter… someone else.

"This is really nice of you," he said, as Davoud ushered him from the shop. They stepped through an inside door into a dimly lit elevator lobby decorated in cracked marble and cherry wainscoting. He instinctively moved to the nearest of the twin elevators.

Davoud took his arm and steered him to the other. "I'm afraid we only keep one running anymore." Keeping hold of Paul's arm, he fished a set of keys from his pocket and fitted one into a slot below the call button. When the elevator arrived, he pointed at the old-fashioned manual control from the period when elevators had operators. "We left the old control lever in place when we renovated, but it docsn't do anything anymore. Just use the buttons like you would anywhere else, but make sure to close the cage first or the elevator won't move."

Davoud's hand was hot on Paul's forearm. He swallowed and tried to distract himself by examining the building. It was, in truth, more than worthy of the attention. The elevator was ornate, with iron grillwork, brass controls, and a tin ceiling. He wondered about the three stories above Avakian Music. Were there private apartments? He knew the building had once been a small hotel. *Hotel Karton* was engraved on the stone frieze above the front entrance. The odd configuration of the first floor showed that nothing in the building had been designed for its present use. Avakian Music had been in Glen Falls for Paul's entire life, but he'd never given its history any thought. "You can't be the first Avakian to run Avakian Music."

"No, my great-grandmother bought the building in the Great Depression, after she moved her family from Iran."

Paul's grasp of Iranian history or culture was sketchy at best. "Was it typical for an Iranian woman to take a leadership role in the family in those days?" The elevator stopped, and Davoud pushed open the gate. He guided Paul to a door marked 2A. Unlocking it, he urged Paul into the foyer of an elegantly appointed apartment straight out of a magazine advertisement from the '50s.

"I don't think anything about my great-grandmother could be called typical. She came from a wealthy, worldly Persian family with ties to the Qajar dynasty. She was educated at La Sorbonne in Paris and eventually became a soprano at the Paris Opera. Before the crash of '29, she toured the United States as a soloist and met my great-grandfather, who was a first violin with the Chicago Symphony. The family legend is that they didn't plan to have a family, but the rhythm method...." Davoud grinned. "Anyway, along came my grandfather. It was something of a scandal. My great-grandmother was forced to marry and quit her career to raise her son. But I'm being impolite. May I offer you a drink?" Without waiting for an answer, Davoud disappeared into the kitchen. "I have red wine and... red wine. I'm sorry, I don't often entertain."

Paul laughed. "I'd love a glass. You were telling me about your great-grandmother. She sounds like quite a woman."

"Yes. I must interject a little Persian history here. In 1921, the Qajar dynasty was overthrown in a military coup. In '25, Reza Khan was established as Shah of Iran, and my family found themselves out of favor. So when my great-grandmother married, she decided to import her family to the States to help her raise her child. I imagine my great-grandfather found it rather overwhelming—all these new Persian relatives with an aversion to speaking English, because they associated it with the British Imperialists."

"How many did she bring over?" asked Paul, amazed.

"Let's see, there were her parents, her brother, and a sister—that's four, plus her sister's husband and two children. You can see why they decided to purchase the hotel."

"I don't suppose you have a picture? I would love to see what she looked like."

"Many, but I'm afraid they're upstairs in my mother's apartment."

It struck Paul as odd that Davoud had not asked his mother for any photographs for his own living quarters. The apartment was furnished with a fortune's worth of worn antique furniture and art, but there was little sign of the rich family history Davoud described. No pictures rested on the mantel of the disused fireplace. The only indications of the family's Persian heritage were the intricately patterned rugs that covered the floor of the sitting room, two-deep in some places. A huge velvet sofa held pride of place in the center of the room.

"How did your family come to settle in Glen Falls?"

"My great-grandmother couldn't bear to give up music, so she accepted a teaching position at the college."

Paul sipped his wine. "That was when they founded Avakian Music?"

"That was my great-grandfather's idea. In the '30s, the symphony didn't pay particularly well. With great-grandmother off the circuit and making only a modest income as a teacher, they had to find some way to pay upkeep on the Music Box." He waved a finger in a circle to indicate the building. "The idea was to use my great-grandmother's fame and reputation to attract private students and sell instruments to them. But the Depression meant very few families could afford to buy instruments."

Davoud caught Paul's gaze and winked. "It wasn't until my grandfather hit upon the idea of renting instruments that the business became profitable."

Paul cringed at the mention of the rental business, embarrassed that he had questioned Davoud's part in that family tradition. He felt like a teenager on a first date, self-conscious and a little giddy. "Was he the one who started the tradition of the annual instrument selection?"

"He and my father sort of fell into that."

"I had no idea your family had such an interesting history."

Davoud didn't answer, but sipped his wine, his eyes on Paul.

"So you took over from your father?"

"I should like to hear something about your family."

Paul felt his family background inadequate in the face of Davoud's colorful history. He didn't normally talk about his parents or grandmother, but he knew it would be impolite to deflect the question entirely. "I was a military brat. Born in Germany. My father was stationed there in the early '60s. I never knew him. He was posted to Vietnam in '72, the year I was born, and died there during his first deployment."

"You were raised by your mother? Did she remarry?"

"No, she… she died when I was ten. I was mostly raised by my grandmother." Paul saw a flash of emotion in Davoud's eyes and looked away, lest it be pity. He did not want to be pitied by this man. "My grandmother was the one who got me interested in jazz."

"I might have preferred her over my grandmother."

Paul was surprised to hear such a statement from Davoud. "Why?" he blurted.

"I was mostly raised by my grandmother as well. Aida chose not to give up her career when I was born, so I saw her between engagements and on holidays. My grandmother Agnes was a music snob. She forbade me listen to or play jazz—or anything too modern." Davoud chuckled grimly. "Stravinsky was too modern for her. She refused to acknowledge the existence of rock and roll, country, or any other form of popular music."

Paul smiled as he pictured a fierce woman leading Parisian rioters over the barricades, after Stravinsky introduced the *Le Sacre du Printemps*, the Rite of Spring. But that had been back in 1913. Maybe the lack of family pictures was a remnant of Davoud's adolescent rebellion.

Davoud waved in the direction of the kitchen. "Are you hungry?" He refilled Paul's wine and rose without waiting for an answer. "It won't take long to make a salad. You really must stay. Make yourself at home while I pull things together."

"All right. You've convinced me."

Davoud grinned and trotted to the kitchen. Paul looked around the apartment while he listened to the cheerful sound of Davoud banging around. The only real concession to comfort was the velvet monstrosity in which he lounged. Outside a pair of large windows, Paul saw the Corinthian-columned streetlamps of Main Street. Rain slanted down through the yellow halos of the flame-shaped glass fixtures.

"Why don't you turn on some music?" Davoud called out from the kitchen.

Paul looked around for a stereo and noticed for the first time that there was no television in the sitting room. A tall bookshelf occupied the wall on one side of the fireplace. Shelves on the other side held CDs and an elegant European sound system. The CDs revealed a surprisingly eclectic mix of classical, jazz, be-bop, and even bluegrass. "Anything in particular you'd like to hear?"

"Pick something you like."

Paul nervously picked out a CD of Leonard Bernstein conducting Aaron Copland's *Symphony No. 3, Quiet City.*

At the first shimmering notes from the violins, Davoud called from the kitchen. "You are a man after my own heart."

Paul laughed silently in relief. It was ridiculous how much he wanted to impress this man. He settled into the sofa to sip his wine and lose himself in Copland's calming tones.

DAVOUD LOOKED up from his inventory at the tinkle of the doorbell and was surprised to see Jonah marching toward the counter. He stared for a second before he realized what was different about the boy: Jonah had put something in his hair to give it bright highlights and combed it with gel too, so it stood in spikes. He glanced at the wall clock above the entrance. It was shortly after noon on a school day. "Hi, Jonah, I didn't expect to see you here at this time of day. What can I do for you?"

"I want my saxophone back."

"Of course, but I haven't had time to clean the case yet. I can give it a try this evening if you'd like to wait until tomorrow."

Jonah's mouth formed a firm line. "I don't want you to clean it. I want my saxophone back."

"You're sure about this?"

Jonah nodded.

"As you wish. Would you mind watching the register while I get it from the storage room? Marta's at lunch."

Jonah's shoulders relaxed visibly. "Sure, Mr. Avakian."

"I thought you were going to call me Davoud."

"Oh yeah. Sure, Davoud."

Davoud opened the hinged counter top and brushed a finger over Jonah's hair as he went past.

Jonah ducked his head. "Hey, no touching the do."

"Sorry, thought you were wearing some kind of fur hat there for a second."

JONAH SHOVED his saxophone through the crowded corridor like a battering ram, Faggot-side out for the world to see. Let the fuckers say something. He came around the corner leading to his locker and saw Billy slumped against the wall.

Billy jerked like he'd put his finger into a socket when he saw the saxophone case. "Dude!"

"Want to make something of it?"

"No way, but...." Billy waved his hands around. "Dude! You've got balls. Aren't you afraid people are gonna think you're gay?"

"What if they do? None of their fucking business."

Billy narrowed his eyes. "You do something to your hair?"

"I figured if I was gonna...."

Billy went goggle-eyed and dragged Jonah into an empty classroom. "Are you coming out, man?"

"What if I am?" Jonah's throat was so constricted he could barely hiss the words.

"Wow!" Billy stared at him like he'd grown a horn in his forehead. Jonah all but stopped breathing. Billy shook his head sadly. "You're gonna need new clothes."

Jonah sucked in a ragged breath. "Maybe you could help...."

"You have got to be kidding, man. I'm way too fond of pointy, squishy parts to help you out there." Billy mimed squeezing something in front of him. "You need someone who bats for your team." He put a hand on Jonah's neck and pushed him down the hall. "Come on, we're gonna be late for Jazz Ensemble."

Jonah hoped his disappointment didn't show on his face. It would have to be enough to have a friend who didn't give a hoot whether he liked dicks or boobs.

When they got to the band room, Jonah was careful to place his saxophone case Faggot-side up. He got his horn out and looked around to see if anyone had noticed. He watched Janelle, the tenor player who sat next to him, catch sight of the word on the case. She glanced at him, eyes wide, but looked away quickly, without saying anything. Mr. G came in and dumped his score on the music stand in front of him and scanned faces to see if everyone was ready. When he reached Jonah, he froze for an instant, almost imperceptibly, his expression unreadable. "Great! Let's get started."

After rehearsal, Mr. G came over and nodded at Jonah. "Would you mind stepping into my office for a second, Jonah?"

Jonah finished putting his sax away and followed his teacher into the office across the hall.

"Have a seat." Mr. G looked at Jonah as if he weren't quite sure where to start. "I just... I don't want to invade your privacy, so you can tell me if you don't want to...." He pushed his hair back. "You know, I really suck at this."

"It's okay. I got the saxophone back from Davoud at lunch. I don't want to pretend that nothing's going on anymore."

"That's good. Actually, that's pretty amazing. I'm proud of you."

"It's not like the shitheads gave me much choice."

"I take it you spoke to your father."

"Yeah."

"You know I'm available if you ever need to—"

"It sucked."

Mr. G puffed out a breath. "I'm sorry. He didn't—"

"Don't worry, he didn't yell at me or anything. He's not like that."

Mr. G watched him for a minute. When Jonah didn't continue, he nodded. "Nice hair. You going for a new look?"

"You know, I've had more comments about the hair than the damn case."

Mr. G grimaced. "It's a whole lot easier to talk about, isn't it?"

Jonah laughed. "Yeah, I guess."

"You know the boys who have been harassing you? Mr. Wong still needs to know who they are."

"Wong can—"

"Jonah! Don't go there. Mr. Wong is only doing his job, and you haven't exactly made that easy." Mr. G waited expectantly. The late autumn light coming through the grimy windowpanes was kind of depressing. Jonah wished it were summer and he didn't have to think about stupid SOBs who couldn't keep their fists to themselves and principals who didn't believe a guy could deal with his own shit.

That morning, his dad had gotten up to cook him his favorite breakfast of blueberry waffles. When Jonah came into the kitchen and his dad saw the new highlights in his hair, he raised his eyebrows, but he turned back to his waffle iron without comment. When the waffles were ready, they passed butter and maple syrup back and forth, still not talking. Finally, Jonah asked his father when his mom was coming home. That was a conversation to anticipate. *Hi Mom, guess what, I'm gay and I'm being bullied at school. Think I've got a civil rights case? Suppose you could stay in town long enough to file a brief?*

"I'm not… I don't know, Jonah. She said she needed a few more days to—"

"Never mind."

That was when he'd decided to get the goddamn case back from Avakian. *What the hell, let's have our own fucking coming-out bash, no invitations required.*

Jonah focused on his teacher's lean face, which already showed red whiskers along its prominent jawline. Faggot or no faggot, there was no fucking way he was telling Mr. G what Antony had said about them. "It's not gonna help, is it?" he answered. "They'll just get mad and the whole fucking shit-bag will get bigger and more stinky."

Mr. G winced. "Jonah, you know me, I'm not one to give students a hard time about their language, but do you think you could at least keep the volume down when you're swearing in my office?"

"Sorry, Mr. G."

DAVOUD STABBED at the inventory form he was filling out and broke his pencil lead. He sighed and rooted around in his desk drawer for a pencil sharpener. The sheet music inventory confirmed what his monthly sales figures had already told him: they were selling very little sheet music. The scores they did sell were mostly bought by four or five regular customers in town who owned pianos and actually played them. Sheet music was definitely not a profit center for Avakian Music. If he counted the overhead and calculated a per-square-foot cost for the floor space, the store was losing money on it. Yet he'd always prided himself on the fact that Avakian Music carried the best selection of sheet music in the state. Doing away with the collection smelled of failure—rather like his mother's dining room.

When he'd talked to Aida about the roof, he hadn't mentioned the larger problem of the shop's declining revenues. His mother's response wasn't encouraging. Davoud thought about breaking it to the whole family after the Thanksgiving turkey. Maybe a dose of tryptophan would serve to keep the discussion civil. Since his mother had returned, Davoud's thoughts had circled around and around the money issue until he was dizzy with the effort, but he still felt unable to strike out in any one direction.

Throwing down the broken pencil, he decided a walk might clear his head. "Marta! I'm going out. Will you keep an eye on things?"

"Who's the lucky fellow?" Marta yelled back.

He shrugged on his overcoat and went out into the sales floor. "I'm taking a walk."

"Okay, chief. Say hello to the squirrels for me." Marta looked up from her novel and squinted at him. "Everything okay?"

"I just need some air."

Davoud stooped to pick up an old burger wrapper in front of the shop. Were people cleanlier in the past, or did he just notice their messes more now? He could not remember ever throwing a piece of trash on the street. What was going on in the heads of people who did that? Did they want to live in a garbage heap?

"Hi, Davoud," said a warm voice from behind. "On your way somewhere?"

He jerked upright. "Paul! You startled me."

Paul, in khaki slacks and a polo shirt, shifted his guitar nervously from hand to hand. "Sorry, I was just coming by to see if I could interest you in a cup of coffee."

Davoud felt the tension slide from his shoulders. "You could." He greedily took in the smile on Paul's striking face. "How about getting it to go and taking a walk along the river?"

"Sure, if I can leave the guitar in the shop."

They each got a latté from the café across Main Street and sipped them as they crunched down the gravel path. Paul seemed less talkative than usual, but companionable in his silence. Davoud's thoughts returned to his financial woes. "Do you suppose there's money to be made in the coffee shops that are springing up all over the place?"

"You thinking of changing businesses?"

"Sometimes I wish...." He trailed off, unsure how to continue.

Paul turned to examine him. "What do you wish?"

Davoud shrugged helplessly. "I love Avakian Music, but it was my father's, and his father's before. I don't know that I'm very good at managing it."

"Rent a 'bone, sell a score, score a sale. What's to know?"

Davoud was sure Paul was just trying keep the conversation light, but the comment stung anyway. "How about how to make money."

Paul winced. "I didn't mean... I'm sorry, Davoud. Are you... never mind, it's none of my business." His confusion would have been endearing on a better day.

"It's okay. I'm just out of sorts today. I don't mean to burden you."

"No, please. I'm just an idiot whose mouth is not always attached to his brain."

Davoud watched a gaggle of geese take flight from the edge of the river. "I've never done anything else but run the shop, and my family is resistant to any change. Sometimes I feel as though they've fitted me with a straitjacket."

"I wouldn't know about family problems."

Davoud laughed in disbelief. "You really must work on your conversational skills."

Paul flushed, but didn't answer. They watched in silence as the geese circled around and splashed back where they'd been before Paul and Davoud had disturbed them with their passing.

"Have you ever thought of having a family?" Davoud wasn't sure what unconscious process generated the question or how it managed to bypass his conversational filter, but he was genuinely curious about the answer. When Paul didn't reply, he continued, "You could have a family if you wanted one. You're young. You could adopt."

"I'm not young. I'm only a few years younger than you."

Davoud watched the realization of what he'd said hit his friend. He knew he shouldn't tease, but he couldn't keep from smiling.

Paul shook his head. "I've done it again, haven't I? I'm hopeless at small talk when I'm nervous."

"Why are you nervous? It's just us ducks out here."

"You were talking about your family."

"They expect so little of me. The shop fell to me as the only son without a music career. Running it is the only thing for which they think me suitable, and I'm failing at that."

"The shop isn't making money?"

"Not enough."

"Why not? The instrument rental business hasn't changed that much, has it? You rent to most of my students."

"Yes, but instrument sales are down with the economy, and sheet music...." Davoud shook his head. "They buy that online now. People used to come from Chicago just to browse the collection. They rarely do now."

Paul grabbed Davoud's arms like he'd found Jesus. "Why don't you open a coffee bar in the store? You're always playing something good on the stereo. I bet people would come to sip and listen."

Davoud laughed. "Why do you think I mentioned coffee shops?"

"Context is everything, man."

"Okay, so where would I put the tables? People would need someplace to sit."

Paul rushed on, clearly energized by the idea. "You could have live music. It might help to sell instruments or inspire people to sign up for lessons."

Davoud couldn't help playing with him a little. "You mean like a trio or a string quartet?"

"Idiot! Rock, folk, bluegrass, jazz—hot local groups."

"My family would never—"

"Stuff your family, Davoud. Who's running the place, you or them? You said yourself the shop's not making money doing things the old way."

"My family aside, there isn't room in the—"

"How much space would the sheet music take up if it were stored in file cabinets instead of the display racks?"

"I don't know."

"It doesn't matter. Stop selling it, better yet, take it online and store it upstairs or in the back. I know people who create e-commerce sites for a living. It wouldn't be hard to expand your website to include the sheet music. Without it, you'd have plenty of space in the front for a coffee bar and stage."

The excitement in Paul's voice warmed Davoud. It wasn't like he hadn't considered the idea, but somehow things seemed more workable coming from Paul. "After Thanksgiving maybe we can—"

Paul skidded to a halt. "We can play together, in the coffee shop. You and me and Jonah. In the evening. We were really good together. People would come to listen."

Davoud savored Paul's excitement, his ferocious grin and gleaming white teeth. He saw the group through Paul's eyes, crammed onto a small stage, an audience of coffee drinkers nodding appreciatively as Paul launched them into the Django Reinhardt version of "It Had to Be You."

"I think I'm falling in love with you," said Davoud.

Paul laughed. "You know it's the only way to keep your mother happy."

Davoud groaned.

CHARLIE PURSED his lips and stared out his office window into the abandoned courtyard. A single student in a wool peacoat and watch cap hunched in the cold and kicked at the yellow and brown leaves cluttering the paving. "He still refuses to divulge the names of the boys who attacked him?"

Paul grunted. "He said it would only exacerbate the situation." He cleared his throat. "I'm paraphrasing."

Charlie smiled briefly. "I bet." He swiveled around to examine Paul. "What do you think? Should we pressure him to give us their names? Or would we be doing more harm than good?"

"We can't force him if we want him to trust us."

"How is he going to react if we let this go on? There's nothing in his file to suggest a tendency to act out, but I have to keep the safety of the school foremost."

"What are you suggesting, Charlie?" Paul wanted to sound calm and reasoned, but he could hear his voice rising. "You're not afraid he'll become violent? Because I can tell you that just isn't going to happen with this kid."

"I'm not suggesting anything, Paul. I'm just asking. If he's internalized the abuse...." Charlie folded his hands on the desk. "We have to ask ourselves how he might react. After Columbine and Sandy Hook and all the others, there's not a school administrator who can see a kid like Jonah without asking himself if he isn't sitting on a time bomb."

Paul started to rake a hand through his hair but stopped halfway and sat on his hand instead. He forced himself to think the unthinkable. "Jonah isn't violent by nature. He's angry, but I think he's more likely to hurt himself than someone else. Isn't that more common in bullying cases, anyway?"

Charlie frowned. "It is, especially with homosexuals, but he admitted he threw the first punch in the parking lot incident."

Paul's tension ratcheted up a couple of cogs with the principal's use of the word homosexual. He let his anger cover his worry. "That term is a bit clinical, don't you think, Charlie?" *What have you been reading, literature from the '50s?*

Charlie didn't seem aware of Paul's discomfort. He was staring out the window again. "He *is* gay, right?"

Do you think we issue ID cards? "What did Winfield say when you called? Do you think he might get Jonah to talk?"

Charlie sighed. "I can't share specifics of our conversation as I didn't ask for permission. However, I can tell you that he'd already spoken to Jonah and that the incident with the saxophone case wasn't a surprise to him."

Paul nodded.

"I told him we'd do everything in our power to see that Jonah isn't bothered again, but it's difficult to act without names."

"Maybe they'll stop now that he's... not pretending there's nothing wrong anymore." He almost said, *now that he's come out*, but it wasn't Paul's place to label the kid. "They'll have less power over him."

Charlie focused dark eyes on Paul. "Does that seem likely to you?"

CHAPTER 5

"LONG TIME no suck, faggot. Ya miss me?"

Jonah turned and tried to run from the boy's room at the sound of Justin's voice, but a drag on his backpack caused him to swing painfully into the cinder-block wall. "Let go!"

Justin laughed and dragged him to the back of the boy's room, where Antony examined himself in the scratched plastic mirror above the row of sinks. "Sorry, Whale Bait. No can do."

It was lunch period, the Monday before Thanksgiving. Jonah had stopped for a pee and to wash his hands before eating. He'd taken care to use a bathroom that wasn't on the way from his last class, just as he varied his routes from class to class in the hope that no one would be able to predict his whereabouts, but his efforts had failed. He swallowed and tried to sound more confident than he was. "What do you want, Antony?"

"What do I want? Faggots like you aren't allowed to question real people. Faggots shouldn't exist, let alone be heard. Show him what happens to faggots who break the rules, Justin."

Justin grinned and tugged on Jonah's pack. "Come here, little boy, time for your punishment." He swung Jonah into the wall causing him to hit his elbow. A burst of agony was followed by numbness that made it difficult for Jonah to lift his forearm or move his fingers. He thought about screaming for help, but with all the noise in the corridors during lunch, it was unlikely anyone would hear anything less than an air raid siren.

"Come on, guys. What did I ever do to you?"

"You were born." Antony finished checking his buzz cut and examined Jonah in the mirror. "Who did your hair, Whale Bait? You find a fag hairdresser to do it for you?"

"I bet he didn't even have to pay for it," said Justin. "You let him suck your cock for it, didn't you?" When Jonah didn't answer, he slapped Jonah on the cheek. "Answer me, faggot! Did you blow him for it?"

"No."

A guy Jonah recognized from the wrestling team came into the bathroom and waved at Antony. "Hey, Antony. Wassup, Justin?" He went straight to a urinal without acknowledging Jonah.

Justin let go of Jonah's pack and leaned against the counter without touching him. Antony grinned at Jonah as he addressed the wrestler. "Caught your last match, Dillon. You gonna make it to state this year?"

Dillon shrugged. "Not likely." He zipped and turned. "See you at lunch?"

"Be there in a few. Justin and I have some business to finish."

Dillon's gaze met Jonah's for the fleetest of seconds, his expression unreadable. Jonah froze, wondering whether Dillon always peed without washing his hands. He wanted to say something, ask for help, but his throat was paralyzed. Dillon left, and the opportunity passed.

Antony laughed, doing a credible jackal impression. "I know. You probably let the hairdresser fuck you for it, didn't you? Did he stick his dick up your ass?"

Jonah tried to push past Justin. "Let me go!" Justin grabbed his pack and spun him into the wall again.

"I think you haven't learned your lesson yet."

"I'll tell Mr. Wong."

"No, I don't think you will, faggot, because you'll be in a world of pain if you do." Antony grabbed Jonah's crotch and yanked up until Jonah scrambled to keep his feet. "You understand me, Whale Bait?"

Jonah tried not to cry out in pain as Antony squeezed his balls.

"Answer him, faggot," said Justin.

"I get it," he gasped.

Antony gave a final yank and shoved him into the wall. The pack saved Jonah from hitting his head against the wall. He slipped in the puddle below the electric hand dryer and landed on his ass in the wet. Antony and Justin slapped hands and laughed themselves out the door.

The water soaked through Jonah's jeans and boxers. He climbed shakily to his feet, doing his best to ignore the numbness in his right arm and his aching nads. Craning his neck to inspect his butt in the mirror, he could see a large wet patch staining his jeans. "Fuck." No way he was going into the cafeteria like this. He might not have an entourage like Antony, but he had some pride. Taking the least populated route he could find, he went to his locker and thumbed the combination with his left hand. Shrugging his pack awkwardly into the locker, he slammed the door and limped for the side entrance onto 4th Street.

"HI, JONAH, I hope you're not going to make a habit of visiting during school because...." Davoud's greeting dribbled to a halt like a closed tap when he saw Jonah's blotchy cheeks and red eyes. Something had happened to him. The boy's gait suggested he'd spent the day on horseback. "What happened to you?"

"Nothing. Can I play the piano, Davoud? Please?"

"Of course. I have to watch the counter until Marta's back, but go on in."

"Thanks."

Davoud watched Jonah limp slowly toward the practice rooms. *Are his pants wet?* When Jonah was out of sight, Davoud lifted the hinged counter top and came out from behind the counter. He hesitated beside a display case of used band instruments: a battered trumpet, two cornets, and a baritone. Jonah clearly hadn't wanted to talk. Pacing, he listened for the Steinway. When the big piano remained quiet, he made up his mind and strode to the front door. He twisted the dead bolt and flipped the open sign around.

Jonah sat at the piano, his back to the curtain that separated the practice area from the showroom. Paper towels from the men's room covered the bench under his jeans. Davoud cleared his throat.

"My fingers won't work," said Jonah, flatly. He held up his right forearm and tried flexing his digits. The fingers barely moved.

Davoud felt a shiver pass down his spine. He suppressed a rare urge to swear and sat down on one end of the piano bench. Taking Jonah's arm, he moved each finger gently. When they flexed normally, he checked Jonah's wrist. When he tried to bend Jonah's elbow, the joint moved, but the boy flinched and pulled away.

"Nothing's broken at least. Do you want to tell me what happened?"

"No."

"Okay, but you should get that arm looked at. Would you like me to take you to the emergency room, or do you want me to call your father? Paul's going to be wondering what's become of you as well."

"I don't need a doctor."

"Okay. What about your father?"

"He'll just worry. He worries too much as it is."

"He loves you, Jonah. When we love someone, we worry about them."

"I'm not stupid."

"I'm sorry. I didn't mean to patronize you." Davoud waited.

"I thought I could handle it by myself."

"I know."

"They said they would hurt me if I told."

"Bullies always say that."

"What did I ever do to them? They hate me, but they don't even know me."

"That's right, Jonah. They don't know you. If they knew you, they couldn't hate you."

Davoud's phone rang in his pocket. He pressed Ignore. Marta would go around the back if he didn't answer.

"I don't want to be gay."

Davoud sighed, his mind going back to the summer after his college graduation. He hadn't wanted to be gay either. His family's acceptance hadn't really helped. His brothers had thrived on being different from everyone else, but they'd always been stronger than him—and content to punch any kid who teased them about the hours they spent practicing or their opera-singing mother.

"You know it's not a choice, right?"

Jonah squirmed impatiently. "I told you, I'm not stupid."

"Okay. Would it help if I told you that I didn't want to be gay, either?"

Jonah's head turned so fast Davoud was afraid he'd get whiplash. "You're gay?"

"Yes."

"Is that why you aren't married? How come you don't have a boyfriend, lover, whatever you call it?"

Davoud was saved from answering by the sound of his mother calling from the front of the store. "Davoud, where are you? Why is the closed sign out? I had to let Marta in from the street. It's no wonder the store isn't making money if you're closing it during…." Aida stopped when she saw Jonah and Davoud together on the piano bench. "Jonah? What's going on?"

Davoud felt Jonah tense. "Jonah's had an accident and hurt his arm."

Aida rushed to see. "Jonah, dear, you must protect yourself. What if you hurt your hands? Your hands are everything, everything. You are a pianist. Let me see. Can you move your wrist? Your fingers?"

"Mother, please, I already checked. Let him be. He just needs—" Davoud's phone rang again in his pocket. He checked the screen. It was Paul's mobile. "I'd better take this. Hi, Paul."

"Davoud, have you seen Jonah? He's not in class. Billy says he saw him in chemistry this morning, so I know he came to school. I'm afraid something's happened again."

"He's here with me."

"Is he okay?"

Davoud hesitated. "Wait, please." He caught Jonah's eye and held out the phone. Jonah took it awkwardly with his left hand.

"Hi, Mr. G. Sorry I skipped class."

Davoud couldn't hear the reply, but he saw Jonah wince and caught his mother's concerned look.

"I know. Yes, I know I shouldn't have… no, I'm okay, I just hurt my arm slipping in the boy's room and couldn't play. Yes, I'm really okay. Yes, I'll call my dad. Okay, here he is." Jonah handed the phone back to Davoud.

"Davoud, I realize you can't talk, so just listen. I know damn well Jonah didn't slip in the restroom—at least not without help. I'm going to talk with Wong and come over after last period. Will you please stay with him until I get there or his father picks him up?"

"Of course."

"Thanks, Davoud. See you in a bit."

Davoud hung up the phone and gave Jonah a significant look.

Jonah patted his pockets. "Fuck, my goddamn phone's in my pack at school. Can I borrow yours?"

Aida raised her eyebrows imperiously. "That would be 'Fuck, my goddamn phone's in my pack at school. May I *please* borrow yours,' young man."

Jonah's eyes widened. "May I please borrow your phone, Davoud?"

Davoud grinned and handed it over.

JONAH CLIMBED into his dad's battered old compact in front of Avakian Music and pulled the door shut. He started right in, figuring a good offense was the best defense. "Hey, Dad. I'm okay. Really. I just hit my elbow on the wall. It's no big deal."

John Winfield put on the turn signal and pulled out into traffic. "You got a story for why you're limping?"

Jonah hadn't really been aware of limping, but his balls still ached. He scrambled for an answer. "Uh, gym class. We did this really heavy workout. I think I may have pulled a muscle in my groin."

His dad didn't answer immediately. Jonah was beginning to hope he'd dodged the bullet when his father made an unexpected turn into the lot at Riverside Park. He pulled the car into an empty spot, put it into park, and sat staring out the windshield toward the river. Jonah felt his gut cramp in anticipation.

"Jonah, I don't know what to say to you. These past few months... until this year you've always been honest with me, always told me what was going on with you. Lately, I don't know whether I can trust anything you say."

"Dad, I told you, it's no big deal. I slipped in the boy's room at school and hit my elbow. Maybe I pulled a muscle, what the fuck do I know? I was embarrassed about being a klutz and getting my pants wet. Why can't you just leave me alone?"

"Mr. Gaston thinks you had another run-in with the boys who've been hassling you." His dad turned to look at Jonah directly. "I don't believe you'd leave school before Jazz Ensemble unless something was seriously wrong. You know I'm not mad, right? I see you hurting, and I want to help."

"Then why won't you listen when I tell you it's no big deal?" Jonah knew it was unfair to ask his dad to ignore his troubles. Some part of him didn't want his dad to ignore them either, but he wanted to solve his own problems instead of adding to his dad's worries.

"You've come back from school twice in the last month with injuries, Jonah. I'm your father. How am I supposed to react to that?"

Jonah felt trapped. "I know you want to help, Dad, but you can't. Nobody can."

"I'd really appreciate the chance to try. Please, Jonah, I'm begging you. Tell me what's happening to you."

Jonah felt the tears he'd been fighting all afternoon flood his eyes. Being made to cry made him meaner than he meant to be. "Dad, you know I'm gay, right? Can you fix that? You can't even find a job, how are you gonna fix that?"

When his dad didn't answer, Jonah peeked and saw that his father was crying too. Great, now they were father and son sissies. After a minute, his dad put the car in gear and backed out. He didn't speak the rest of the way home.

AFTER A dinner conversation consisting of "Pass the butter," Jonah
went up to his room and threw himself on the bed. He punched the
pillow. Why did he have to hurt his dad? He wasn't only a pervert, but
a mean one. Why couldn't he do anything right? After a moment his
phone beeped, the tone indicating someone had texted him. The event
was rare enough to spark his curiosity. He rolled over and checked the
display.

> *Billy Preston: U ok? Y did u skip class?*

This was new. Somebody actually checking up on him beside his
parents?

> *Jonah Winfield: Didn't feel good*
> *Billy Preston: Cafeteria shits?*
> *Jonah Winfield: Slipped hurt hand*

There was a break as though Billy were distracted or thinking
about his answer. Jonah pictured him listening to gangsta rap on his
headphones while walking home from basketball practice.

> *Billy Preston: U slip or pushed?*
> *Billy Preston: Mr. g worried 4 u*
> *Billy Preston: Xd me if i knew y u gone*
> *Jonah Winfield: If i tell, u cant say*
> *Jonah Winfield: Secret*
> *Billy Preston: Ok*
> *Jonah Winfield: Antony justin*
> *Billy Preston: Tell me*
> *Jonah Winfield: Called names pushed*
> *Jonah Winfield: Nbd*

Billy Preston: Fuckers
Billy Preston: C u 2morrow
Jonah Winfield: Ok

Jonah must've fallen asleep after that, because the next thing he heard was his dad's angry voice coming from the hot air vent near the head of his bed. He had to be on the phone in the den below his bedroom. Jonah didn't need to make out the words to know who his dad was speaking to—or the topic of conversation. He wondered if his dad had told his mom about her gay son yet. He wasn't sure if he wanted him to or not. Maybe his dad would wait and make Jonah do it when she got home.

"… come home!" The words were loud enough to understand, even if their context wasn't. So his dad was calling for reinforcements. He must be pretty upset to ask his mom to come home early. She didn't like interruptions when she was arguing a case. They'd fought about it before. She said that asking a judge for a continuance for family business was incurring a debt. It could cost you that case or the next one. Jonah wrapped a pillow over his head and tried to block the sound of his dad's voice.

Would his mom come home? What would she say if she did? He felt like a gnat wrested suddenly from flight by a spider's web, the bonding silk quivering as fate loomed.

CHAPTER 6

PAUL ARRIVED at Avakian Music shortly after five. John Winfield had already retrieved his son. Davoud ushered him into the music store anyway. "You look like you could use a drink."

"I'm worried about Jonah."

"Me too." Davoud flipped the Open sign around and locked the door to the shop. "He wouldn't tell me about it, but something certainly happened. His elbow was badly bruised, and he was limping."

"Damn it. I admire his spirit, but I wish the hell he'd tell us who's doing this."

"He's afraid, Paul. He told me they threatened him. You mustn't be too hard on him." He led Paul into the elevator lobby. "Come upstairs. It'll do you good to talk." He was pleased when Paul followed without hesitation. In the apartment, Paul dropped into the sofa and dived in with his usual lack of small talk.

"I don't know what to do. Julie, our guidance counselor, wants to have an all-school assembly to talk about bullying. Maybe it'll help...."

Davoud mimed drinking and raised his eyebrows.

Paul nodded and continued. "It can't hurt, and I offered to help, but it's not enough. We need to stop this now."

Davoud got a bottle of Cabernet Sauvignon from the rack he kept in his pantry. Plucking a corkscrew from a drawer, he found glasses and bustled back to the living room.

"It's not enough," Paul repeated. "I know it's not. Jonah's not the type to go Columbine, but even I can see how this is hurting him. He's missing school now. Maybe his grades start to go down so he doesn't get into a good college or get the music scholarship he deserves. Maybe he just misses out on the good stuff, like Jazz Ensemble. That's harm enough."

Davoud handed Paul a glass of wine. Paul shook himself and sipped. "I can't bear to think about the things kids have done in his place."

Davoud sat next to Paul on the sofa. "I'll invite him to practice with me after school. You come too, when your work allows. He feels safe here. And what do you mean, *even you* can see?"

"It's good of you to help."

"How could I not? You would do the same, were our positions reversed."

Paul leaned forward, elbows on knees. "I don't know. I'm not always as sensitive to other people's problems as I should be."

"I don't believe that."

"You don't know me very well yet. Hey, Aida likes Jonah, doesn't she? Maybe she'll want to coach him a little."

"So long as she doesn't scare him off."

Paul smiled for the first time since he'd arrived. "She likes me too."

"She has a soft spot for shameless flirts."

Paul laughed. "Yeah, well, she's not the one I want to flirt with."

Davoud felt himself stiffen.

Paul sighed, his mouth apparently having gotten ahead of his brain, but he soldiered on. "Your mother wasn't wrong to ask, you know. I am attracted to you."

"I can't imagine why."

"Why not? You're kind, handsome—"

"Come on, I'm not—"

"For Christ's sake." Paul leaned over and pressed his mouth to Davoud's. For a second, Davoud's surprise made him stiff, but then Paul shifted closer and pushed his wine-flavored tongue into Davoud's mouth, and the muscular thrust of it overwhelmed his reserve. Heat flashed through him, his lips parted, and his tongue danced with Paul's until the need for oxygen forced him to turn his mouth away. He panted, out of control as though drugged, and slid his hand under the lapel of Davoud's jacket to pull them closer together.

Davoud pulled back, trying to regain his composure. "I'm not sure this is a good idea."

Paul froze. "You're not seeing someone?"

"No, nobody. I want... it just feels a little fast. I'm out of practice."

Paul nodded, wide-eyed. "We can go slower."

"Are you hungry? We can eat, get to know one another."

Paul settled deeper into the plush sofa as though he'd been afraid Davoud would ask him to leave. "I could eat a horse. Well maybe a pony. A small donkey? It's not like I'm a pig. Although, come to think of it, a pig sounds pretty good."

Davoud laughed as he got up. "You want another glass of wine? I do."

ESMÉ WINFIELD perched on the edge of a plastic chair in the luggage claim, as though relaxing might expose her to germs. As usual, her golden-blonde hair was pulled tightly back and bound behind her head. Her legs were clamped together and aimed to one side, finishing school style. Jonah watched her smooth the gray wool of her skirt as she watched the baggage carousel. Was she as nervous as he was about their upcoming reunion and the conversation that must follow, or was her mind on the case she'd left behind in Washington? He went to get his dad, who was scanning the crowd in the wrong direction. He grabbed his dad's arm and turned him toward his wife.

"There she is, Dad, by Carousel 3. Go say hello. I'll get her bags."

His dad's brow wrinkled. "Sure, thanks Jonah."

Jonah wove his way into the center of the cluster of people waiting for bags where they slid down from the top of the metal cone to hit the rubber bumper lining inside the carousel. He knew it was silly, but he never could wait for his bag to circle around to a less crowded position. His dad always picked a spot on the other side and announced that he would catch anything Jonah missed, but it was a point of pride for Jonah that his dad never hoisted a bag from the rotating slats.

All too soon, Jonah saw the second of his mother's battered set of matching luggage slide to the bumper. He snaked an arm in between a couple of tired-looking businessmen and yanked the bag out. One of them turned to give him a look. "Careful there, fella, or you'll give someone a bruise to remember you by."

"Sorry, man," Jonah called over his shoulder as he dragged the bags toward his waiting parents.

"Hi, Mom, how was the trip?"

"Jonah, come here. It's so good to see you." Reluctantly, he let go of the bags and let himself lean into his mother's embrace.

"You too."

"I'm so glad to be home for Thanksgiving. I've missed you so much."

Jonah really wanted that to be true. He really did. His mother must have felt his uncertainty, because she pulled him in tighter.

"Oh, Jonah. You know I'd stay home if I could."

"Sure, Mom."

On the drive home, they spoke of unimportant things, like seats in coach that were so tightly packed you could hardly put your seat back without jamming it into someone's face. It wasn't until they reached their block that Esmé asked about dinner. "Who'd you invite for Thanksgiving dinner, John? Anyone I know?" Thanksgiving at the Winfield house had always been a big deal, with Jonah's dad preparing a feast for as many family, friends, and coworkers as he could persuade to come. This year, however, was their first in Glen Falls, and if his dad had invited anyone, Jonah didn't know about it.

The answer was uncharacteristically brief. "Just us this time."

Jonah couldn't see his mother's face, but he could imagine the tightening around her mouth that he associated with parental strife.

"You didn't have to do that, John. I told you I'd make time."

"When does the judge want you back?"

"Next week, but my flight's not until Monday morning."

"Four days."

"Four and a half. You know I can't afford to bow out of this one. It could make a real difference. I need the billable hours if I'm going to make partner."

Jonah's dad pulled into their driveway without answering. He pressed the button on the garage door opener clipped to the visor. The door was barely high enough to clear the roof of the car when he revved the engine and accelerated in, jamming on the brakes at the last second, almost hitting Jonah's old bike.

"You'll stay home and help me cook tomorrow, Jonah." It wasn't a question.

"Sure, Dad."

THANKSGIVING MORNING, Jonah pulled a bathrobe over his boxers and went downstairs for some orange juice. His dad was already chopping celery for the stuffing.

"I would have done that for you."

"I got up early."

No kidding. Did you even sleep? Jonah had heard his parents' angry voices through the wall of his bedroom until he fell asleep. He went to the refrigerator and poured himself a glass of juice while he watched his dad's precise motions. "Do you like to cook?"

"I like to cook for you."

"You're good at it. Billy told me his mom usually brings take-home for dinner, and his dad won't even make coffee."

His dad's knife hovered in the air over the stalks of celery. "Thank you, Jonah. You know there isn't anything I wouldn't do for you."

"I know, Dad. Mom still in bed?"

The knife fell on a cluster of stalks. "She was very tired last night."

Jonah finished his orange juice and rinsed out his cup in the sink before putting it into the dishwasher. His dad's voice stopped him before he reached the stairs. "I told her you're being bullied at school. I didn't tell her *why* I thought you were being bullied. I figure that one's for you."

"Oh." That answered one question.

"She loves you very much, Jonah. You know that."

Did he know that? Either way, it didn't help, did it? His dad ought to know. Sometimes love made things hurt more. "I've gotta take a shower. Save me something to do, would you?"

"You want to make the sweet potatoes?"

"Sure."

After his shower, Jonah tucked a more or less unwrinkled button-down into his jeans, feeling the occasion required something better than a T-shirt. He poked his head into the kitchen. His mom cradled a cup of coffee while his dad prepped a huge turkey. "Wow! You invite an army I don't know about?"

"You two are too damned alike," his dad complained. "That's the first thing she says to me. I can freeze what we don't eat. Anyway, I'd probably burn a little bird. I've never made one before."

"Don't give him a hard time, Jonah," said Esmé. "I don't want to be eating pizza on Thanksgiving."

Like Dad would do that to us.

"Why don't you guys go into the living room and get out of my hair? I've got a few more things to do before the bird goes into the oven, and then we can relax."

Thanks a lot, Dad. He followed his mom into the living room and flopped onto the couch.

"How's the case going? You gonna win?"

"It's too soon to be sure. We've only just started oral arguments."

"The judge okay?"

Esmé smiled. "The judge, my handsome son, is a misogynist who thinks that women should stay home and raise children, not argue civil rights cases. If he had his way, we'd still be marching for suffrage. He likes me even less because he's afraid I'm going to win."

Jonah warmed to the man. "But he granted you a continuance, right, so you could come home."

Esmé cocked her head. "Whatever gave you that idea? The courts always shut down for the holiday."

Meaning you didn't even ask him. Jonah jumped up. "I've got a history paper to work on."

"Jonah! Come back here, please. I'd like to talk with you."

"You gonna depose me like a fucking witness?"

"I haven't seen you in weeks and you want to run away and do homework?"

"What do you care?"

He got her with that one. Her face didn't change, but her eyes glinted. "I know I'm not the mother you'd like me to be sometimes. But do you suppose you could at least give me a chance? Your dad told me there's something going on at school. Will you tell me about it?"

"There's nothing to tell. Some kids don't like me. Big whoop."

"John told me you came home the other day with a bruised elbow and couldn't play the piano. I know how that must have hurt you." She didn't specify whether she was referring to the elbow or not being able to play the piano. Maybe she meant both. He *had* been scared the damage would be permanent.

"I told him. I slipped and fell in the bathroom."

"And somebody wrote 'Faggot' on your saxophone case."

"Yeah, so what? Kids do crap like that all the time."

Esmé raised a carefully plucked eyebrow and waited.

"Jesus, I'm not a fucking witness."

She continued to wait. He knew she would wait as long as it took. Resistance was futile. She was worse than the Borg. He might as well tear off the bloody Band-Aid.

"So I'm gay and some kids figured it out and they don't like me and keep doing stupid shit."

"Okay." Esmé took a breath and counted off, flicking her manicured fingers as if she were trying to get a booger off. "One, I love you. Two, I don't care if you're gay. Three, no one has the right to bully you, no matter what the reason. Four, use condoms."

She had to have planned this like she planned her arguments in court. "Dad said he didn't tell you. He said I had to tell you myself."

"He didn't tell me."

"When did you figure it out?" She'd probably had his DNA analyzed the first time he picked up a pink toy or something.

"I knew it was a possibility when your dad told me about the 'Faggot' thing. You... it wasn't obvious, Jonah."

So this was only one possibility for which she'd prepared. He wondered what other speeches she'd memorized. Maybe she'd tell him later if he asked.

"Are you sure?" she said.

"I know I like dick—and Billy Preston's butt is *fabulous.*" Esmé winced. *Got ya!* He knew he was being a jerk, but what did she expect?

"I'll take that as a yes."

"It's nobody's damn business but mine."

"Are you and Billy...?"

"Again, nobody's business—"

"Whoa there, cowboy, so long as you're living in this house, it sure is my—"

"This house? You mean the one Dad inherited? The one you visit once a month? *This* house?"

"Jonah, you know that's not relevant to—"

"Relevant?" The word offended him so deeply he couldn't begin to voice his objection. "Relevant?"

"I need to know that you're being safe. If you're having sex, you have to be safe. That means using condoms and practicing safe sex."

Jesus! He was so not ready to have this conversation with his mom. "I'll be safe. I'm not stupid. Can't you just drop it?"

"No, you're not stupid." Esmé brushed her designer jeans as if she were pushing a skirt over her knees. "What about the bullying? Your dad says you won't tell the principal who's bothering you."

"It'll just make it worse if I do."

"Are you sure about that? Mr. Wong will have to suspend or expel them if you give him any names. The school board approved a no tolerance policy last year. He'll have no choice but to act."

When the hell had she found time to look up the school board policy on bullying? "They'll just wait for me after school."

"If they bother you after school, we can get the police involved. Charge them with assault."

"Right, then the entire world will know I'm gay instead of just the whole school."

"It's your decision, Jonah. I want you to know that I'll back you up no matter what you decide."

In all his rehearsing, Jonah had never considered the possibility that she'd allow him to make his own decision. In his confusion, he allowed her to put an arm around his shoulders and envelop him in the sweet musk of her perfume.

"Anyone want any eggnog?" said his dad from the kitchen.

"Not now, John," said Esmé.

To: davoud@avakianmusic.com
From: rasul@avakianmusic.com
Subject: Thanksgiving

Hey Bro,

Mother's been on my case about Thanksgiving. Sorry I haven't been in touch. We're in our eighth week of nonstop performances. I can't tell you how exhausted I am. Swear to God, I wake up in hotels and have to check my phone to figure out what city I'm in. Thank goodness Martin keeps track for us. We'd probably forget gigs if he didn't remind us—wake up some morning in the wrong town. Thank God we're nearly done. One concert in Chicago—I'm so glad I insisted he book us something close to home for the last—then we'll go our separate ways for the holiday. You'll have 2B ready for me, won't you? I'm so looking forward to a familiar bed.

Rascal

To: rasul@avakianmusic.com
From: davoud@avakianmusic.com
Subject: Re: Thanksgiving

Hey Rascal,

I'm delighted to hear you'll be joining us for Thanksgiving. I'll see what I can do about getting 2B fit for habitation. A warning, I gave the workmen who put in the new windows this summer permission to use the sitting room as a staging area. It'll need some work to make ready. It would help to know when you're going to arrive. Your e-mail didn't mention a date or time.

I'm fine. Thanks for asking.

Davoud

To: davoud@avakianmusic.com
From: rasul@avakianmusic.com
Subject: Re: Thanksgiving

Davoud,

Sheesh, Davy, no need to get snotty! I'm arriving Wednesday night, the day before Thanksgiving. We've a concert that evening, so I won't be in until late, probably after midnight.

I'm sorry I didn't ask after you. You know I love my little brother, right? I'm just so tired, I'd forget my head if it wasn't attached. It's no picnic, this business. The constant travel really gets to you. Sometimes I think you got the better end of the stick, with nothing to worry about but who's going to cover the cash register.

Anyway, I'm looking forward to hearing all your news on Thursday.

Rascal

To: davoud@avakianmusic.com
From: amir@avakianmusic.com
Subject: Thanksgiving

Davy,

Rascal says you're a bit anxious about the holiday. I plan to drive down on Wednesday afternoon with the girls. Is 1B habitable? We'd appreciate its use. No need to make any special efforts to get things ready for us. Dorothy and I can change the sheets or vacuum if we have to. I know you've got your hands full. Unfortunately, we'll have to head back into town on Friday. I've got a concert Saturday, and the girls want to get back to their friends. You know how it is.

Listen, don't be too hard on Rascal. He told me last month he was thinking about quitting the quartet and finding a steady job in Chicago or New York. I guess the travel's getting him down. He won't admit it, but I think he's lonely. The girl in every port thing gets old after a while. You know he's not like you, content to be alone.

How is the old place holding up? Rascal says you had the windows replaced. That must have cost a pretty penny. I'm glad to hear the shop is doing well. With the economy so bad, I would have thought the music business might see a downturn, but I guess people need their tunes more than ever, huh?

Anyway, I'm looking forward to seeing everyone on Wednesday.

Amir

Davoud moved the cursor over the Reply button, but stopped without clicking. *Davy!* His brothers were the only ones left in the world who called him that. As a kid, Davy had been preferable to Davoud. His real name made him no friends, even in the years before 9/11. Only Amir had gone by his real name throughout his childhood, his genuine kindness and affability carrying him through when Rasul and Davoud wanted the protection of names more familiar to English speakers.

Content to be alone. The words burned in Davoud's chest. Did Amir think of him as the bachelor uncle who would never marry, the middle-aged eccentric content to stay home and lavish gifts and affection on his niece in place of the child he would never have? Or worse, did Amir imagine him to be some kind of eunuch, sexless and comfortable in his solitude? He shifted uncomfortably in his swivel chair. Amir was wrong. He wasn't content by himself, but there was a kernel of truth in the observation. What had happened to Davoud was simple enough: he'd lost hope. As a young man it had been easy to imagine meeting someone, courting them—yes, courting, an old-fashioned concept, but one he believed in fervently—and settling down to make a life together. It was why he'd waited to make significant changes to his apartment, leaving it largely as originally decorated by the great-aunt who'd first lived there. It might even be why he'd delayed making changes to Avakian Music. He was waiting for a partner. Then his father had died. Avakian Music had become a heavier burden. Davoud had started seeing gray on the barber's floor. The creases and seams in his face had taken up permanent residence rather than appearing for limited engagements, and one day he'd lost hope. It was not gradual. There was no warning. It was like he'd fallen asleep one night with a limb pressed beneath him. Instead of waking to pins and needles, he'd roused to find it withered.

But all that had changed just as suddenly when Paul kissed him.

The crippling loneliness that was both cause and result of his inaction on Friday and Saturday nights faded. He could hardly remember his last date, but his time with Paul was vivid, however brief. The softness of Paul's lips, his eager tongue, the faint scent of chalk dust that clung to Paul's jacket had stayed in his thoughts and continued to pop up at odd moments ever since. What had prompted him to stop Paul at one kiss? He wasn't a prude. He'd had one-night stands. The rush of emotion—oh, treacherous hope—had unsettled him. He knew he wouldn't be satisfied with a one-night stand. Paul was dangerous because he could hurt Davoud.

Should he tell his brothers about Paul? Should he feign anger at Amir's assumptions and throw his imaginary relationship with Paul in his face? In truth, he was more chagrined than angry. He could tell

Amir the truth: he had a crush on a local teacher who might or might not have any real interest in him. Neither approach would touch the real miracle in his life, the miracle he wouldn't share with his brother or anyone else—that he had lost hope, and in the autumn of his 40th year, regained it.

To: amir@avakianmusic.com
From: davoud@avakianmusic.com
Subject: Re: Thanksgiving

Amir,

    I'm looking forward to seeing you and the girls at Thanksgiving. Thanks for sharing your plans. You may certainly use 1B. We'll be celebrating in 3B. Mom's place has some unfinished work. I vacuumed and dusted this morning so no asthma attacks for Zhara, I hope. How is my little girl? Does your pediatrician think she'll grow out of it?

    Your mention of the Music Box is timely. The family must discuss the building soon. I wish you could stay another night, so we could avoid doing it on Thanksgiving Day. Perhaps Dorothy could take Zhara home on Friday and you could stay over? I'd be happy to drive you to Chicago Saturday morning. It's vital we talk soon, and I'd rather do it while all the shareholders are here.

    I'll bear in mind what you say about Rascal. If he wants to settle down, I think fatherhood might actually suit him. For some reason the phrase "nobody kids like a kidder" runs through my mind.

    I should mention that I've invited a friend to Thanksgiving dinner. I don't know if you ever met Paul Gaston, the high school music teacher. He grew up in Glen Falls, but I think he would have been away at school when you last lived here. He's a fantastic guitar player who has done wonders with the school's jazz ensemble. Do you remember when we used to risk Grandmother's wrath and sneak down to jam together at night? Paul, and

*a student of his, Jonah, who is a talented pianist, have
come over a few times recently to practice with me.
Between the two of them, they've awakened my
slumbering bow.*

  Love,

  Davoud

To: davoud@avakianmusic.com
From: amir@avakianmusic.com
Subject: Re: Thanksgiving

Davy,

  *I can stay another day if it's important. You've got
me wondering: this isn't another harebrained scheme to
rent out the Music Box, is it? You know Mother won't go
for it. She thinks of the old place as her home, not a
business.*

  *Zhara is fine. Our doctor says it's too soon to know
whether she'll grow out of the asthma, but she responds
well to the new inhalers, so we're all breathing better.*

  *I'm looking forward to meeting this Paul fellow
who's got your bow taut. Ha, ha. Seriously though, if I'm
reading you right, someone's finally caught your eye, and
I'm delighted. Rascal's not the only one who needs to find
a partner. Mother and I agree on that at least.*

  *I put this aside to finish in the morning, and I've
kept Dorothy awake with my thrashing around since, so
I'm back in the kitchen to say what's been keeping me
awake. I think I've asked too little about your personal
life. I think it fair to say we've both been embarrassed to
discuss some aspects of your lifestyle. At the risk of
voicing a cliché, let me just say this: since I left home,
I've come to know a number of gay men and lesbians.
Whatever I might have thought or said in the past, I
believe they're no different than anyone else. Hard as it is
for anyone to truly connect with another human being, I
believe we are all happiest in a long-term relationship.*

*Dorothy and I have had bad times—none worse than
when we've let our fears get the better of us—but never
doubt that what I have with her and Zhara is the best part
of my life. I want the same joy for you, little brother. If
I've shied away from asking about your personal life, it's
not because I don't care. I apologize for my stupid
squeamishness. Please don't be afraid to share.*

I'm looking forward to meeting Paul.

Amir

To: amir@avakianmusic.com
From: davoud@avakianmusic.com
Subject: Re: Thanksgiving

Amir,

*I owe a reply to your last note, but I think my
feelings are too fresh to the pot. Will it suffice to say that
I'm touched by your comments, and that I'd welcome a
little more curiosity on your part, even if it should prove
uncomfortable for us both? I'll try for a fuller answer
when you visit, or when I'm better able to sort myself out.*

I love you.

Davoud

PAUL REACHED the entrance of the Avakian Music building and pressed the buzzer for 3B as instructed. Davoud had been vague about the time, suggesting that Paul should show up whenever he liked between one and three in the afternoon. He said family would be in and out until four, when they'd settle down to eat. Not knowing how to respond to such an invitation, Paul had gotten showered and dressed by one and then paced his apartment for half an hour, not wanting to arrive too early. At 1:30, his impatience had overwhelmed his anxiety over meeting Davoud's family, and he'd headed for his car to make the short drive.

The anemic rattle of the electronic door lock interrupted his thoughts, and he grabbed awkwardly at the door. Finding his way to the elevator, he remembered to close the cage behind him before pushing the button for the third floor.

He wasn't prepared for the disembodied voice that greeted him when the brass floor-indicator dial pointed to three and he shoved the cage open. "Hello, you must be Paul, Uncle Davy's friend. I'm Zhara. I'm supposed to take you to Uncle Davy. He's in the kitchen. I'm not usually allowed in there when he's cooking, but he said he would make an *exception* if I got you. Do you think he might give me a carrot? I like carrots and I'm very hungry."

Paul stepped into the hall and looked around to find the source of the soft, high-pitched voice. Sitting with her back to the corridor wall and her knees pulled close to her chest was a little girl with big brown eyes, dense eyelashes, and long black hair.

"Hi, Zhara, I'm Paul."

"I know that. Uncle Davy said you were a strawberry blond. I know what blond means, but does strawberry blond mean you color your hair with strawberries? That might be kind of fun, but I think I would rather eat strawberries than put them in my hair." She stopped for breath, hopped to her feet, and examined him closely. "We don't have any blond people in my family, although my daddy's hair is dark brown instead of black."

Paul blinked as he tried to keep up with the rapid stream of information. "A strawberry blond is someone who has blond hair with some red in it. What do you think? Do I qualify?" He knelt so she could look more closely.

"Yes, I guess so, but I don't know why they call it strawberry blond, because strawberries are much redder."

Fortunately, Zhara didn't seem to require an answer, because she took his hand and pulled him down the corridor toward an open door from which he could hear the sounds of music and laughter. Inside, a sharp-featured, slender, raven-haired man leaned against the arched entrance to the living room. He produced a brilliant white-toothed grin and waved. "You must be Davy's Paul. Welcome! I'm Rasul, but you'll hear everyone call me Rascal. You might as well too."

"Nice to meet you, Rascal."

Paul slowed and would have offered a hand to shake, but a determined tug from his guide prevented him. "Come on, Paul, I have to take you to Uncle Davy. He made me promise. You can say hello to Uncle Rascal later. He lives here now, so you can talk to him forever." Paul waved apologetically and allowed Zhara to drag him into the kitchen.

"There you are, Paul. I'm so glad you could come." Davoud held out his arms for a hug, which he carried out entirely with the sides of his forearms, holding his wet hands away from Paul's suit coat. "Thank you, Zhara."

"I believe you owe Zhara a carrot for her efforts."

"Is that so? I guess I might just be able to find a carrot somewhere around here for a little bunny."

"I'm not a bunny. I'm a girl."

"Yes, I know, but you eat carrots like a bunny." Taking a carrot from the vegetable crisper, he washed it in the sink and cut the greens off the thick end. "There you go, bunny," he said, kneeling to present it, a proud courtier presenting a bauble to his princess.

"Thank you, Uncle Davy," said Zhara.

"Hey, I've got an idea. Why don't you see if you can get Uncle Rascal to give you a pony ride?"

"Yay, a pony ride, a pony ride!" Zhara ran off to find Rascal.

"She's adorable. She's one of your brother's, I take it, Uncle Davy?"

Davoud grinned. "Amir's daughter and the baby in the family." Drying his hands, he took Paul's arm. "Let's get you introduced."

AFTER INTRODUCTIONS, Paul found himself with his back to the mantelpiece, wineglass in hand, listening to Rascal tell his brother Amir about the tour he'd just finished. He was pretty sure the life of late-night interstate hauls, sterile hotel rooms, impatient music directors, and chilly rehearsal halls wouldn't have suited him. It was hard to conclude that the nomadic life of the touring artist would have made finding a partner easier. At least Paul's teaching career gave him a chance to get to know his students and fellow teachers.

"I gather you're a member of the fraternity, Paul." Paul must have looked startled, because Amir raised an eyebrow, much like Paul had seen his mother and brother do. "Davy said you're a talented guitarist—as well as teacher."

"He did?" Paul said, still recovering from his initial impression that he'd been asked to confirm he was gay. Was the man playing with him?

Amir leaned close and whispered, "Rascal suggested we might jam a little later. Don't mention it in front of Aida."

Paul shifted his gaze across the room. Aida was telling Amir's wife Dorothy a story, her hands moving gracefully in time with her expression and posture.

Amir followed his look. "She's not as bad as Agnes. That old bat *really* made us sing the blues if she caught us practicing anyone beyond the romantics."

Hadn't Davoud said Amir was a cellist? Well, why not? "I'd love to, but I didn't bring my guitar."

"Davy'll scare something up," said Rascal. "He's bound to have something sitting around. So you'll do it? Don't worry, we're not exactly into bebop. We mostly stick to old standards."

Something predatory in Rascal's grin had Paul feeling there was something more than a casual jam in the offing. Was this the Avakian brothers' way of checking out the prospective boyfriend?

"Sure, why not?" he answered, quelling the faint uneasiness in his gut.

AT THE dinner table—a huge Victorian cherry antique with enough extensions to seat everyone together—Paul sat with Davoud to his left and Dorothy, Amir's wife, to his right. Dorothy was a tall, elegantly coiffed woman in an Armani suit and red pumps. Between delicate bites of turkey breast, she told him the story of her first visit to the Music Box to meet Aida and Farhad Avakian, a small smile playing at the corners of her mouth as though she were revealing a secret.

"Farhad was warm and welcoming, but not overly talkative. He listened to everything I said, smiling and nodding as though I'd just complimented his children, which I guess I had, since I was head-over-heels with Amir and I imagine I talked about him more than me." She laughed. "I must have sounded like a real groupie. Anyway, Farhad was easy. Aida, on the other hand, examined me from the other side of the table like she was measuring me for a gynecologist's stirrups. When we finally talked, her first words were to ask me if I'd like an introduction to her hairdresser." Dorothy brushed back a strand of gleaming shoulder-length hair. "I was certain it was a backhanded criticism."

"It was, not that you deserved it, Dorothy. You were gorgeous even in your Birkenstocks-and-granola phase," said Davoud. "Aida was convinced you would follow Amir from gig to gig and never stay home long enough to have babies. God knows what she'd have bribed that hairdresser to do to you."

Dorothy laughed out loud and called down to the head of the table. "Aida, your son is dissing you over here. You'd better come defend your honor or Paul will get the wrong impression."

"Oh, Paul's already corrupt, Dorothy. He flirts shamelessly when he's less nervous."

"Aida, be nice," said Davoud. "Paul's doing fine, isn't he, Dorothy?"

Dorothy patted Paul's hand. "Yes, he's doing just fine."

WHEN PAUL excused himself to visit the bathroom, Davoud cornered his older brother in the kitchen, where he was opening a bottle of twenty-year-old port.

"What did you say to him?"

Amir looked about as innocent as a choirboy. "What do you mean?"

"I saw you and Rascal talking to him."

"A little paranoid are we now, Davy? Isn't talking what we're supposed to do at parties?"

"Come on, you asked him a question, and he looked surprised. I know you're up to something."

"I merely asked if he'd like to join us for the jam session tonight. Since I'm staying another day, I thought we could have a little fun and get to know him."

Rascal sauntered in. "What's holding up the port?"

"I'm not your sister, and he's not some horny teenager for you to check out."

"Of course we have to check him out, little brother. It's our duty. Plus it'll be a gas."

"For you, maybe."

"Come on, Davy. All we're going to do is play with him."

"Play as in cat with mouse or play as in boy with puppy?"

Rascal smirked. "We'll leave the boy parts to you."

Davoud glared. He knew he protested too much, but he couldn't help himself.

"We can tell you're interested. We always could, you know. Even in high school. You're not exactly George Smiley—"

"Or Charlie Chan," said Amir.

"Remember Andy Miller, that kid who played the tympani in orchestra? You drooled every time you saw him."

"Oh look, Rascal. You've got him flustered," Amir chided. "Stop that or Mother will swoop in to defend her turf. She's the only one allowed to give baby a hard time."

"Give me one of those." Davoud snatched a glass of port from Amir's tray and downed it.

"That's no way to treat a good port," said Amir.

"Shut up and pour another."

RASCAL UNZIPPED the outer cover of his violin case. "We like to make a game of it. Don't worry, the rules are simple. We take turns choosing something we all know or we've found in the sheet music collection. When it's your turn, you pick and start out. Everyone else finds the groove as best as they can. We trade off solos. That's all there is to it."

Sure, nothing to it. Paul could smell testosterone in the air along with the alcohol fumes. "Right. You said something about a guitar?"

"That's Davy's department."

Davoud gave Paul a direct look. "You know you don't have to do this, Paul."

"It's fine. Should be fun." Paul tried to sound more confident than he was.

"Rhythm or electric?"

"Both, if ya got 'em."

Davoud grinned.

That's a point won, at least. Davoud came back a few minutes later with a couple of cases and a guitar stand under his arm. He rolled an amp from the corner and plugged it in. The first case contained a beautifully made, unusually shaped acoustic guitar with a rosewood back and sides, cedar top and neck, small oval sound hole, and high action. Paul strummed a few chords, pleased. He set the guitar aside, opened the second case, and burst into delighted laughter. The electric was a phosphorus-white, 1959 Gibson Flying V, with sparkles baked into the finish and a wah-wah bar.

Rascal smirked.

Davoud shrugged apologetically. "For some reason, I've been having trouble moving this one. Had it forever." He handed Paul a cable and foot-operated volume pedal.

"Not the kind of thing we're known for," said Amir.

"No problem," said Paul. "I'll make do." He plugged the guitar into the amplifier and strummed a few test chords, adjusting the dials until he had a mellow tone that felt suitable for the strange ensemble. When he looked up, he found Amir with his cello at the ready. Davoud was adjusting the tension on his bow. Rascal leaned against the piano. Paul caught his eye and nodded. Rascal raised his bow and produced a clear, warm *A*. Amir matched his pitch a couple of octaves down and rapidly made adjustments. Davoud followed suit. Paul tuned the acoustic first and then the flashy Gibson.

"Guest's choice. You want to start, or you want one of us to?" said Rascal.

Paul glanced at Davoud. "Why don't you go first, Rascal?"

"Your wish is my command." Rascal stared into the distance for a moment, and then started a slow glide through the opening of "Mood Indigo." After a few notes, Davoud joined in with a steady *thunk* from the double bass. Paul snatched up the acoustic guitar and strummed a steady rhythm, choosing the chords from memory. He looked up to see Amir nod as he added a harmony below Rascal's high sweet line.

Point.

When it came time for what, in Duke Ellington's version, would have been a muted trumpet solo, Amir stepped in with a surprisingly credible effort on the cello. If there'd been any signal between the brothers, Paul had failed to pick it up. Amir brought his solo to a finish. Paul caught Davoud's attention and raised his eyebrows. Davoud nodded. *Go for it.* Paul switched from strumming to picking, bringing a grin to Rascal's saturnine features. They made their way through the same chord changes as Amir's solo, and Paul prepared to switch back to strumming. He glanced up to see Davoud grin.

Game.

He finished with a flourish, and Davoud took over as though they'd planned it from the start. For his go-around, Davoud stuck with pizzicato, but moved up the neck of his bass to pluck a line at the high end of his range before sliding back down afterward. Rascal repeated the opening phrases and brought them to a finish.

"Well," said Davoud, a proprietary gleam in his dark eyes belying his bland expression, "who wants to go next?"

For his turn, Paul swapped the acoustic for the Gibson and launched into Django Reinhardt's "Appel Direct," picking the opening scales at a blistering tempo. Davoud joined within a few bars, pacing him with a steady bass line. Rascal came in with harmonies to match the chord changes. He was delighted when Amir began strumming rhythm after the opening phrases, cradling his cello as if it were an overweight guitar.

And set.

He raised an eyebrow at Rascal. Rascal didn't so much as twitch, but took over the melody at the end of Paul's phrase, shifting into a subtle variation after a few bars. Paul shifted back to rhythm and Amir to bowing while they listened to Rascal's elegant phrases. Paul couldn't remember the last time he'd had so much fun. The only thing that would have made it better was if Jonah had been there. He caught Davoud's eye and glanced at the abandoned piano. Davoud nodded. *He should be here.*

CHAPTER 7

RASCAL AND Amir sank into the velvet monstrosity in Davoud's living room. Aida planted herself firmly on a hard-backed chair from the kitchen. Davoud cleared his throat. "I've asked you to come because we need to talk about the Music Box and Avakian Music." He took in Amir's noncommittal smile, Rascal's atypically serious expression, and his mother's frown. "I don't imagine any of you are fully aware of how hard Glen Falls has been hit by the economic downturn."

"It's hard times all around, Davy," said Amir.

Davoud nodded, thinking of the ongoing fight between the musicians' union and the Chicago Symphony, which had been in the Chicago papers for months.

"Come on, man, there's no point in beating around the bush," said Rascal. "What's this about?"

Davoud sighed. "The fact is that the store is not doing well. Instrument sales are down. I expect sales for the year will be 40 percent below those of 2008. Sheet music sales are almost nonexistent."

"Two thousand-eight? What about last year?" Amir asked.

"Last year was just slightly worse, but it's too soon to tell if the trend has turned yet. I mention 2008, because we've seen a steady downward trend since then."

"Wait a minute, the store's been losing sales since 2008? Why are we just hearing about this now?" said Rascal.

Because I was embarrassed to tell you. Because I thought I could fix it by myself. Because you were gallivanting around the globe with the quartet. It would have helped if Rascal could be relied upon to check—or better yet answer—his e-mail. Maybe Davoud would have shared more. Amir was another story. He and Dorothy had experienced a rough period about the time of the crash. Davoud had been reluctant to add to Amir's worries.

"It's not like I've been hiding it. The information is in the annual statements none of you read. The fact is, I expected some downturn given the housing crash and recession. I didn't anticipate it would last this long or get this bad."

"That isn't what I asked."

"If you're asking why I didn't bring it to your attention more forcefully... I didn't want to bother you. You have your own lives and concerns."

"What's with the windows, then? If the store is doing so badly, how did you pay for that?" said Rascal.

This was the question Davoud dreaded but knew he couldn't avoid any longer. He took a deep breath.

"He took it from his own salary," said Aida suddenly. "He tried to tell me when I got home, but I wasn't... I didn't want to listen."

"Don't worry, Mother. We'll find a way to deal with—"

"We're not hurting for money, Davy," said Rascal. "Apparently, you—"

Davoud bristled. "How would you feel if—"

"You don't know a damn thing about how I feel."

Amir clapped his hands together, the sharp sound bringing silence in its wake. "Let him speak, Rascal. Is Mother right, Davy? Have you been shorting yourself to pay for the Music Box?"

"I thought it was just a loan at first, but there hasn't been enough...."

"How much?" said Amir.

Davoud's face warmed. He took a printout from the briefcase he'd set on the coffee table. "This year was particularly bad, what with the windows and other repairs... about twenty-one."

"Twenty-one what? Hundred?" asked Rascal.

"Thousand."

Rascal's jaw dropped. "Dammit, Davy. Why didn't you say—"

"Twenty-one thousand, this year alone." Amir's eyes narrowed. "How much altogether, Davy?"

"Nearly fifty thousand since 2008."

Amir was relentless. "And what do you normally pay yourself?"

Davoud couldn't get the words out. Silently, he handed over the budget summary he'd prepared before the holidays. His salary was listed first under the personnel expenses.

"What about benefits? Health, dental. You've not shown...."

Amir handed the budget to Rascal.

Davoud tried to explain. "They've gotten so expensive now that we've only got two full-time employees. We don't qualify for much of a discount."

"Jesus, man. Why in hell didn't you say something?" Rascal was red-faced now.

Aida, who had been silent since figuring out what Davoud had been doing, spoke with a quiet intensity that filled the room without apparent effort. "That's enough, Rasul. Davoud was only doing what he thought best for the family."

"How much is it going to take to fix this?" said Amir.

"The money I've spent isn't really the point," said Davoud. "I don't care about—"

"Well, I do!" Rascal yelled. "We're your fucking brothers. You didn't think enough of us to—"

"Please, Rascal!" said Amir. "Can't you understand why Davy would—"

"No, frankly I can't."

"Boys, please," said Aida. "Let Davoud have his say. We'll have time enough for recrimination later. What is your plan, dear?"

IN THE end, it was the tour of 3A—Aida's apartment—that quieted Davoud's brothers enough to listen to his ideas. The musky smell in Aida's dining room, the real reason they had to use 3B for

Thanksgiving dinner, left Rascal shell-shocked and Amir grim. "What will it cost to fix this?" Amir asked again. Davoud told them about the roof. The hurt expression on Rascal's face and the resignation in Amir's were painful to see. Aida was uncharacteristically withdrawn throughout the discussion. He'd expected an explosion, an operatic outpouring. This was far worse. She simply looked tired.

It didn't help when he let slip that he'd discussed the family business with Paul. "What are you doing talking to him before family?" Rascal asked. Before Davoud could answer, Amir physically dragged Rascal into the next room. The closed door did not entirely muffle the urgency in their whispers. Amir returned stone-faced. Rascal's expression wavered between chastened and resentful.

Davoud was surprised Aida said nothing about bringing in local bands to play in the store. Instead, she focused on the café. "I don't like the idea of bringing food into the building. A café will attract vermin."

Amir had other concerns. "I accept that the sheet music has to go, or go online anyway," he said. "But you can't afford to pay yourself now, Davoud. How are you going to pay for baristas and a new roof at the same time? Not to mention the cost of getting the permits, espresso machines, and power for the stage. How do you propose to pay these groups you want to bring in?"

"I can apply for a loan. I've started writing a business plan." Davoud chose not to respond to the vermin comment. He wasn't totally sure if Aida was more concerned about rodents or the quality of the customer who would enjoy bluegrass with their coffee. While she and their grandmother had taught them tolerance for different-colored people, neither had expressed anything but contempt for what they considered lowbrow music.

"Do you know how to write one of those?" asked Rascal.

Davoud suppressed a flash of anger. It wasn't like he hadn't gone to college. He wasn't entirely ignorant. "Have you forgotten that I minored in business administration?"

"Did they teach you to pay for the business out of your own pocket?" Rascal countered. "Even I know better than that."

"I thought it was temporary. Am I supposed to apologize for not wanting to bother you with my problems, Rascal? Or are you just mad because you're afraid I was right in thinking you'd be more trouble than help?" As the words emerged, Davoud felt an unholy alchemy of satisfaction at the injured look on Rascal's face, and shock at the depth of his resentment and its capacity to ambush him. He was ashamed to have said something so hurtful to his brother. He and Rascal had shared everything in school, not least his dawning realization that he was attracted to boys. When Rascal had abandoned him to study at the Curtis Institute of Music less than a year later, he'd been lost.

"I guess you were right, Davy. You can fix this yourself."

"Rascal, wait," Davoud called, but Rascal stamped out of the apartment, slamming the door on his way.

"That was helpful, little brother," said Amir. "You want me to go after him?"

Aida stamped a foot. "Why are you hurting the people who love you?"

Davoud sighed. "I didn't mean to hurt anyone. I'll talk to him."

Amir sighed. "You'd better give him a few minutes to cool down."

DAVOUD KNOCKED for a third time. "Come on, Rascal. Please let me in. We need to talk."

"Maybe you need to talk. I need not to see your face for a while."

Davoud turned and slid down with his back to the door. Talking through wood was better than nothing. "Listen, I'm sorry about what I said. I didn't mean it. I'm stressed out. My feelings got the better of me."

"Which feelings would those be? Your resentment about me getting into music school and you not?"

"Is that what you think? That I was jealous?" Davoud let his head thump against the door.

"Isn't that what this is about?"

"I admit I was hurt, but I never resented your success at getting that scholarship. You left me behind. You were my guy, the one person I could always talk to. Amir was at college. Mom was on tour. I couldn't talk to Dad about it. When I came out after college, Dad…

Dad had no clue what to say to me. He loved me, but he didn't understand the gay thing and couldn't deal with the mechanics of it. It disgusted him. *I* disgusted him."

"No, that's not true. He would never say—"

"He didn't have to," Davoud interrupted. "I could see it in his face every time I said anything… pretty soon I didn't say anything."

"You were always so close. You and he were like coconspirators in a heist film, always putting your heads together. I wanted that, but all he did was yell at me."

"I'm sorry…. He and I were close when I was little—and again before he died. I can't tell you how grateful I was for that. I suppose he got used to the idea…."

"He told me I was self-centered," Rascal said bitterly.

Davoud closed his eyes. "You are, a little bit. But we… I know it's not the important part of you."

"Thanks a lot."

"Rascal, I love you. I've always loved you. That's why I was so hurt when you left. I was proud of you, but I missed you terribly. I was lost and I didn't know how to tell you."

There was a pause during which Davoud could hear Rascal breathing.

"I need you, Rascal. I need you to support me with Amir and Mother. Avakian Music is going under—and the Music Box with it—unless I take action, and I don't think I have the strength to do it if I have to fight with everyone. I love them both, but Mother's ideas about music are Paleolithic, and Amir is too conservative to accept these changes on his own. He'll want to plod along one step at a time while we're slipping downhill at twice that rate. You're the risk taker in the family. You always have been. Please help me do this."

Davoud heard the deadbolt slide and nearly went sprawling on his back when the door opened wide behind him. "What are you doing out there in the hall, bro? Didn't you say something about changes to plan?"

CHAPTER 8

THE CONVERSATION with his mother confused Jonah. He was relieved to have told her, but he'd expected her to force him to give her Antony and Justin's names. Charged up for a fight like a wrestler on *WWE Smackdown*, he'd not expected a choice. He'd been ready to lose. Now he'd have to find another way.

After Thanksgiving, lounging on his bed trying to decide what to do with his vacation day, he texted Billy.

Jonah Winfield: U free
Billy Preston: How t-day
Jonah Winfield: Told mom
Billy Preston: U ok
Jonah Winfield: I guess
Billy Preston: She flip out
Jonah Winfield: No
Jonah Winfield: Why am I still mad
Billy Preston: Want 2 hang
Jonah Winfield: Where
Billy Preston: R park
Jonah Winfield: Ok

THE DAY was gloomy and fresh, with dark clouds whipping by at low altitude under a pale-gray cover. The river was choppy, with whitecaps forming in the wide parts. Jonah wore a yellow rain parka his mother had bought him a few years before that was long and loose, but which he liked anyway because it reminded him of deep-sea fishermen and wicked waves, and it suited his mood.

"Dude." Billy arrived in a pant like he'd been running. He wore a gray fleece hoodie with a white skull and crossbones on the back.

"Hey, Billy."

"You want to check out the dam?"

"Sure."

Jonah hunched against the wind and fell into step with Billy, stretching his stride to keep up with the basketball player, their feet crunching on the gravel path that led to the low flood control dam that backed up the river south of town.

"What did she say?"

"My mom? She's a fucking calculator." He counted with his fingers. "One, she loves me. Two, she doesn't care if I'm gay. Three, no one has the right to bully me—like that makes any difference." He bounced on the balls of his feet just to feel the shape of the stones under his sneakers. "Oh yeah, four, use condoms. Like I'm gonna need them anytime soon. Who the hell's gonna want a scrawny shrimp like me?"

Billy cleared his throat. "You're not scrawny, just compact."

"I'm the smallest guy in gym class."

"You probably got a few more inches coming."

"That's a relief. I might make five foot six."

"Sorry, I'm not so good at this."

"Good at what?"

Billy punched him on the arm. "Support. Encouragement."

Jonah didn't know what to say, but he had a nearly uncontrollable desire to unzip and bury his head in Billy's hoodie. He'd find the intoxicating scent of warm male there. "Fuck. You don't... I mean that isn't...."

"Don't hurt yourself, squeaky. I'm just trying to be a friend." Billy skidded to a stop like a demented snowboarder at the end of a run. "Hey, have you heard that new mix by Marco Loco? You probably don't listen to shit like them."

"I don't live in a cave."

"So you know the one?"

Jonah felt blood warm his face.

"Never mind. I just like it."

"You got it on your phone?" Jonah tapped his phone through his pants pocket. "Send the file."

"Okay. You never told me what your dad said when he found out."

"What do you... oh. He was okay, I guess. I'm pretty sure he thinks it's his fault. That's how he is."

"Isn't it like... supposed to be genetic or something?"

"Careful you don't get a paper cut from all that reading."

"Hey, I'm just trying to be a good—"

"Friend. Right." Jonah kicked at the gravel. They'd reached the dam. Billy led the way up a short stair to a locked gate on the top of the dam. "You sure this is okay?"

"Everyone does it." Billy pulled himself up and threw a leg over the iron gate. "Come on."

Jonah scrambled over the gate. Billy led the way onto the concrete walkway at the top of the low dam. They stopped at the guardrail where a spillway cut a channel through the top of the dam, and Billy rested a size twelve on the bottom rung of the railing.

Jonah leaned over the railing. The current hustled flotsam over the top of the spillway and into the foaming maelstrom at the base of the cascade. "I get you're just palling up when you ask about the gay thing. Sometimes I just don't want to talk about it, okay?"

"Whatever." Billy hunched his shoulders and stared into roiling water at the bottom of the spillway.

"It's the only fucking thing people see anymore, like I'm some kind of windup doll labeled 'Jonah the Gay Boy.'"

"Before I knew you were gay, I saw this fucking amazing musician who could play like I'm never gonna—no matter how much I practice."

"Yeah, well, I'm special," Jonah lisped like a little kid.

Billy winced. "Fuck you, Whale Bait."

A gust of wind brought a sprinkle of rain, spotting the concrete dam with freckles. "Let's walk some more," Jonah said. Billy followed as Jonah led the way back to the gate and pulled himself over. Jonah watched Billy drop to the gravel, his long legs practically reaching the ground as he hung from the iron bar at the top of the gate. "Do you have to be so tall?"

"The better for catching shrimp like you." Billy grabbed Jonah around the middle and hoisted him off the ground, laughing.

"Lookee here! Whale Bait's got a boyfriend," Justin taunted, sickly sweet, from behind them.

Jonah's whole body flinched, and he wanted to pee. Billy's arms loosened, and Jonah dropped to the ground. He spun to face Antony's sidekick, relieved to see Antony wasn't there. A fight would be two against one in their favor. "Shut up, fuckface."

The wrestler bounced in place on the gravel path. "Make me, faggot."

Billy faced Justin more slowly. "Jonah isn't my boyfriend."

"That's not what it looked like to me."

Billy glared, hands in fists. "Fuck off, dumbshit. You wouldn't know *what* it's like to have a friend, since you don't have any." He stepped toward Justin.

"Let's see what everyone thinks when I tell 'em about you and Pretty Boy." Justin danced backward, grinning. "This is gonna be fun." He turned and jogged upriver, waving a hand over his shoulder like a member of the royal family.

"Crap." Billy sounded worried.

"I'm sorry, Billy. It's my fault. I should have never—"

"Shut up, shut up, shut up. Don't apologize for that asshole." Billy vibrated with fury.

Jonah fell silent.

"Shit. I gotta go home," said Billy. "My dad...." He took off jogging toward the parking area.

"Right." Jonah didn't bother to hide the anger in his voice. Billy was just like everyone else. He might be a friend in private, but when push came to shove…. Jonah took off running as fast as he could, passing Billy.

"What are you doing?"

"Fuck off."

"Jonah, wait!"

Billy sped up and pulled alongside Jonah, Jonah's short legs no match for his long ones, even when Jonah pushed himself. Billy didn't say anything, but Jonah felt him looking every so often as they sprinted back to the parking area. Jonah steadfastly ignored him, refusing to acknowledge Billy's wave when they split in opposite directions to catch their buses home.

JONAH HELD himself together until he reached the house. No car blocked the driveway, so his mother must be out. Unlocking the door with keys that didn't seem to fit, he finally got the door open. His dad slumped on the living room couch with his hands in his lap. He looked up at Jonah, his wavering smile hopeful. "Hi, Jonah, didn't expect you back so soon. Are you hungry? I could make a cheese-grilled sandwich."

Not wanting to burst into tears in front of his dad like a fucking baby, Jonah brushed past without saying anything and rushed up the stairs to his bedroom. After slamming his door, he stopped to lock it for good measure. He'd thought Billy was different, but he wasn't. Billy was driven by what people thought just like anyone else. Jonah's saxophone case leaned against the windowsill, the hateful word on its side glowing like a neon sign. He kicked the case as hard as he could. The sharp pain in his toes opened the floodgates, and he threw himself on the bed, sobbing.

Sometime later, he heard his doorknob rattle, but his breathing still wasn't under control, so he ignored it.

"Jonah? Please talk to me. I need you to talk to me," his father called from outside the door.

Jonah knew he was a bastard for shutting his father out, but he wasn't prepared to talk about Billy or the hopelessness that overwhelmed him. His father would only stare at Jonah with the swollen features and puffy eyes of a defeated boxer and spout something stupid like "I'm sure things will work out eventually, son." The rattling stopped and Jonah heard his father's footsteps recede to the master bedroom.

ON SUNDAY, Jonah found the courage to go online and check Billy's home page. The comments there ranged from supportive to nasty.

> *Justin's a shit. Ignore him.*
> *Wow, I didn't know you were gay!*
> *Now I know why you broke up with Jessica.*
> *Quit the basketball team or die, cocksucker.*

At the end of two pages, Billy had posted a reply. "I AM NOT GAY. JONAH IS NOT MY BOYFRIEND." Jonah didn't bother to check his own page. He'd stopped friending people or responding to posts after the incident with the saxophone case. When a well-meaning student offered to pray for him even though he was going to burn in Hell, he'd unfriended everyone who wasn't a member of Jazz Ensemble. He turned off his computer and tried to read a book on the War of Independence for Mr. G's American History class. When that didn't work, he put on his headset and practiced piano on his electric keyboard.

Jonah's mom tapped him on the shoulder to get his attention around five o'clock and asked if he'd like pizza for dinner. He shrugged and agreed that pepperoni was okay, even though he hated it. He wondered why his dad hadn't said anything. He would have known what Jonah liked without having to ask.

That evening, he stayed downstairs to put the dishes in the dishwasher. He and his dad usually cleaned up together, even though it was technically Jonah's job to do the dishes after his father cooked. His dad was uncharacteristically quiet, staying in the living room to watch television with his mom. When he was finished, Jonah went out the back to chuck the pizza box into the recycling bin beside the garage.

When he came back, shivering in his T-shirt, his mother and father were waiting in the kitchen.

"Jonah, it's time to say good-bye to your mother. She's going back to Washington tonight. I'm sorry. I asked her to stay for a few more days, but she wouldn't—"

"John!" his mom snapped. "We agreed not to discuss this again." She turned to Jonah, her expression softening. "I'm sorry, honey, but I'm the lead attorney. I have to be there for the arguments. You understand, don't you? I'll come home as soon as I can."

What the fuck was he supposed to say? He understood all right. The house could be burning and she'd call the fire department and the insurance company and a fucking hotel, too, but she'd still be in that taxi when it left for the airport. "Whatever."

His mother pulled him into a hug. "You know I love you, honey." Jonah allowed her to envelop him in her warm scent, wishing he had the strength to pull away and stand with his father, but he didn't. Instead, he let her hug him until a honk from the front announced that her taxi had arrived. She pulled away. "See you soon."

His dad turned and went upstairs. Jonah heard the door of the bedroom click shut.

MONDAY MORNING, Jonah lay in bed until it was time to catch the bus. At the last second, he grabbed a random T-shirt, jeans, and dark-blue hoodie from the heap of mostly clean clothes that covered his dresser. Leaving his saxophone where it was, he grabbed his pack and ran for the door.

His father called from the kitchen. "Jonah! Don't you want some breakfast? Hey, take your winter coat!"

"No time," he called, rushing into the heatless winter sun.

At school, he went to the library and waited until just before the bell rang before sprinting to his first-period chemistry class. Billy, in a red sweatshirt with *WHAT ARE YOU LOOKING AT?* printed in block letters on the back, leaned against the row of lockers outside the classroom. He was talking to a tall African-American basketball player from the varsity team. Jonah brushed past without giving Billy a chance to say anything. When the period was over, he was up and out of his seat before the bell stopped vibrating.

He was halfway to his next class when someone grabbed his arm. "Wait up!"

"What do you want, Billy?"

"What do you think? I wanna talk to you."

"Be careful or you'll catch a disease."

"What's your problem? I tried to call you all weekend. All I got was this message saying your phone was turned off."

"What's my problem? You're my goddamn problem, Mr. I-got-to-go."

Billy tightened his grip on Jonah's arm. "Hold up, for fuck's sake."

"Don't touch me!"

A teacher Jonah didn't know called out to them from a classroom doorway. "Hey, what's going on?" Billy let go of Jonah's arm. "Nothing, sorry." Jonah took off, checking over his shoulder to see if Billy was following. Billy watched him go with a frustrated look. He held a hand to his face with forefinger and pinkie outstretched. *Call me.*

PAUL WATCHED Jonah plod into the band room empty-handed. "Where's your sax?"

Jonah wouldn't meet his eyes. "Didn't bring it today. Do you mind if I go to the nurse's office? I don't feel so well."

"What's wrong, Jonah?"

"Nothing, I don't feel good. Can I go?"

Paul felt his stomach drop. "Please, if something happened—"

"Fuck this! I told you I'm sick." Jonah yanked the door open.

"Hey, Jonah." Billy started to enter but stopped when Jonah stalked past without speaking and slammed the door behind him.

Paul followed him out into the corridor. "Billy, has something happened I should know about?"

"This day sucks." Billy rolled his neck. "What the hell, might as well tell you. Everyone else has heard by now. This guy saw me and Jonah in the park last week and decided to tell everyone that me and Jonah are boyfriends. He posted it all over the net."

Paul's energy drained faster than a battery abandoned on the arctic tundra. "I'm sorry, Billy."

Billy flinched when the bell for fifth period rang. "I should get my trumpet."

"Do you want to talk about it? I can ask someone to fill in for a moment."

"Not really. My friends get that it's only Justin's bullshit, but Jonah's acting really crazy and won't talk to me."

"Wait, is Justin one of the boys who's been harassing Jonah?"

Billy paled and closed his eyes. "Fuck me."

"What?"

"Sorry, I didn't mean you, Mr. G. I was just…. Jonah's never going speak to me again. I told him I wouldn't tell."

"But you know this Justin?"

"Yeah, he's on the wrestling team." Billy bounced in place, distress coming off him in waves. "Does Jonah have to know you got it from me?"

Paul thought of the last time he'd been asked to keep something quiet. "I can't make any promises, but I'll do what I can."

"I'm so fucked."

"Listen, I'm going to check on Jonah. Would you do me a favor and get the band started? I'll be back in a minute."

Billy nodded. "Tell him I'm sorry, would you?"

Just around the corner, Paul found Jonah sitting on the floor with his back against the wall. "I thought you were going to the nurse's office."

"If I go there, she'll call my dad."

The ragged sound of tuning instruments drifted down the corridor. Paul slid down the wall next to Jonah. "This wouldn't have anything to do with Billy and Justin, would it?"

Jonah banged his head against the cinder-block wall.

"Jonah! Stop that right now." Paul used a tone he normally reserved for the marching band practices and class clowns.

Jonah's head jerked to a halt.

"You know Billy doesn't blame you for what Justin did, right?"

"He told you about Justin?"

"I'm pretty sure he didn't mean to. It kind of slipped out. It's not my place to speak for Billy, but I really think you ought to talk to him. I know he wants to talk to you."

"He couldn't get away from me fast enough after Justin saw us in the park. Are you going to tell Mr. Wong?"

"Yes."

"Butt custard! He's going to tell my dad, isn't he?"

"Probably."

"Can I go home now?"

"We have to call your father."

Jonah pulled his phone from his pocket. "I'll tell him," he said, tapping the touchscreen on his phone. Paul waited while Jonah held the phone to his ear, the sound of ringing audible in the quiet hallway. "He's not answering. He must have gone to the grocery store or something."

"Doesn't he have a mobile?"

"Mom made him cancel it when he…." Jonah stopped, coloring.

Paul heard the Winfield's answering system kick in. "You've reached the Winfield residence—"

Jonah ended the call. "I don't have a clue what to say."

Paul stood and held out a hand. "Tell you what. Why don't you hang out in my office until sixth period? Then we can go down to Mr. Wong's office together."

Jonah rose slowly. "Whatever."

PAUL BYPASSED a pair of sullen miscreants outside Charlie's office and stuck his head in the door. "Charlie, can Jonah and I speak to you for a moment? I've got some new information."

Charlie pointed at the waiting area. "I suppose they've cooled their heels long enough. Send them in, would you? Stick around, this won't take long."

Paul motioned to the waiting boys. Jonah didn't look much happier to visit the principal than they did. "I know you wanted to deal with this on your own, Jonah. I respect that."

"So why won't you let me?"

"You know the school can't let this go, right?" Before Jonah could answer, Paul heard uncharacteristically sharp tones coming from Charlie's office.

Jonah grinned suddenly. "Great day for it."

The door opened and Charlie ushered the boys out. "I'll be speaking to your parents this evening. My suggestion is that you talk to them first." The boys filed out, unconcerned. "I hope you've got something better to say for yourself, Jonah."

"Jonah has confirmed the name of one of our bullies."

"Bravo." Charlie returned to the desk and folded his hands on the desk like an offering. "Now you can give me the name of the other one."

Jonah rolled his eyes at Paul.

"What's the point of giving me one and not the other?"

"I didn't give anyone anything," said Jonah.

"Billy Preston told me about Justin," said Paul.

Charlie glanced at his watch. "Do I have to pull Billy from basketball practice? You might as well tell me the name of the other boy, Jonah. At this point, all you're doing is wasting my time."

The possibility of involving Billy apparently convinced Jonah to cooperate. Jonah listed a set of incidents when Antony and Justin had teased, hit, or bullied him. Charlie pressed for details.

"Tell me what they said to you."

To Paul's ears, Jonah's account of Antony and Justin's actual words seemed vague and evasive, but Paul said nothing. Jonah was withdrawn, his voice barely audible. Paul guessed his focus was on the upcoming conversation with his father.

"Do you have to call him? It's time for me to go home. I'll talk to him when I get there."

"I think it's best that I call, Jonah. I promised that I'd inform him personally if there were any further incidents."

"Whatever."

Charlie asked Jonah for his home number and dialed it on his office phone, but it rang until the voice mail picked up this time as well.

"I guess you get it your way," said Charlie. "Would you like one of us to give you a ride home? I know this has been a difficult day for you, Jonah."

"I'll be happy to do it," said Paul.

THE WINFIELD house was a two-story box with white vinyl siding and nonfunctional black shutters. If it was consistent with similar homes Paul had visited, it would have a kitchen, combined living and dining area, and den on the first floor. The second floor would have a master bedroom suite on one side and two bedrooms sharing a bath on the other. It had one atypical feature: someone had replaced the twin dormers on one side with a raised roof, probably to create a more airy master bedroom. The front yard was trim, but the grass was faded and brown, and the shrubs that bordered the driveway had lost their leaves. A dense row of late-blooming roses divided the Winfield's property from their neighbor's, the spiny stems still supporting pink or yellow petaled flowers.

"Your dad must be fond of roses," said Paul, jamming his shift lever into park.

"I guess. He spends a lot of time on them. Do you wanna come in?"

"Do you mind if I say hello to your dad?"

"I'll get him for you."

Jonah led Paul to the front door and fished his keys from his backpack. He motioned to Paul to follow him in. "Dad, I'm home!"

Pointing to the couch, he dropped his pack on the coffee table. "Do you want some water or something?"

"No, thanks."

"He must be taking a nap. I'll be right back." Jonah ran up the stairs to the second floor calling out, "Hey, Dad! Mr. G's here."

Paul heard the swish of a door brushing carpet. "Dad!" Jonah's voice cracked high and frantic. "Oh no, you didn't. You didn't. Dad!"

Paul ran up the stairs and through the open door to the master bedroom. Jonah was locked in a gruesome embrace with his father. John Winfield was hanging from an exposed beam in the middle of the room, a coil of nylon climbing rope at his feet, his face swollen and purple, his head cocked to one side. A dining room chair lay on its side on the beige-and-brown carpet.

Gagging at the stink of human excrement, Paul ran to Jonah's side and reluctantly touched Winfield's wrist. The skin was cool. He wasn't surprised to feel no pulse. "Jonah, I'm so sorry." He tried to pull Jonah away from the body, but the boy screamed incoherently and clutched his father's legs with one arm, flailing at Paul with the other. Paul backed away and retrieved his phone. He dialed 911 with shaking fingers.

CHAPTER 9

TWENTY MINUTES later, Paul stepped into the yard and was bathed in the red and blue flashing lights of the police car and EMT vehicle. He dialed his phone.

"Hello?"

"Davoud. Is that you?"

"Hi, Paul. What's wrong? You sound terrible."

"Listen, I'm at Jonah's place. Can you write down the address? I'll wait." Paul hadn't even considered calling anyone else. Davoud and his family would help.

"I'm getting a pen." Davoud's voice faded for a moment as he stepped away from the phone. "Okay."

"The address is 411 Piedmont Place."

"Right. I've got it. What's going on?"

Paul kept clearing his throat, the impulse to gag strong even out of the house. "It's Jonah's father. He's hung himself. Jonah's hysterical. I need help."

"Have you called the police?" said Davoud.

"They're here with the EMTs, but they want to take Jonah, and I don't know what to do."

Davoud's purr became a growl. "What do you mean, take him?"

"He's a minor. They can't leave him here alone. They want to call Child Protective Services and have them meet us at the hospital."

"Where's his mother? Is Jonah okay? Why do they want to take him to the hospital?"

"Jonah's not hurt physically, but he isn't coherent. I guess they'd keep an eye on him at the hospital until CPS shows, but I think he'll do better with family. Unfortunately, his mother's on a business trip. He's been repeating something about Washington."

"Get his phone and use it to call his mother."

"Right."

"Have her tell the police to let you take care of Jonah. You can come here. Aida and Rascal will help us with him. We'll be his family as long as he needs us."

"Got it." Paul disconnected and ran to the living room, where a middle-aged female EMT had an arm around the hysterical teenager. Her partner was upstairs with the police officers.

"Jonah, where's your phone?"

Jonah's response was buried amid a barrage of sobs, gasps, and hiccups. Looking around the room, Paul's gaze fell on Jonah's pack, which lay on the coffee table where Jonah had dropped it. He rummaged around inside. An internal pocket held what he was looking for. He was grateful it was the same type he used. Pulling up the address book, he looked under M for mom or mother. Nothing. The addresses were sorted by last name. He paged to W. There was only one female listed, Esmé Winfield. He dialed the number.

"Hi, honey. What's up?"

"Is this Esmé Winfield?"

"Yes." The woman's tone changed instantly to brisk. "Why are you calling on my son's phone?"

"This is Paul Gaston, Jonah's music teacher."

"Where's Jonah? Has something happened to him? What's that noise in the background? It's hard to hear you."

"I'm sorry, Mrs. Winfield. Jonah's okay, but your husband— something has happened to your husband. You need to come home right away."

The older of the two police officers, who'd arrived after the EMT unit, came down the stairs. Paul motioned him over and pressed the mute button on the phone. "I've got Mrs. Winfield on the line. Do you want to speak to her?"

Esmé's tinny voice sounded from the tiny speakers. "What do you mean, something's happened to my husband? Where is he?"

The officer glared at Paul for a second, and then took the phone as if it were the remote control for an explosive device. "Mrs. Winfield? I'm Officer Mitchell of the Glen Falls Police Department. Yes, that's right. There's been an accident. We need you to come home right away and take care of your son. Your son is fine, ma'am, but he needs you. How soon can you get here?" He listened for a moment and took a measured breath. "Ma'am. You're not listening. You need to come home *now*."

Paul motioned to the officer to mute the phone.

"Hold on a second, ma'am."

"Ask her if it's okay if Paul Gaston watches her son until she gets back."

The officer frowned. "Are you Gaston? What is your relation to the Winfields?"

"Yes, I'm Paul Gaston. I'm the music teacher at the high school. I'm a friend of the family."

"You were the one who called it in, right?"

Paul nodded.

"Don't go anywhere until I've gotten a statement from you." The officer pressed the mute button again. "Mrs. Winfield, there's a Paul Gaston here who says you know him. The music teacher?" He paused, listening. "Right, at the high school. He says he'll watch Jonah until you arrive. Is that okay with you?" He nodded at Paul as he listened. "Thank you, Mrs. Winfield. Now, when you get back into town, I want you to call this number." He recited a number from memory. "It's very important that you call. We'll send someone to pick you up. Yes, that's right. Call and we'll pick you up. Just like the rental company." He ended the call and examined Paul. "Right. I hope you know what you're in for, buddy."

Jonah had quieted and lay in a fetal position on the couch. He didn't seem aware of anything happening around him. Paul swallowed. "I'll make sure Jonah has whatever he needs."

"Right. The coroner will come for the body. Don't touch anything until he arrives." The officer pointed to Jonah. "He going to be okay, Panowski?"

The EMT raised her eyebrows. "What do you think, Officer Mitchell?"

Mitchell spoke with exaggerated precision. "Does he need to go to the hospital?"

"No, he doesn't."

"Okay." Officer Mitchell looked at Paul. "He's all yours as soon as we get that statement."

"Will you stay with him until I'm done?" Paul asked the EMT.

She nodded, rubbing Jonah's back. "I'll stay with him."

DAVOUD TURNED onto Piedmont Place to find the dead-end street clogged with vehicles. Flashing red, white, and blue lights made for a disco effect and brought to mind a club he'd visited once in Chicago that had an outdoor dance floor surrounded by colored strobes.

"Don't park too close. You don't want to get blocked in," said Aida.

"Okay, Mother." Davoud stopped a few houses down. "Why don't you wait in the car? Rascal and I can get them."

"Don't be silly. You may need me." Aida climbed stiffly from Rascal's black SUV. Davoud's car couldn't fit five, and Davoud hadn't been sure that Paul would be fit to drive, so he'd asked for Rascal's help. Aida had heard Rascal on the phone and insisted on coming too.

At the front door, Davoud knocked. When no one answered, he pushed the door open.

"Who the hell are you?" said the female EMT on the couch.

"I'm Davoud Avakian. This is my brother, Rasul, and my mother, Aida." He gestured to encompass them all. "We're the cavalry."

THAT NIGHT, as Paul listened to the ticking of a radiator and watched Jonah sleep, he wondered at his dual decisions to call Davoud instead of Charlie or another teacher and to follow Davoud's instructions without question. He'd come to trust Davoud without realizing it. He was sure that meant something, but he was too tired to think what.

A FACELESS man in an undertaker's suit chased him down the hall at Martin Luther King High School. His bare feet slapped past lockers with doors askew. He slammed into a stairwell, feet barely touching the steps until he stumbled and fell, tumbling wildly and twisting his neck at the bottom. A purple-faced corpse extended a fat tongue to lick his mouth.

Jonah woke with a cry. The corpse had looked like his dad. No, the corpse *was* his dad, hanging from the beam in his parents' bedroom. A dark-haired man in a black sweater and gray wool slacks rose from a chair in the corner of the room and approached the bed cautiously. "Hi, Jonah. I'm Rasul Avakian, Davoud's brother, but everyone calls me Rascal. You were dreaming."

Jonah swallowed and croaked, "Where?"

"You're in the Music Box—in one of the apartments above Avakian Music. Paul asked me to keep an eye on you."

Someone had substituted jellyfish for Jonah's brains. "Mr. G?"

Rascal's brow furrowed. "I don't—oh, you mean Paul. He was here all night, but he had to go to school this morning."

School. Mr. G and the principal questioning him about Antony and Justin. His dad telling Mr. Wong it was wrong to hit. That was before, before.... No, he didn't want to think about that.

"Here, drink this." Rascal helped him sit up and held a glass of water while he sipped. He looked around, head clearing a little. The room was lifted from a Lemony Snicket story. Light from the window was blocked by midnight-blue velvet drapes with sheer inner curtains. The walls were protected by dark paneling extending about four feet from the floor. Blue-and-gold wallpaper rose in vertical stripes to a pressed-tin ceiling. The solid bureau and chair would require a crane to move.

"Who decorated this place?"

Rascal chuckled. "My great-aunt Suri lived here, but I imagine the decor is mostly turn-of-the-century hotel."

Jonah would have sunk back into the warm bed, but he had to pee. He struggled to swing his legs from under the bedclothes.

Rasul moved nearer to the bed. "You may be a little groggy yet. The doctor gave you a pretty strong sedative last night."

"I need to pee."

"It's down the hall. I'll show you."

When they returned, Jonah climbed back into the bed. "Where's Davoud?"

"He went down to open the shop. He'll be back to check on you when Marta arrives." Marta reminded Jonah of his mother, and he began to cry silently without knowing exactly why. The expression of dismay on Rascal's face was comical, but he sat down on the bed and patted Jonah's hair.

WHEN JONAH next woke, Davoud's mother, Aida, sat by the bed. The opera diva's beauty-shopped hair caught the window light, limning her head. She turned her face, and he saw the lines around her eyes and mouth. She was old. How did she feel when her father died? Was she angry too, or was she a better person than he was?

Aida smiled. "I see you're awake. Are you hungry?"

"No." He looked away. "Is my mother here?"

"She arrived this morning. Davoud said she went—she's with the police. She'll be here soon."

"Will I have to… I don't want…." He started to cry again.

"Shh, or you'll scare Rascal." Aida patted his hand.

"Rascal?"

"Never mind. It's time he thought about someone besides himself. He's a very pretty violin player, but not so good at dealing with feelings when they come attached to people. I think you frightened him."

Jonah stammered out a reply. "I didn't mean to."

"Of course not, dear. None of this is your fault. You have a good cry, and I'll sit here and hold your hand."

HOURS LATER, when the light behind the curtains was golden, a violin played something sweet and sad. Jonah listened carefully so he could remember it later. After a while, it was interrupted by a knock on the apartment door. He heard hushed voices, and then his mother was there in the doorway with Rascal. Her suit was rumpled and her blond hair was loose on her shoulders, but her eyes were dry until they found his.

"Jonah?" She rushed to the bed. "Oh, honey. Are you okay?"

Dad hanged himself in your bedroom because you weren't there and I wouldn't talk to him. His dad wasn't okay. Nothing would ever be right again.

He rolled onto his side and squeezed his knees to his chest.

AIDA STAMPED, the effect muted by the thick layer of Persian carpet covering the hardwood floor of her apartment. "She cannot go back to that place, Davoud. Most of all, she cannot take the boy back there. He'll see his father every time—"

"It's not our place to interfere, Mother."

"You must talk to her. She knows who you are, at least. Jonah has spoken of you. Convince her to stay with us. We have room in the Music Box."

Oh, Mother! We have room, all right. I may not be able to pay the heating bill, but we have room. In our hearts we have room. He stroked his mother's cheek with a knuckle. "I'll try."

Esmé Winfield was still in 3B with Rascal and Jonah. When Davoud had slipped out, Jonah was still refusing to acknowledge his mother. "Paul will be back soon. We'll talk to her together. She knows him better than me."

"You must not take no for an answer."

"We can't hold her child against her will."

"She'll listen. If she has any sense at all, she'll listen." Aida went to a roll-top secretary and slid the top up, revealing a small writing surface and set of wooden cubbyholes. She plucked a leather-bound checkbook from one and a fountain pen from another. "You know I'm angry with you."

Davoud swung a kitchen chair around to straddle and rested his arms on the back. "What have I done now?"

"You'll cut your salary until you're living like a scullery maid on scraps from the kitchen, and you'll transform Avakian Music until it's unrecognizable to your own family...." She finished writing out a check and signed it with a flourish. "But you refuse to ask your mother for help." She handed him the check. "The roof is a solvable problem. Jonah and his mother have so much more to contend with...." She stamped again, in frustration. "It's just stupid for us to waste time arguing about nonsense like loans and business plans when we could be doing something important."

A scullery maid? She'd been watching too much public television. Davoud read the dollar amount and sighed inwardly. The check might cover this month's heating bill, but it wasn't anywhere near the cost of a new roof.

Aida watched him carefully. "I'll hear no arguments. If you tear that up, I'll hire the contractor myself. Although God help us, we'll probably end up with a pagoda on the roof or something."

"Thank you, Mother."

"You're welcome, dear."

The door buzzer rang. "That'll be Paul."

Aida glared. "You know your duty."

"Yes, Mother, I do."

THE ELECTRONIC door lock buzzed. Paul pushed the door open, needing very much for this nightmarish day to be over. He'd told himself he was visiting the Avakian Music building to check on Jonah, but in truth, he didn't want to be alone. He'd walked to school that morning hoping the routine of classes and bells would calm him like the steady clicking of his grandmother's clockwork metronome.

Instead, he'd been unable to shake John Winfield's bloated face from his mind. He'd repeatedly lost his train of thought, his strange behavior in class a spreading ripple not unlike the quiet that follows an earthquake. He'd hardly known Jonah's father. It was beyond imagining how Jonah felt.

After fifth period, he'd visited Charlie Wong's office to ask for a few days off. Charlie blinked at him and suggested he take the rest of the week. Paul didn't mention his temporary role as Jonah's caretaker, so he was caught by surprise when Charlie called out as he left. "Paul, you're going over to the Avakian building, aren't you?" Charlie said he was suspending Antony Scarelli and Justin Amberson for the remainder of the term. "Pass that on to Mrs. Winfield and to Jonah, if you think it will help. I'm sending a letter, but...." It was not until Paul was crossing the Martin Luther King High School parking lot that the import of Charlie's words caught up with him. The end of the term wasn't that far off. Antony and Justin might actually be back in school before Jonah was. He drifted to a halt, wanting to go back and argue, an impulse he finally rejected as unwise.

He slid the cage open on the third floor. Davoud's lean form rested against the wall opposite the elevator. The sight calmed him like a touch. The time was coming when he'd have to examine his feelings for the man. For now, he allowed himself to be comforted.

Davoud's expression shifted to concern. "You look exhausted."

"No kidding. How's Jonah?"

"He's awake but refusing to speak to his mother. I'm afraid he blames her for being away when it happened. Rascal's with Esmé now."

"What does she plan to do? Has she said anything?"

"Aida wants me to invite them both to stay with us until she's figured something out."

Paul pressed his palms to his forehead. "I've been seeing Winfield hanging from that beam all day. I can only imagine what Jonah's feeling. There's no way he should return to that house."

Davoud nodded. "I was hoping you'd help me convince Esmé of that."

"Of course."

Davoud led the way to 3B. He tapped quietly on the door and pushed it open. "Esmé? Paul Gaston is here."

Esmé perched on one side of the couch, a mug cradled in her hands. Her eyes were dry, but a tremor formed ripples in the surface of the liquid. Rascal had planted himself on the other side, his hands on his thighs, thumbs beating time on the sharply creased wool of his slacks. He leapt to his feet. "Paul, thank God you're here!"

"Mrs. Winfield, I'm Paul Gaston. We met last year at the parent-teacher conference."

"Yes, of course." Esmé rose, placing her mug carefully on a coaster, and presented an unsteady hand. "Jonah speaks well of you. Thank you for helping... thank you all. I don't know what I would've done if you'd not been there."

"I just called for help, Mrs. Winfield."

"Please call me Esmé," she said automatically. She gestured at the apartment. "Mr. Avakian, I'm so grateful to you and your family for giving us a place to stay."

Davoud nodded, smiling hesitantly. "You must call me Davoud. We're very fond of Jonah. It was the least we could do. My mother, Aida, wants you to know you're welcome to stay if you'd rather not return to the house."

"Oh no, Mr. Avakian. I couldn't—"

"Davoud, please."

"Jonah can't go back there," Paul said. "You don't know what it was like. I've been seeing John hanging there all... shit."

Esmé paled, the tremor in her hands spreading to the corners of her mouth.

"I'm sorry, I wasn't thinking," said Paul.

"What my brother and Paul are trying to say, Esmé, is that we think it might be less traumatic for both of you if you stay here for a while, rather than go home," said Rascal quietly. "That is, if it's okay with you. My family owns the building. You're welcome to use this apartment as long as you need it."

Esmé looked around the plush sitting room. "You're very generous, but I must think what to do. The coroner said they would release my husband's body tomorrow. I must call the funeral home. There is John's family to inform... and Jonah's school."

"You can do all of that here, Esmé," said Aida, making her way briskly from the hall. "I'll help. Davoud and Paul will look after Jonah. Paul can deal with the school. Rasul will mind the store. You see, it's all very simple."

"I gather you've met my mother, Aida," said Davoud.

"I'll need some clothes," said Esmé, hesitantly.

Paul felt for his keys. "I can take you."

"Don't be silly, dear," said Aida. "You've just come from work, and Davoud's going to feed you dinner. Rasul will drive Esmé." Rascal's eyes widened. Aida glared until Rascal acquiesced silently. If Esmé noticed the exchange, she showed no sign.

"TAKE A load off, Paul. I need to put something in the oven, and then we can relax."

Paul flopped onto the plush cushions of the velvet monstrosity Davoud referred to as a sofa, his feet dangling off the side. Davoud disappeared into the kitchen. Paul heard the refrigerator door swish open and other kitchen sounds he associated with Ethel, the grandmother who'd raised him from age ten. "You really don't need to keep feeding me. I'm perfectly capable of taking care of myself."

"Of course you are, but I enjoy feeding you. Consider it a favor to me."

Paul laughed. "How could I refuse when you put it like that?"

"Indeed, I'd be terribly hurt. Would you like some wine?"

"Yes, please."

Davoud brought him a glass of something white. "Chardonnay all right?"

Davoud set the glass on the coffee table and patted Paul's knee. "Take off your shoes and relax. Take a nap if you like."

"I'm not sure what I've done to deserve you, Davoud, but I'm grateful."

"I like having you around." Davoud smiled warmly before returning to the kitchen. "Do you have school work?"

"No, thank goodness. I asked Charlie for a couple of days off. That reminds me...." Paul hesitated, suddenly reluctant to continue.

"Yes? Did Charlie say something?"

Paul rose and paced over to the window overlooking Main Street. It was fully dark, the streetlights throwing long shadows that faded in the headlights of oncoming cars, only to return after they'd passed. "I'm so angry, I'm not sure I want to talk about it."

"Tell me the news, anyway, would you? Then we can drop it if you like."

"Sorry, I guess Jonah is your concern now too."

"He is."

Paul sighed. "Wong suspended Antony and Justin until the end of the term. They'll probably be back in school before Jonah is."

"I thought the school has a no-tolerance policy?"

"That just means there must be disciplinary action and/or counseling for the participants in confirmed incidents. The policy doesn't specify expulsion for bullies."

Davoud stuck his head out of the kitchen. "There isn't anything we can do?"

"Not unless Jonah is willing to press assault charges. Of course, if they try it again...."

Davoud disappeared and more sounds drifted from the kitchen. "I have vegetarian lasagna and garlic bread. Are balsamic vinegar and olive oil okay for the salad?"

"That's a whole lot better than I'd be getting at home."

"Good! I want to impress you."

"It's almost as if you were trying to seduce me."

When Davoud didn't reply, Paul wanted to groan out of sheer frustration. *I've gone too far.*

"Dinner is served," Davoud called. "Come to the dining room."

JONAH WOKE at the sound of the apartment door opening. The bedroom was dark. Low voices moved into the living room. After a moment, muffled footsteps approached the bedroom door. He closed his eyes and steadied his breathing. The door opened and he smelled his mom's distinctive perfume. He kept his eyes closed, hoping she would go away. A touch so light he wasn't sure if he imagined it brushed the hair over his ear. After a moment, his mom moved away and the door closed. He knew he'd have to speak to her soon, but he wasn't ready yet. *Maybe tomorrow.*

Sometime later, it could have been minutes or hours, he heard the violin again, practicing the same sad music he'd heard earlier. Humming to himself, he began to work out an accompanying part on the piano, his fingers twitching over an imaginary keyboard. Tomorrow he would go down and visit the Steinway.

THE STEINWAY'S ivory and ebony keys were cold to the touch, but Jonah was eager to hear the music he'd composed in his head the night before. He'd woken early and taken the elevator to the second floor to knock on Davoud's door. Davoud answered in a bathrobe and slippers, his dark hair on end.

"Jonah, you're up early. Are you looking for breakfast?"

When Jonah explained about the Steinway, Davoud simply nodded and handed him a set of keys he lifted from a hook beside the door. "Come up when you're hungry."

Having no violin, Jonah hummed the slow melody he'd heard from his bed. He wasn't sure what to do in a couple of spots, but he thought he had the key and the chord changes, so he worked in the silence between the notes, and on the bridge.

"Hey, kid, I think I've heard that somewhere before."

Jonah startled, clenching his fingers above the keys. Rascal didn't *sound* angry.

"No, don't stop. I need to work on the second part anyway. Do you mind if I join you?"

Jonah twisted around on the bench. "I was just... you know. I liked it, and I wanted to see if I could figure out a piano part. You're not mad?"

Rascal blinked. "God no, you've paid me a great compliment." He set his violin case on the floor and lifted out his instrument. "Give me an *A*, would you?"

Jonah faced the piano and tapped a key while pressing the sustain pedal with his foot.

"Thanks." Rascal made quick adjustments to his *A* string and checked the others against it, tweaking the pegs. Finally, he ran through a rapid set of scales and stopped. After a few seconds of silence, he closed his eyes and began the piece. Jonah waited, unsure whether Rascal wanted him to play. Finishing the first part, Rascal stopped after a few bars of the second. "Hear that, right at the transition? It's not right, but I'm not sure how to fix it. Maybe if I hear the piano part, I'll get an idea. Let's take it together from the top."

Jonah played the part he'd worked out in his head the night before. When they reached the transition, he thought of Count Basie and tried to fill with a few perfect notes.

"That's it," Rascal murmured, modifying the original melody to match Jonah's improvisation. "Lovely."

Jonah flushed with pleasure.

THE E-MAIL Jonah received from Billy the following Monday was the first Jonah had ever gotten from another student. Kids texted or used a chat room. E-mail was for old people like teachers and parents. His mom and dad e-mailed him. Only Dad wasn't sending any more messages. Maybe if he'd sent one before he decided to off himself.... His father's swollen tongue intruded on his thoughts, and he pinched himself on the arm hard enough to bruise. After a moment focusing on the pain in his arm, he returned to Billy's e-mail. He hadn't responded to any texts since the day his father killed himself. Maybe the e-mail would distract him.

To: jonahwin784@gmail.com
From: trumpeter0923@gmail.com
Subject: Sorry

I asked Mr. G where you were today, and he told me about your dad.
I'm really sorry. I can't imagine how I would feel if my dad died, let alone if he did what yours did. I started

to put in that I hope you're okay, but then I thought that's pretty stupid. I sure as shit wouldn't be okay, so I'll just say that I'm thinking about you, and I hope you'll want to talk to me again soon. I'm so mad your dad hurt you. I get that he must have been feeling pretty crappy, but I never met him, so I can't work up much sympathy. I'm probably not saying the right things, so I'll stop.

Please don't give Mr. G a hard time for telling me what happened. I threatened to skip all his classes and chain myself to his desk if he didn't tell me what was up with you. You know how he hates it when you cut his classes. I got your e-mail from the history class list.

I don't know if you'll read this, but I don't know what else to do since you won't answer my texts. I don't understand why you went dark on me after we met Justin in the park. What a bastard that guy is! Did you hear he was suspended until next term for bullying? Anyway, I guess I did something to piss you off. Even though I don't know what it was, I'm sorry. I'll try to give you a better apology if you tell me what I did.

I was going to send this, but then I remembered what you said in the hall after Justin's shit hit the fan. You called me Mr. I-got-to-go. Maybe I'm off base, but did you think I left the park because I was embarrassed to be seen with you? Or that I was mad at you because people were going to think I'm queer?

I don't know what's going on in your head. I wish the fuck you'd tell me. If it helps, I took off because my dad makes me friend him on everything online. He says it's to protect me, but I think he's just nosy and doesn't believe in privacy. Anyway, he sees everything people post about me, so I had to go home and do damage control before he saw anything. Okay, maybe I was a little worried about what people were going to think, but there's no way I'm going to let a fuck like Justin control who I'm friends with. I'm your friend, Jonah, even though you're kind of a jerk when you're mad.

Crap. I'm screwing this up, but I don't even know if you're going to see it or if I'm just shooting it into fucking space like those messages they sent with Voyager. Please read this!

To: trumpeter0923@gmail.com
From: jonahwin784@gmail.com
Subject: Re: Sorry

Hi Billy,

I guess Mr. G told you I'm staying with the Avakians. Did you know that Davoud's—Mr. Avakian's—family owns the whole building above the music store? They call it the Music Box. His mother is this famous opera star, Aida Kazmi, although she's retired now, and his brothers are both professional musicians. Rascal and I—that's Rasul Avakian, Davoud's brother—are working on this piece together. It's modern, like classical modern, not pop, so you probably won't like it, but he's helping me write out the piano part.

You didn't do anything wrong. I'm sorry I'm such a jerk. I don't even know why you want to be my friend, but I guess it's okay with me. I haven't turned on my phone yet, so don't text me.

My dad's funeral is on Friday if you want to come.
Jonah

THERE WEREN'T many people at his dad's funeral. Jonah didn't know whether to be sad there weren't more people or gratified that his dad had gotten what he deserved for abandoning him and his mom. He felt out of control, like he was being swept downstream on a logjam. They weren't in their usual church, St. Mary's, where his dad had always taken them for Mass on Sundays, because his dad had committed suicide and that was a sin, and the priest was being a jerk about it.

Instead, they were holding the service in a Universalist Unitarian church, where the minister was a friend of his mom's and could be counted on not to say anything mean. His dad was going to be cremated afterward so there wouldn't be any question where to bury him. Jonah wasn't sure he liked the idea. He couldn't see himself visiting an urn to talk to his dad, but nobody asked him, so that was that.

His mom leaned over and pointed out a couple of old college friends who'd driven over from Chicago. A few childhood buddies and some of his mother's colleagues from her law firm were scattered around the pews. Davoud and his family took up a whole pew, Rascal and Aida looking very stiff in dark clothes Jonah suspected they usually wore for concerts. Billy looked really uncomfortable in a blue corduroy jacket and black jeans as he slid into the back row. Jonah asked his mom if he could invite his friend up to sit with them. She acted kind of surprised, but she agreed, so Jonah got up and went to get him.

"Hey, Billy. Do you want to sit with me? My mom says it's okay." Jonah knew it was probably mean to put Billy on the spot, but he wanted Billy next to him.

Billy blinked and grinned. "Sure thing, Piano Man."

Jonah felt himself grinning back, but then he thought he shouldn't be happy at his dad's funeral so he glanced around to see if anyone had noticed. "Come on, you want to meet Davoud?"

"After the service, dude. The minister looks like he's gonna have a cow."

"Oh, right." Jonah felt stupid, but he grabbed Billy's arm anyway and dragged him to the first row. "Mom, this is Billy Preston. He's first trumpet in the jazz ensemble at school."

Billy performed a sort of jerky half bow. "I'm sorry for your loss, Mrs. Winfield."

"Thank you for coming, Billy."

They sat, and the minister began the service. Before coming to the church, Jonah's mom had asked him if he wanted to say anything, but she said he didn't have to if he didn't want to, so he didn't. When his mother got up to speak, she held the podium for a moment like she didn't know what to say either, but then she told the story of how she'd met his dad at an antiapartheid rally at college and how they'd cared about the same things. She talked about him like he'd died of a heart attack or something normal, and Jonah must have looked upset or maybe made a little sound or something, because Billy reached over and took his hand. The heat of Billy's hand was pretty distracting, so Jonah just sat there and concentrated on that until the service was done, and it was time to go back to the Music Box.

CHAPTER 10

PAUL WAS grateful for the help with Jonah, but Davoud's family could be a bit overwhelming. Flirting with Aida was fun, but she sometimes left him feeling a little small, like his choices in life hadn't taken him far enough from home. And while he would have paid for tickets to see Rascal escorting Esmé Winfield like he was dancing on ice, jamming with the brothers was like doing wind sprints with a pair of greyhounds. The core of his discomfort, however, had to do with Davoud. On the one hand, Davoud was clearly delighted to entertain and feed him. On the other hand, he shied away when Paul flirted. Paul knew he was no prize, but after some weeks of getting to know each other, he was pretty sure he'd read the signs right, and that Davoud was attracted to him. If they'd met in a bar, Paul wouldn't have hesitated to pursue the tall man with messy black hair and warm eyes. Surrounded by Davoud's family, Paul was less confident that an overt expression of interest would be appreciated.

It was these thoughts that prompted Paul to invite Davoud on a formal date. Maybe the man would be more comfortable wrested from the arms of his family. While Paul couldn't fault the brothers' behavior toward him, there did seem to be some residual family business that was making Davoud skittish. When Paul asked him out, Davoud hesitated a fraction longer than Paul would have liked, before accepting gravely. He nearly asked if Davoud wanted to reconsider, but that would have been catty, and he was determined to move their relationship forward, so he swallowed his tongue.

Blind dates had been less nerve-wracking. He'd barely shoved the shift lever into park at the Music Box, when Davoud slipped out of the building and pried open Paul's battered sedan.

"Paul. It's so good to see you."

The gravel slurry of Davoud's greeting was enough to prompt an immediate expression of interest from Paul's dick. Climbing into the car, Davoud leaned over as if for a kiss, but instead ran a finger over the soft fabric of Paul's shirt collar. "That's lovely. Where did you get it? Surely not around here."

It was like Davoud to say just the thing to make Paul feel better about himself. Paul had spent a ridiculous half hour deciding what to wear before heading over. He'd finally gone with the clothing equivalent of comfort food. The shirt was a prized favorite from his time playing gigs in Chicago, from his life before becoming a frumpy schoolteacher. It was Egyptian cotton with a green-and-violet pattern. "I got it from a shop in Chicago—Boystown actually."

"You must tell me where. Someday, I'm going to have to replace some of these old rags."

The old rags in question consisted of a loosely cut, pristine white, button-down shirt and fitted black slacks. Paul licked his lips at the thought of how they would show off Davoud's tight round posterior. "You look hot tonight, Davoud."

"That's kind of you, but we both know who's the handsome one."

Paul put his car into drive and pulled into traffic. "We'll have to agree to disagree about that." He glanced over and was relieved to see Davoud's smile. "Have you been to Café Boeuf? You didn't say on the phone."

"No, I haven't. I don't eat out much. This is a big treat for me."

"I hope you like it. It's a bit funky. The décor looks like it came from Rick's Café, but the name's taken from the *Prairie Home Companion* sketch. The food's good—if you can get the tongue out of your cheek."

Davoud laughed, a soft baritone rumble. "I hardly get to listen anymore because my mother insists we eat dinner together on Sundays, but I love that show."

"I would never have guessed. The music—"

"Isn't my family's thing. Nevertheless, I like it."

Paul glanced away from the traffic. Davoud had lost his smile. "I'm sorry, I ought to know better than that. You have your own taste."

"Drive the car, would you."

At the restaurant, they were greeted by scents of garlic, fresh basil, and roasted lamb—despite the place's name. After the host seated them, an enthusiastic teenager recited daily specials in an outrageous French accent. Davoud laughed out loud, and Paul marveled at the pleasure he took in the sound. Nevertheless, he was relieved the joke only lasted until they'd ordered. After that, the waiter was attentive but unobtrusive. Clearly, somebody had trained him well.

When they were sipping tiny glasses of ruby-red port, an after-dinner habit Paul had quickly adopted from the Avakian family, Paul's thoughts returned to Jonah and Esmé. "How was Jonah this morning? Do you think he'll be ready to return to school? I miss him in Jazz Ensemble."

Davoud tilted his head. "He seems better. Rascal's got him working on the accompaniment for one of his violin compositions, but Esmé says he's still up at night."

Paul shuddered involuntarily. "I don't need to ask why. I'm still seeing Winfield in my dreams. You talked to him. Would you have guessed he'd do something like that?"

Davoud's expression was unreadable. "I only spoke to him once. He was concerned about his son."

"Then why the hell did he kill himself?"

"I imagine he was desperate."

"Yeah." Paul was silent for a moment. He knew what that was like. He was sure Davoud did too. "How's Esmé taking it?"

Davoud spread long fingers on the tablecloth and examined his hand as if it were a tarantula he'd found in the garden. "It's hard to tell. She doesn't say much. Rascal's been spending more time with her than I have. I've got the shop to run, so I see her mainly when Aida makes everyone eat together." He glanced at the bar like he was thinking of ordering another drink. "She's talking about selling the house. I expect she's no more eager to go back than Jonah is."

"Jonah will be off to college soon. I'm trying to convince him to apply for Juilliard or the Curtis Institute, but he's not ready to think about it."

Davoud glanced up. "He can stay with us so long as he wants—until the roof falls in anyway."

"That reminds me," said Paul. "Don't you think it's time we started working on the riser for the corner stage?" Actually, stage seemed too big a word for the tiny space they'd marked with chalk in the front room of Avakian Music.

Davoud drained the last of his port. His tongue flicked into the tiny glass to extract the last drops. Paul laughed, and Davoud shook his head ruefully, realizing he'd been caught. "I can't imagine what you see in me," he said. "No manners at all."

Paul licked his lips salaciously. Davoud bit his lower lip, but he didn't lower his eyes or look away. It was progress. "Will you come home with me for a drink?" Paul asked. "We can talk about the shop on the way." Davoud battled visibly to repress his laughter and lost, his shoulders shaking. Paul joined in when he realized what he'd said. Talking shop was not what either of them wanted.

AFTER FILLING an old backpack with makeup work, Paul walked over to the Music Box. He found Jonah in the sitting room of 3B, surrounded by sheets of staff paper—the kind Rascal used for composing—covered with handwritten notes. "Okay, chief, I got assignments and handouts from all your teachers. Next time I'm going to rent a flatbed. It's amazing what piles up in a couple of weeks, isn't it? I think everyone's trying to catch up to their lesson plans before Christmas."

Jonah poked the stack of papers as if they might spontaneously animate as a brain-sucking monster. "Sorry, Mr. G, I didn't realize there'd be so much."

"You're lucky they're letting you work at home. Some school districts would make you repeat the year with this many days missed."

Paul picked up a random sheet of music. "What are you working on?"

"Rascal's showing me how to write out my ideas. How to do it right, I mean, with all the parts."

"You mean he's got you doing his arrangements. You know, people actually get paid to do that."

"I know. Rascal said he'd hook me up when I'm good enough."

"He did, huh?" Paul examined the sheet in his hand. "You've added guitar and bass parts to this."

Jonah managed to look simultaneously smug and nervous. "I was hoping you and Davoud would try it with me and Rascal." Watching Jonah's open face, Paul thought about what it would be like to have a child of his own—what he'd missed. Diapers, he told himself. He'd missed diapers, and waking up at five in the morning, and plastic plugs in the electrical sockets that you had to pry out of the wall before you could power up the amp for your guitar, which you couldn't play anyway because the baby was sleeping.

"What's wrong? I thought it would be okay. Butt custard! Nobody's making you—"

Paul shook himself. "Relax, potty mouth. I'd love to try it with you. And Davoud will be thrilled."

Jonah examined him suspiciously. "You're kind of weird, you know that?"

"I've been told. Listen, Davoud's invited me to dinner tonight. You mind if I hang out with you until it's time? Seems silly to go home. I won't bother you. I've got papers to grade."

Paul was ridiculously pleased when Jonah shrugged and pointed at the couch. "Suit yourself. It's not my place, anyway."

Paul drew a folder of ungraded papers and a red felt-tipped pen from his briefcase.

"You know I hate that red shit." Jonah didn't look up from his music.

"What do you mean? Red makes the corrections easy to see."

"Yeah, and you feel like a twit when you see your paper covered in it."

"It isn't meant to make you feel bad."

"My dad always checked my assignments whenever he saw any red."

It was the first time Jonah had mentioned his dad to Paul since the funeral. Paul tried to keep his expression neutral. "He probably wanted to know if there was something he could help you with."

"Whatever."

Paul put a large B− on the top of the essay he was reading and placed it in the finished stack.

"He liked to watch me eat," said Jonah. "Especially when it was something he'd cooked. He never said anything. He just watched with this goofy smile on his face."

He loved you, kid. Just like I do. That's why I'll never understand what he did. "I probably look pretty goofy too when I'm conducting."

Jonah grimaced and dropped the staff paper he'd been holding and picked up another sheet. "Tomorrow, after school."

"What?"

"I'll have this done by then. I want to try it. Will you tell Davoud?"

"If you want. Don't forget you've got all that homework—"

"Don't you fucking dare tell me what to do!"

It seemed Paul had overstepped some boundary. "Okay."

"I'm going to get all As this term," Jonah announced.

They worked in silence, Jonah humming as he wrote out the parts. He never glanced at the homework.

"Are you and Davoud having sex?"

Paul was deep into untangling a student's convoluted syntax. It took a second for Jonah's question to sink in. "What? What kind of question is that? I'm your teacher. You're not supposed to ask me things like that."

"We have to be friends if we're going to play together," said Jonah, as if that explained everything.

"It's still none of your business. I'm an adult and you're my student."

Jonah crossed his arms defiantly. "If we're going to play together, I have to know where everyone stands."

This was about safety and stability. It made sense in a weird kind of way, but Paul still couldn't go with Jonah where he hadn't with Davoud.

"It's early, Jonah. We're still getting to know one another." Maybe Jonah wouldn't catch the evasion.

"Most people have sex first. Then they get to know each other."

"Is that so? I hope you won't take that route."

"Why not? Some people think I'm pretty. What's wrong with having a little fun and finding out if you're compatible up front?"

Pretty. The word struck Paul as out of character for Jonah to use to describe himself, even if someone else had. "I'm sure plenty of people find you attractive, Jonah, but that isn't the point. Having sex is a big step, with big potential consequences. I don't take it lightly. I hope you don't either."

"It's all everyone talks about online: who's banging who. Crystal's doing Travis, even though he's seeing Danielle. Max popped Cindy's cherry in her parents' bedroom while they were out of town. Jannel is an ejac vac. Who gives a flying fuck? I'm sick of it."

Ejac vac? Paul wondered if he should be having a conversation with Jannel's parents—or Cindy's. "I get that, and I'm saying I'm not ready to share yet. Can't I have any privacy?"

Jonah was silent. Paul picked up an essay and cringed. The first sentence contained three misspellings and a grammatical error. Nor did it appear to have an end. He flipped the page, curious whether there was a period somewhere.

"Okay, but you have to tell me if you and Davoud start fighting."

"Deal."

Paul broke up the run-on sentence and began working through an extended explanation of why King George was a fool.

"My mom wants to sell the house and move to Chicago."

Paul's heart stuttered in his chest before shifting into overdrive. Jonah would be leaving soon enough without a move to Chicago. "How do you feel about that?"

"What the purple fuck do I know? At least Antony and Justin won't be in Chicago."

Other bullies might be. Paul said nothing. Maybe there was a kernel of truth in what Charlie had said—or not said. He felt like this brief moment when Jonah needed him might be his only taste of something he'd never expected to have at all. Was it wrong of him to hate Esmé for threatening to take Jonah away?

"I like living at the Music Box," said Jonah. "I fit in with Davoud and Rascal and Aida."

So do I.

"We would miss you." Paul cleared his throat. "I would miss you."

"Fuck. Why is my life always so screwed up?"

"I'm sure your mother is trying to do what's right for you."

"Yeah, that's why she's never home."

"Tell her what you want, Jonah. She'll do the right thing." Paul wished he could believe his own words.

JONAH WAITED by the elevator for Billy, who was coming by after school to drop off the latest handouts and assignments. When the elevator stopped, he pulled the cage open and led Billy to 3B. "Rascal likes us to leave our shoes by the door. He says it's more civilized. I think he picked it up when he toured in Japan."

Billy shrugged and kicked off his high-top trainers, revealing a distinct absence of socks. "Which one is Rascal? He was in Japan?"

"The middle brother. His real name is Rasul, but everyone calls him Rascal. He plays violin with this famous string quartet."

"Which one? Maybe I've heard of them."

Jonah felt his face heating. "I forget the name." He was lying. He'd never thought to ask the name of Rascal's group.

Billy gave him a look that said he wasn't buying it. "Seriously, dude. If you're gonna have friends, you gotta pay attention to this stuff."

Was Rascal his friend? Jonah had not really thought about it that way. He turned hastily and took off for the bedroom.

Billy followed. "Whoa, dude. I was just shitting you. It's no big deal."

Jonah got himself under control and waved at the room. "You wanna hang out?"

"Sure." Billy dropped his pack on the floor and flopped facedown on the bed, pale toes waving like underwater growths.

Jonah grimaced at the pile of books and papers on the little desk that Paul and Davoud had moved over from the old house so he would have a place for his laptop. "Why can't I just stay here? It's not like I gotta hear the stupid lectures to figure this crap out."

"Come on, Jonah. You can't hide in the Music Box forever."

"I'm not hiding, I'm taking a break."

"Whatever, dude. Jazz Ensemble isn't the same without you."

"You could come over and practice with us here."

Billy flopped over and gave Jonah a squint-eyed look. "Thanks, but you know I'm not good enough to hang with the likes of the Rascals and Mr. G."

"Hey, that sounds like a real band."

"Tell everyone I came up with it after you're famous."

"Aida will have a cow."

"Who's Aida?"

"Davoud and Rascal's mom, Aida Kazmi. She's this famous...." Christ, he must sound like a real jerk-off calling everyone famous, even if they kind of were.

Billy laughed. "You really gotta chill, man."

Jonah couldn't look at his friend. "She really is famous."

"Aida Kazmi? You know, I think my mom has one of her records."

He was pretty sure Billy was just saying that to make him feel better, but it worked anyway. "Really?"

"Sure. She's really Davoud's mom?"

CHAPTER 11

JONAH MIGHT have gone back to school sooner if it hadn't been so close to Christmas. He was usually a Christmas enthusiast, fond of tiny white lights, the scents of pine and cinnamon candles, peppermint candy canes, and, when he got tired of sweet, his dad's cloved ham. This year he wished the Santas hanging out in front of the shops on Main Street would pack up their annoying bells and return to the frozen North from whence they'd come. If he had to get up Christmas morning and open presents under the tree with his mom and without his dad, he was totally gonna lose his shit.

He wasn't sure his mom would do much better. They were talking again, sort of. She'd gone back to work the week after his dad's funeral, telecommuting first, and then taking off for Washington. Before she'd left, she'd installed video conferencing software on her laptop and on his. She made him promise to load it every night at eight. The one time he'd gotten wrapped up in his composing and forgotten, Rascal had come knocking at his door.

Rascal pointed at the laptop. "It's 8:10. Turn that on or she'll have both our asses."

He'd looked up at Rascal from the bed, where he was sinking in a pond of staff paper. "Huh?"

Rascal opened the laptop. "Your mom? Esmé? Am I going to have to tattoo the schedule on your forehead?"

"Oh shit. Sorry."

"Don't apologize to me. Talk to your mother."

When he got connected, his mom's face reminded him of a nature special about volcanoes, in which some foolhardy scientist poked a smoking black lava tube and its surface cracked to show the molten red inside. After that, Jonah set a reminder on his smartphone. It wasn't worth the heat.

He wasn't much relieved, a week before Christmas, when Davoud asked, in typical roundabout fashion, if there was something special he'd like for Christmas dinner. It seemed they were having dinner with the Avakian family. Nice of Mom to mention it.

"Aida will roast a leg of lamb. I'll make rosemary potatoes, green bean casserole, and a green salad. Paul is bringing some kind of dessert, but if there's something special you'd like, I'm sure we can work something out."

Jonah's head went to his dad and the family dinner rule.

Davoud put a hand on his shoulder and squeezed. "You think about it and get back to me. We've got a few days before we do the grocery shopping."

"Mr. G—Paul's coming?"

"Of course. Everyone will be here. Paul, Rascal, Amir and his family—you haven't met Dorothy and Zhara yet—your mother, mine."

He still didn't look forward to Christmas, but Jonah figured losing himself in a crowd would be better than being alone with his mom.

BILLY STARED at Jonah like he was speaking Basque. "No, I don't know what kind of music Thomas Jefferson would have listened to. Who says he listened to anything? It's not like they had MP3 players then."

They were on their way to Billy's locker before Jazz Ensemble. Jonah had returned to school after the winter break and was feeling silly—probably a post-holiday stress reaction. "I think they sang a lot and played the harpsichord. Rich people like Jefferson would have had a harpsichord in the conservatory."

Billy was skeptical. "I thought a conservatory was like a greenhouse. Wouldn't they have a music room for the harpsichord?" He thought for a moment. "Did they have a music room in Clue?"

"That's where you learn about rich people's houses?" Jonah giggled. "Colonel Mustard did it in the Conservatory with a harpsichord."

"Right. Rascal's been slipping you little blue pills, huh? Who plays board games anymore? That's old school."

Jonah didn't answer. Clue had been a favorite in his dad's collection of old board games, which he'd dragged out for camping trips and holidays. He turned away from Billy. He hated feeling so volatile, like any little thing could set him off. Fortunately, no passing students paid him any attention. Not that undue attention had really been a problem since he'd returned to school. He might have been invisible, if it weren't for Billy. Not even his friends in Jazz Ensemble wanted to deal with the kid whose dad had killed himself.

Billy threw his pack into the locker and thumbed the combination. "Good thing I wasn't born yet. I sound like the frog that ate the cricket when I sing. I just lip-sync at church."

"I thought your family didn't go to church."

"We don't, normally. But my dad likes Christmas carols, so we go to the Christmas Eve Mass at St. Mary's."

"We didn't go this year. My mom was pissed off about Dad."

Billy sounded wary. "I don't...."

"St. Mary's is Roman Catholic. Suicide is a sin?"

Billy shouldered his trumpet case and took off down the corridor. "Right."

"She says Dad was sick and nobody realized how bad it was, and it's not fair to punish the family for something he did anyway."

"That makes sense." Billy looked like he wanted to ask something, but he didn't speak until they got to the band room and started getting out their instruments. "Did he say anything before he...."

Jonah must have looked funny or something, because Billy's eyes widened, and he backtracked fast.

"Shit, I'm sorry. I shouldn't have.... It's none of my business. Are you and Mr. G going over to the Music Box after school?"

Billy had started calling the Avakian building the Music Box. Jonah thought it was kind of presumptuous of him, but he didn't say anything.

"Mr. G's coming over later."

"You wanna hang out after school?"

AFTER JAZZ Ensemble, they dropped off their instruments at the Music Box and crossed the street to get French fries at the café. The café was crowded with high school and college students, many with open laptops on their tables. Davoud and Paul had the right idea for Avakian Music. They could really use another coffee shop downtown.

Jonah dragged a fry through the pool of ketchup on the platter. "So why doesn't anyone play the harpsichord anymore?"

"What is it with you and the harpsichord? I have no idea. Maybe people don't like the sound of them."

"That doesn't keep people from listening to oboes. I'm writing a paper for Mr. G's American History class on music during the Revolution."

Billy licked the salt off a couple of fries before stuffing them into his mouth. "What's wrong with the oboe? I like the oboe. Actually, I think harpsichords aren't loud enough. That's why they don't use them so much anymore."

Jonah swallowed a sudden rush of saliva at the sight of Billy's agile tongue. "I like the oboe too, but it's not exactly modern, is it? Did you know that oboe players have a reputation for going mad? I mean like...." Jonah circled a finger by the side of his head. "They have to blow so hard they pop blood vessels in their brains."

Billy grimaced and took another fry. "Gross."

Jonah heard the front door open behind him and saw Billy's expression harden. "Oh shit." He didn't have to look to know who had come in.

"Lookee here. It's the faggots. Just like old times," said Justin. He and Antony sauntered over to the booth.

Antony leaned over to snag a fry off the patter. "Mind if we join the party? Scooch over." He slid onto the bench next to Jonah and pressed himself against Jonah, digging Jonah painfully in the ribs and shoving him into the wall.

Billy's face darkened, and he spoke loudly enough to be heard at adjacent tables. "Get out of here, Antony. You're not wanted." The only person who seemed to notice was a twenty-something guy in a Michigan sweatshirt who just looked away like Billy'd cut a fart.

"Look who's jealous. Afraid your boyfriend might like a taste of real man?" said Antony.

"Get off me, asswipe!" Jonah shoved Antony as hard as he could, but he was too tight against the wall to get any leverage. Antony grinned and shoved back.

"Getting feisty, Whale Bait? Hey, I bet you like it rough, don't you?"

"Probably not getting enough from his boyfriend," said Justin, grabbing his crotch. He made as if he was going to sit next to Billy, but Billy slithered out of the booth and faced off with him. "Shut up, fuckface. You wouldn't know a man from a stick up your ass."

Justin stepped backward involuntarily, his eyes narrowing. "Who you calling fuckface, pansy ass?"

Billy took out his phone and held it up. "Get off him, Antony, or I'm calling the police."

"Don't trouble yourself," their waitress called from behind the lunch counter. "I already done it."

Justin's eyes slid to Antony, who was still engaged in a silent shoving contest with Jonah. Antony shrugged. "Well, if that's how you're gonna be about it." He rammed his elbow into Jonah hard enough to knock the air from Jonah's lungs and splash Jonah's root beer over the table, and then he slid out of the booth. "Unlike faggots, we know when we're not wanted."

When the door slammed behind them, Billy slid back into the booth. "You okay?"

Jonah took a cautious breath. His ribs hurt, but he didn't think they were broken or anything. "What's another bruise from Asswipe?"

The waitress came over to wipe off the table and set a fresh root beer in front of Jonah. "You boys okay? You want I really call the police?"

"I thought you already—"

"Nah, I knew them creeps wasn't gonna stay around long enough to find out."

"No, but thanks for helping out," said Jonah.

She shrugged, but her eyes were hard. "I seen those two in here before, hassling folk. It's bad for business. You need anything else?"

"We're good," said Billy.

"Shout out if y'all change your minds."

When she'd gone back to wipe down the counter, Jonah had trouble meeting Billy's eyes. "Thanks for standing up for me."

Billy shrugged. "Assholes."

"You don't have to. I wouldn't blame you if you didn't want to see me anymore."

"That's lame, dude."

Maybe it was because he was tired, or maybe it was because his ribs felt like they'd been hit with a sledgehammer, but Jonah said what he was thinking for once. "I don't get it. You can have anyone you want for a friend. Why do you put up with this shit for me?"

Billy popped another fry into his mouth and grimaced. "Blech, cold. I dunno. Maybe I got my reasons."

Billy's face seemed redder than usual. Jonah wanted to press him, but he figured Billy'd earned a pass. "Whatever. Hey, you want to go over to the Music Box and hear the piece we've been working on?"

"Sorry, I've gotta get going."

Jonah fished for some money, wincing at the pull from his aching ribs. He tried not to think about what would have happened if Billy hadn't been there, or if they'd been in a less public place. Maybe he should tell his mom he wanted to move to Chicago. It was probably some stupid delayed reaction, but his hands began to shake. He threw a five on the table and jammed the offending appendages into his pockets. "I'm gonna head over."

Billy poked at a French fry without actually picking it up. "See ya."

"WHAT DO you think, bro?" Rascal's light tone didn't match his eager expression.

Davoud examined the score gravely, running through the opening phrases in his mind. "It's not your usual sort of thing." They were waiting next to the Steinway for Jonah and Paul to show up. Rascal had persuaded Davoud to help him move an old love seat from 1A so they'd have someplace comfortable to sit during breaks.

"It hardly would be, given my collaborator." Rascal waggled his fingers. "And yet I really…."

Davoud stretched out his legs and leaned back. "I'm looking forward to trying it."

"You're not fooling me. Your fingers twitch when you're thinking about your bass. Come on, I know you've got something to say."

Davoud tried to keep all expression from his face. "I should probably reserve judgment until we've played it."

"You can read a score as well as I can." Rascal was vibrating like a crack baby on Christmas morning.

Teasing his brother was fun, but Rascal would need a defibrillator soon. Davoud let a grin take over his face. "With a little work, it'll be your best yet."

Rascal released a long breath. "You're a bastard, you know that, bro."

"Yeah, but you love me anyway."

"Love or hate, sometimes I can't tell the difference. Shouldn't they be here by now?"

Davoud checked his watch. It was 4:08. "They should be."

"So you really like it?"

"Now you're just fishing."

They heard the front door tinkle. Paul stuck his head through the curtain. "Anyone home?"

Rascal waved him over. "Hey, Paul, how're they hanging?"

Paul pushed through the curtain, shedding watch cap, scarf, and coat as he went. "Sorry I'm late. Charlie wanted to talk about next year's schedule."

"I know that's been on your mind. What did you tell him?" said Davoud.

Paul unceremoniously shoved Davoud's knees apart and sank to the floor between his legs with the self-assurance of a dog looking for affection. He laid his head on Davoud's thigh.

Davoud combed his fingers through Paul's strawberry hair and then glanced up in alarm to see Rascal's smirk.

Paul closed his eyes and moaned. "Oh, that feels wonderful. Don't stop."

Davoud stuck out his tongue at Rascal and resumed his touch, loving the softness of Paul's hair and the warmth of his scalp. "What did you tell Charlie?"

"I put him off for another week."

"Why? You aren't really thinking of quitting? Just tell him you'll take the AP English."

"I don't know what I'm thinking. I feel as though I'm suspended like a cartoon character who's stepped off a cliff. Gravity's got to kick in soon, but I'm not in any rush for it."

"You make it sound worse than it is." Davoud glanced at his brother. "They've cut the music budget again at the high school. Paul's been asked to cut a music class and teach a new subject. I think he would be good at teaching English."

"I haven't told you the worst of it."

Davoud's hand stopped moving of its own accord.

"I have to cut Jazz Ensemble."

Davoud groaned. He knew what Jazz Ensemble meant to Paul. "That's Jonah's favorite class—and yours."

Jonah's brittle voice cut across the silence like a blade. "You have to cut Jazz Ensemble and you didn't tell me?" Jonah marched into the room and kicked his saxophone case, wincing as he did so. *Faggot* gleamed in the overhead lights.

"Shit, Jonah." Paul leapt to his feet. "I'm sorry you had to hear about it this way. I was going to make an announcement when the schedule is finalized. We can still make it an after-school activity." Davoud got to his feet as well, unsure what to do.

"Whatever. Maybe I should go to Chicago with my mom. Nobody gives a shit anyway."

Paul sounded anguished. "Please don't—"

"I expect you to finish your work on my piece, Jonah," said Rascal, his tone businesslike and calm. "The arrangement."

Jonah jerked and went from near hysteria to calm as if Rascal had flipped a switch. "Oh."

Rascal nodded. "That's settled, then. Let's give this thing a whirl, shall we?"

"Close your mouth and pick up your bass," Paul whispered to Davoud.

THE FIRST phrases reminded Davoud of the opening to Copland's clarinet concerto, with its slow melodic line and delayed harmonies, like the call and response of new lovers. The first section consisted mostly of back-and-forth between Rascal and Jonah. Hearing them together was startling, like coming across a couple on a blanket in the woods. Later, Davoud and Paul repeated the theme in a variation with guitar on the melodic line and bass responding.

The pizzicato snap of Davoud's bass at his entrance at the start of the second section was a twig snapping—it signaled a retreat from intimacy and a cacophonous return to the public realm. The remainder was a long tumble downhill, with a shriek from Rascal's violin at the bottom like a plunge into cold water. The closing section returned to the simplicity of the first bars, each instrument taking a turn with the melody until Rascal finished in solitude.

When Rascal's last notes faded, Paul set down his guitar and slipped his hand into Davoud's. A shimmer of excitement lit Davoud's nerves from scalp to fingertip.

"Well, Rascal, I don't know whether to buy you flowers or light a cigarette," said Paul.

Rascal laughed and lowered his violin. "What do you say, Jonah?"

Jonah's face pinked. "I think we need to work on the bridge. It seemed a little rough."

"Whatever you say, boss."

They started it again. Davoud didn't need to concentrate quite so fiercely the second time, and he noticed Jonah holding his right arm oddly, close to his body, with his shoulder hunched.

"Hold up, Rascal." He set the bass down. "Jonah, are you okay?" he said, catching Paul's concerned look.

Jonah's hands dropped from the piano. "I'm fine. Why are you stopping?"

"I stopped because you look like you're in pain, and I want to know why."

"It's a bruise. I slipped by the pool in swimming class."

Davoud felt his excitement and joy congeal into a painful knot. He and Rascal exchanged looks as Paul moved over to kneel by Jonah's side.

"Jonah, if you've been attacked again, please tell us," said Paul. "We want to help."

"Can't we keep going? I'm okay."

Paul's tone was gentle but firm. "Not until you show us, and we can see for ourselves that you're all right."

Jonah appealed to Rascal. "Can't you make them leave me alone? We're supposed to be rehearsing."

"Sorry, pal. I'm with them on this one."

Jonah raised his eyes to the ceiling and lifted his T-shirt. The bruise on his ribs had bloomed round and dark. It was accompanied by a lighter set of bruises up and down Jonah's side.

"Tell us the truth, Jonah," said Paul, his voice tight. "This is not from a slip by the pool, unless the pool has elbows. Did Antony do this to you?"

"Yes."

"When?"

"This afternoon, at the café. Billy and I were just sitting there and Antony and Justin came in and started giving us shit."

Davoud had not felt so angry or helpless since his father died. "This has got to stop."

"We're taking you to the hospital," said Paul to Jonah. "Get your jacket."

"I'll call Esmé," said Rascal, unexpectedly.

"Fuck," said Jonah, not moving.

PAUL SHIFTED uncomfortably on the hard plastic chair. The waiting room smelled unpleasantly of floor cleaner. Davoud seemed to be meditating, breathing slowly and steadily, with his eyes closed. The only other residents of the waiting area were a harried mother with a red-faced, whimpering baby in her arms and a middle-aged woman in a business suit holding the hand of her white-nimbused mother. Paul's phone vibrated in his pocket, and he fished it out and checked the display before tapping Answer. "Rascal, what's up?"

"I talked to Esmé. I don't think she's going to come home this time. Her team is scheduled to resume arguments tomorrow, and she's afraid she'll lose her job. She'll call you back in an hour, when she's back at the hotel."

Paul made no effort to keep the anger from his voice. "The hospital staff will be talking about bringing Child Protective Services into it."

Rascal was silent.

"I told the nurse it was bullying, but they'll have to report this to the police."

"That can only be good, right?"

"If they don't arrest me and Davoud for child abuse. I have to go. The nurse is coming over."

Paul hung up and stood to meet the tired-looking woman in pink scrubs. "How is Jonah?"

Parallel lines formed between the nurse's eyebrows. She was a middle-aged black woman with an ID badge hanging on a lanyard around her neck. The badge was turned around so he couldn't see her name.

"What exactly is your relationship to Jonah, Mr....?"

"Gaston, Paul Gaston. I'm Jonah's music teacher and a friend of the family."

The nurse looked at Davoud. "And you are?"

"Davoud Avakian. Jonah is staying with my family while his mother is out of town."

The nurse examined them coolly. Paul was certain she suspected them of membership in a white slavery ring. "Is there anyone here from Jonah's family?"

"Jonah's father died recently, and his mother is out of town," said Paul. "We're Jonah's family."

The nurse sighed. "Not as far as the law is concerned, you're not. I'm afraid I can't release any medical information without approval from a parent or guardian."

"Fine. When will he be ready to go home?"

"The doctor has finished with him now, but I'm afraid he can't leave just yet."

Paul's level of agitation rose. "Can we at least talk to him?"

The nurse pursed her lips and met his look with an assessing one of her own. "In cases like this, it's hospital policy to make a police report. I'm afraid you'll have to wait until they arrive."

"You think we're responsible for hurting Jonah." Paul felt Davoud's hand on his shoulder, whether to comfort him or keep him from strangling the nurse, he wasn't sure.

The nurse stepped back. "I'm sorry, but we have strict rules concerning minors."

"Come on, Paul," said Davoud, "let's sit down. Ms....?" He smiled at the nurse expectantly.

"Brown."

Davoud stuck out his hand. "I'm pleased to meet you, Ms. Brown."

Brown looked as though she might refuse to shake hands, but she relented when Davoud stubbornly held out his hand.

"That would be Nurse Brown to you," she said, softening infinitesimally.

"Of course. Nurse Brown is only doing her job, Paul."

"I have work to do. Please stay until the police arrive. They'll want statements from you as well as Jonah." Brown turned and started back to her station.

"Nurse Brown?" said Paul, "I'm expecting a call from Jonah's mother. Do you want to speak to her?"

"Yes, come to the Admissions window when she's on the line," said Brown, without breaking stride.

"That was fun," said Paul.

Davoud massaged the back of Paul's neck. "I know you're upset, but patience and calm will help—especially when the police arrive."

Paul closed his eyes and leaned into Davoud's touch. "I don't think I could cope without you."

"Yes you could, but I'm glad you don't have to."

PAUL AND Davoud met at the school first thing to inform Charlie Wong about the incident in the café. Charlie's secretary ushered them in with a warning. "He's not feeling well today. I told him to go home, but...."

Charlie appeared to have dressed after a workout without a shower. Sweat beaded on his forehead, which he patted with a tissue from the box on his desk. "Where is Mrs. Winfield?" he asked, when Paul explained why they were there.

"DC. She's arguing a case today."

"I see. Mr. Avakian, forgive me, but why are you here?"

"Please call me Davoud. Jonah is staying with my family. I'm concerned about his well-being."

"I would feel a lot more comfortable discussing this problem if Jonah's mother or guardian were here."

"Well, she isn't," said Paul. "Are we supposed to ignore the problem until Jonah gets his head bashed?"

Charlie pulled a new tissue from the box and folded it into a square. "If Jonah has no guardian present, perhaps it's time we consider involving CPS."

"Child Protective Services," said Paul, not trying to keep the contempt from his voice.

"Do you think that would be in Jonah's best interests?" said Davoud. "Jonah has a family looking out for him. It seems to me the question is how to keep Antony and Justin away from him. Can't you expel them, at least?"

"I'm sorry to say it, because it would make my life a lot easier if it were different, but bullying problems are rarely resolved through punishment."

"What do you suggest?"

"Again, I'm not sure that I should even be speaking to you about this issue, Mr. Avakian. While I appreciate your concern for Jonah—"

"Davoud is here, Charlie, and Mrs. Winfield is not," Paul interrupted. "Doesn't that count for anything?"

Charlie turned to stare into the courtyard where the first snowflakes of the season were wafting to the cement. Paul took a breath, determined to press, but Davoud shook his head.

Charlie sighed and patted his forehead with the tissue. "Very well. I would appreciate it, Mr. Avakian, if you would keep... if you would be discreet."

"Of course." Davoud gave Paul's thigh a pat.

Charlie followed the movement expressionlessly. "In the short term, if I receive a police report or statement confirming Antony's role in the latest incident, I will take action in accordance with our policy. I cannot act on an uncorroborated report from you."

Paul began to feel as though he were underwater. "Jesus, Charlie! I took him to the hospital yesterday. What more do you need?" Davoud lifted his hand and rested it on Paul's.

"I need paper. You know how it works. A note from Jonah's doctor describing his injury, plus a statement from Jonah would do. A police report would be even better. Something that's not hearsay."

"The hospital won't release medical information to us, because we aren't Jonah's parents or guardians," said Paul.

"But you said his ribs were only bruised, right? What about the police? A statement from a witness?"

"I can't believe this." The warm weight of Davoud's hand was the only thing anchoring Paul to his seat.

Charlie relented a little. "I have Mrs. Winfield's cell number. I'll ask her to request copies of the necessary documents."

"What about a longer-term solution, Mr. Wong? How do you recommend we address the problem?" said Davoud, leaning forward slightly.

"I will speak to Mr. and Mrs. Scarelli about Antony's behavior. I will suggest that Antony receive counseling. I believe I will be justified in making the counseling a condition of Antony's continued enrollment at Martin Luther King High School." Charlie paused. "Is Jonah seeing someone? I don't believe Julie—our guidance counselor—has spoken to him."

"You think this is Jonah's fault," said Paul. Davoud's grip tightened painfully, and he snatched his hand away.

Charlie frowned. "Absolutely not, Paul, but counseling might help him to react differently to Antony's provocations. It could help him to keep these incidents from escalating." Charlie seemed to be channeling Jonah's dead father.

"We will discuss it with Esmé," said Davoud.

"What about Justin?" said Paul. "He's been involved too."

Charlie stood with a grunt and came around the desk. Paul and Davoud followed suit and stood automatically. "I don't think we need worry about Justin. He was arrested for auto theft last Sunday. His parents have withdrawn him from school. I believe they plan to enroll him in a private institution." He produced a wry smile. "I'm considering a letter of condolence for the dean." He stuck out a hand for Davoud to shake. "Thank you for taking an interest in Jonah, Mr. Avakian. Paul, could I have a word with you, please, before you go?"

"I'll wait outside," said Davoud. He touched Paul's shoulder on the way out.

"Paul, I'll be frank with you. Your behavior today has been worrisome. I'm concerned that your feelings... that your attachment to Jonah may be clouding your judgment."

"What are you saying?" Paul realized his hands were clenched into fists. He clasped them behind his back.

"Your interest in Jonah could be misinterpreted."

"By whom?"

"Is Mrs. Winfield aware of the nature of your relationship with Mr. Avakian?"

"Davoud and I are friends, that's all."

Charlie pursed his lips.

"Esmé asked for my help with her son."

"Would she have done so had she known you're gay?"

There it was. Finally out in the open. Paul felt himself shiver, but he wasn't sure if his reaction was more of relief or fear. The back of his neck felt hot, as if Davoud's hand still rested there.

"I'm pretty sure she knows I'm gay, Charlie."

Charlie turned to peer out at the falling snow and wiped his brow. "I suggest you make sure, and that you prepare for the possibility that she will not want Jonah to remain in your and Mr. Avakian's care."

"You're wrong, Charlie. She's not a bigot."

Charlie continued to stare out the window. "Make sure, Paul. You tread a fine line. Jonah's troubles are bad enough. You don't want to make them worse."

THE CAFETERIA was out of bounds. Jonah hadn't eaten there for days. There were too many jerks who'd welcome the chance to call him a fag or tease him about his size. They didn't seem to need a reason. Sometimes it was stupid stuff like the T-shirt he was wearing—today's was light blue with *Eat me!* printed on the back. Students who didn't actively participate in the teasing shunned him, either because they shared his tormentor's contempt or because they feared similar treatment. He was Jonah the Magic Busboy. He sat, the table cleared. The lobby near the principal's office was safe, but it wasn't exactly a hotel lobby. There was no place to sit, and he was open to random acts of kindness from passing Good Samaritans. Unused classrooms were problematic, because it was against the rules for students to hang out in unsupervised areas and teachers mostly locked them. He'd discovered that the auditorium could be a good choice if a rehearsal was scheduled, so long as nobody noticed him lurking in the back and threw him out. Some days, he just wandered, chewing as he walked.

Deciding to check out the auditorium, Jonah shouldered his pack. Ironically, since he'd been staying at the Music Box, the lunch problem had become more acute. Davoud didn't believe in simple sandwiches. Instead, he packed healthy stuff like vegetarian lasagna or yesterday's fresh baby spinach salad, with toasted almonds, dried cranberries, real bacon bits, and a tiny Tupperware container of dressing hand printed with instructions for heating the homemade mix in a microwave. There was no fucking way that Jonah was going to tell him that he didn't dare to go into the cafeteria to heat stuff, even though they had a microwave for the students, so he told Davoud that he liked salads. He could deal with cold dressing. At least he wasn't going to get fat.

A paper notice on the auditorium door announced that today's rehearsal of the school play was canceled due to illness. Jonah held his breath and tried the door. It opened with a well-oiled whisper. *Fabulous.* Glancing around to make sure no one was watching, Jonah slipped into the dimly lit space, giddy with the prospect of a comfortable, undisturbed lunch. He was only mildly disappointed to discover that his lunch consisted of an earthenware container of cold cassoulet. He only knew what that was because he'd watched Davoud make it the weekend before. Picking beans out of the congealed mess with a plastic fork, he tried to imagine what it would taste like warm. It had smelled richly of roast duck and bacon when Davoud took it from the oven Sunday afternoon.

A few minutes before the bell for next period, Jonah left his auditorium sanctuary. Trotting to his English class, he detoured at the last second for a pit stop in the boy's room. He didn't know he'd made a mistake until he was facing a urinal with his back to the door, and he smelled cigarette smoke.

"I thought I recognized those ratty shoes. Hi, Whale Bait. How's life treating you?"

Jonah zipped up and turned slowly to see Antony step from an open stall. "Where's Justin, Antony? Your sidekick abandon you?" For some reason, that was a bad choice of topic, because Antony's face clouded and he got in Jonah's face, forcing Jonah to tilt his head back or talk to Antony's bulging pecs. Asswipe wasn't as tall as Davoud, but he was built. Next to Jonah's five foot four, he was a fucking giant.

Antony flipped his cigarette into the sink. "Shut up or I'll stick your head so far up your ass, even a fag like you won't be able get it out."

Jonah knew he wasn't supposed to resort to violence—like that would work anyway. Past experience taught him that name-calling just spurred Antony on. He tried to step around the football player. Antony sidestepped into the puddle that always seemed to form under the electric hand dryers. Starting to sweat, Jonah tried a Socratic approach. "What did I ever do to you, Antony?"

"You're a slow learner, Whale Bait. We've been over this. You're a fag. I don't like fags. Therefore, I don't like you."

Jonah couldn't fault his logic, and banter was better than punching. "Nope. Still doesn't work for me. You need new material."

Antony smirked. "How about this? Your dad killed himself because he couldn't stand that his son was a faggot."

Jonah didn't think about hitting Antony. He didn't think about anything at all. He tucked his head down and barreled into Antony like a boxer training with the heavy bag. His attack would have only resulted in another beating if Antony hadn't been standing in the puddle. But the sudden ferocity of Jonah's rush caught Antony off-balance, and his feet slipped in the wet. Antony went down hard, his head bouncing on the hard tile. Jonah landed on top of him, the animal part of him gleeful he could reach Antony's face to pound the expression off it. The fact that Antony wasn't defending himself was an unexpected bonus. Jonah must've landed a blow on Antony's nose, because the copper stink of blood filled Jonah's senses, and he screamed in triumph.

Jonah didn't see or hear the teacher who pulled him off Antony. Someone grabbed him around the middle and swung him around to slide across the wet, pink floor. Before he could catch his balance, his arm was twisted behind his back and he stopped resisting.

CHAPTER 12

DAVOUD CHECKED his mobile and saw it was Paul.

"Hey, guy. You at lunch?"

"Davoud, I need your help. Jonah's gone berserk and beaten up Antony. It's pretty bad. I need—"

"Jonah's beaten up Antony? You're kidding!"

"Yeah, I don't know what happened exactly, but Antony's been taken to the hospital. There was a lot of blood."

"How in hell…." Davoud sank onto the stool behind the counter. "Is Jonah okay?"

"The teacher who pulled him off Antony said he was screaming like a banshee. The police have taken him to the station, so I guess he wasn't physically hurt. Charlie wouldn't let me talk to him. I need you to go to the police station and make sure he doesn't say anything until Esmé can get a lawyer."

"I don't know if they'll let me—"

"Just try, would you? I'd go, but I can't abandon my class."

"Of course. Paul?"

"What?"

"You can't blame yourself."

"Yes, I can. I'm calling Esmé now."

Paul disconnected. Davoud slid his phone into his pocket and started to collect his keys and coat. "Marta?"

"I'm coming." Marta swept the curtain aside and stepped into display area. She'd taken to eating her lunch on the love seat in the practice area.

"I've got to leave for a while. Can you keep an eye on the place?"

"Jonah again?"

He nodded and went for the door.

THE GLEN Falls police station was an unfortunate mix of 1960s clean lines and fifty-year-old grunge. Stepping into the lobby with its fiberglass molded chairs, Davoud's eyes were drawn to the cracks and gaps in the linoleum tile, which were black with the soil of countless rubber-soled shoes. Heading to the chest-high counter, he hesitated behind a balding, middle-aged man in a blue oxford shirt with a frayed collar and a business suit. The man gesticulated at an officer who sat impassively behind the Plexiglas shield that topped the counter. The bald man's agitation was obvious in the tension of his shoulders and the flush of his exposed scalp. Davoud stepped closer to hear what he was saying.

"I don't care if he's only sixteen. He broke my son's nose and gave him a concussion. I want him put away."

Davoud's stomach knotted as he realized who the man was. The officer's answer wasn't audible, but it must not have been satisfactory, because the man continued his tirade.

"My son is in the hospital with a concussion and broken nose. If the runt is old enough to be queer, he's old enough to be charged as an adult."

How did the man know Jonah was queer? Had Antony actually bragged about the bullying? "Excuse me, you're Mr. Scarelli, aren't you?"

"Yeah, what's it to you?"

"I'm Davoud Avakian. Jonah Winfield has been staying with my family since his father died. I wonder if I might speak to you for a moment?"

Scarelli turned to glare at Davoud. He ignored Davoud's outstretched hand. "He's staying with you? Why?"

"He and his mother didn't wish to return to the house where his father died."

"Can't say as I blame 'em. She needs a real man to take care of her, and that boy needs someone to set him straight."

"Mrs. Winfield is an attorney in the firm of Franklin, Stone, and Rathmore. She doesn't need anyone to take care of her, Mr. Scarelli."

Scarelli's eyes narrowed. "She's a lawyer? How 'bout that. Why isn't she here to get her boy? Something wrong with her?"

Davoud had to breathe for a moment before answering. He could sympathize to a degree with Scarelli's anger, given his son's injuries, but the man seemed to go out of his way to be offensive. "I believe she's arguing a case in Washington at the moment."

"You gonna do something about that boy for her?"

Davoud sidestepped Scarelli to move closer to the counter. He was aware the police officer was listening with interest from behind the plastic panel. "I'm not quite sure what you mean, Mr. Scarelli, but if Jonah has done something wrong, I'm sure Mrs. Winfield will take appropriate action. I know you're aware that your son Antony and his friend Justin—the one who was arrested for car theft—were bullying Jonah. I believe Principal Wong spoke to you about the problem."

Scarelli pushed into Davoud's space, although the effect was diminished because he was at least seven inches shorter than Davoud. "My son didn't break anyone's nose."

"He certainly seemed determined to break Jonah's spirit."

Scarelli shrugged. "Kid's a faggot. You gotta expect he'll be teased."

"Are you aware that the use of that term to intimidate or label a person may be considered hate speech, and that it's a crime?"

"I'm just telling it like it is. Pansy-ass mayor. I can't believe people bought that liberal bullshit. What do you care, anyway? You some kind of pervert too, Avakian?"

Davoud felt a weight in his chest like the air in his lungs had solidified. He'd never before denied he was gay, but he didn't go out of his way to tell strangers either. He'd never faced a situation like this. Should he confront Scarelli with the truth? He should focus on what was best for Jonah? But what was that? He tried to keep the heat from his voice. "I'm concerned about the well-being of both boys, and I find your use of the term faggot offensive."

"So you're a fag too. That Winfield gal sure knows how to pick 'em. No wonder her boy's messed up."

"You go out of your way to be offensive, Mr. Scarelli. Why?"

"Gentlemen, I think it's about time we break this up." Davoud had been so focused on Scarelli, he hadn't noticed the police officer had left his perch behind the counter and come around to the lobby.

Davoud held out his hand. "I agree, Officer...."

"Sergeant Haskel."

"Sergeant. Pleased to meet you. I'm Davoud Avakian, here to pick up Jonah Winfield."

"I gathered. Please have a seat. I'll be with you in a moment." The sergeant pointed to a seat on the other side of the lobby.

Davoud stepped back, but not so far that he couldn't hear what Scarelli said.

"You're not going to let the kid go, are you?"

"As I told you before, Mr. Scarelli, the Winfield boy is a minor. So is your son. Principal Wong's statement suggests that the fight was not an isolated incident—or unprovoked. Under the circumstances, I think it would be best if everyone just took a big breath and cooled down while we sort this out."

"Jesus Christ, you are going to let the little faggot get away with it."

Haskel stared at Scarelli for a second. "Mr. Scarelli, I don't know if the boy is gay or not, but we do have a hate speech law in this community, and your language is not helping your case. Why don't you get your son from the hospital and go home? I understand his injuries are minor, all things considered. If you still feel strongly about it in the morning, you can come down and file charges."

"I knew this would happen when that pansy-ass liberal mayor was elected. Everything's going to shit in this town."

"The pansy-ass mayor is my boss's boss, Mr. Scarelli. I think it's time you go home."

Scarelli grunted. "Fucking pansy-ass liberal." But he moved toward the exit. "I'll be back."

When Scarelli was gone, Sergeant Haskel sighed and rubbed between his eyes with a middle finger.

Davoud watched carefully. "He's a piece of work."

"Maybe, but if he pushes, the Winfield boy could end up charged with a felony. What did you say was your relationship with the kid?"

"I'm a friend of the family. Jonah's staying in our home while Mrs. Winfield is out of town."

Haskel frowned and closed his eyes. "Our policy is to release minors to a parent or guardian. Has he no family in the area?"

"We are his family, Sergeant."

Haskel snorted. "Family is who you make it, or so I've heard." The sergeant seemed to make up his mind. "Short of calling CPS, I suppose we don't have much choice. Still, we'll have to get Mrs. Winfield's permission. You have her number?"

"Thank you." Davoud followed the sergeant to the back of the lobby and watched as he punched in a key code to open a door. The room beyond contained a number of metal desks of the sort purchased by public institutions. A '90s-era computer monitor hogged the real estate on each desk. Jonah slumped next to a buzz-cut uniformed officer whom Davoud assumed must have been the one called to the school. Jonah's light-blue T-shirt was covered in dark splotches— drying blood from the smell. Jonah's hands clenched in his lap, his knuckles scratched and swollen. The officer typed on his computer with two fingers.

"Hey, Butch. This guy's come to pick up your boy." The sergeant jerked his head at the officer to follow him. "Wait here a moment," he said to Davoud. He resumed his post at the counter, speaking quietly to the uniformed officer.

"Hi, Jonah. You okay?"

"I guess. I fucked up, didn't I?"

Davoud nodded. "Running would have been better. You know not to say anything without a lawyer, right?"

Jonah rolled his eyes. "My mother is a lawyer."

"Right. So you haven't made any kind of statement?"

"Watch. My. Lips. My mother is a lawyer." Jonah smiled sourly. "I told them I wanted my mother."

Davoud lowered himself into the officer's swivel chair, knees popping. "What happened?"

"He wouldn't let me leave the bathroom."

"Did he attack you?"

Jonah looked away.

"Okay. He say something to set you off?"

"I don't want to talk about it."

"You might feel better if you did."

"All everyone wants to do is talk about everything. What fucking good does it do? I should have run away or ignored him or something. I know I fucked up. End of story."

"The principal is going to want you to talk to a counselor. You might as well get used to it."

"Fuck."

Davoud waited, keeping an eye out for the return of the officer or anyone else who might hear anything Jonah said.

"If I tell you, you can't say anything."

"Of course."

"If you really want to know, I lost it when he said that my dad...." Jonah cleared his throat. "My dad killed himself because he couldn't deal with me being gay. It isn't true! He never even said anything...."

"It isn't true, Jonah. Your father didn't kill himself because of who you are or anything you did. We can't know exactly what was going on in his head, but there's one thing I'm certain about. He loved you. It was his own value he was confused about."

Davoud brushed his fingers over Jonah's swollen and cracked knuckles. Jonah shivered and remained silent until Haskel came to tell them they were free to go.

PAUL REACHED a milestone watching Jonah being escorted to a police cruiser parked with lights flashing at the main entrance to Martin Luther King High School. Behind the cruiser, Antony pressed a gauze pad to his nose and protested groggily as he was loaded into a waiting ambulance. Trudging the familiar corridor to the band room afterward felt like going uphill. He wanted to cancel Jazz Ensemble and let a student lead the group through practice, but the hushed voices and the fits and starts of conversation as he passed down the hall convinced him that he had a duty to stay.

Billy cornered him in the band room. "What's gonna happen to Jonah?"

"I don't know, Billy. I suppose it depends whether Antony is okay." *And whether his parents file charges.*

"It's not fair. Antony hit Jonah all the time. Jonah fights back once and the police drag him off?"

It didn't seem fair to Paul either, but he couldn't say that. "Violence is never a solution."

"That's lame, Mr. G. We spend more on our military than any other nation on earth—and we use them too—because violence is *never* the answer?"

"A badass military keeps us from being attacked by terrorists," said Rafael, one of their trombone players.

"Does it really?" Billy was vibrating like a bell. "Switzerland has a tiny army compared to ours, and they don't get targeted like we do. I think the way we act makes us a target for everyone who thinks there's something wrong with the world."

Paul tapped his baton on his music stand. "Guys, interesting as this is, it might be more appropriate to discuss in social studies or history class."

"When do we get to talk about bullying, Mr. G? Jonah isn't the only one to get hassled around here." The speaker was a jumbo-sized alto saxophone player named Sheila. "I think Antony got what he deserved."

Paul had been focused on Jonah. Had he been missing other traumas? He put down his baton and slumped on the stool. Maybe Charlie was partly right about his feelings for Jonah. He'd certainly been distracted. He looked around the room. "Okay, show of hands, how many of you have seen someone bullied in the last year?"

Sheila raised a hand. Carol followed suit immediately. Billy snorted. "Come on guys. Everyone saw what happened with Jonah's saxophone case. You don't think that was bullying?" More hands went up.

Noah, the trumpet player next chair over from Billy spoke up. "I never saw anyone touch Jonah."

"You don't have to get hit for it to be bullying," said Sheila. "How do you think I feel when they call me fatso on my home page. Or when nobody picks me in gym class?"

"You're not exactly the fastest thing on two feet, Sheila."

"Thanks."

"Well, I wouldn't pick you. Not if I wanted to win," said Noah.

"Whoa!" said Paul. "That might be true, Noah, but did you need to say it?"

"Jerk," Sheila muttered.

Paul tapped his music stand. "No name-calling, please."

"What about the shit people put on my wall after Justin posted about me and Jonah? That was bullying, wasn't it?" said Billy.

"It's not bullying to call you gay if you really are," said Noah.

"What if he didn't want anyone to know?" someone else asked.

"I'm not gay," said Billy, his voice tight.

"Justin's an asshole," said Sheila.

"What did I say about name-calling, Sheila?"

"They give me shit, I give them shit."

A throat cleared, and Billy's eyes widened. Paul looked around to see the principal framed in the doorway.

"Okay, everyone, simmer down for a moment while I talk to Mr. Wong."

"That's okay, Paul. I just came by to ask you to stop by my office before you leave today."

"Will do."

"Hey, Mr. Wong. Do you know if Antony is okay?" asked Noah.

Charlie hesitated. After a moment, he marched to the front of the class and took a stand like he was at parade rest. "His mother called to say that he had a mild concussion and a broken nose. They'll probably keep him at the hospital overnight for observation."

Paul had expected Charlie to refuse to share any medical information—even if he had it. The principal caught his expression and shrugged. "His mother said to tell the football team, so I figure it's public knowledge."

"He deserved to have his skull caved in, as far as I'm concerned," said Sheila.

Charlie frowned. "I couldn't help hearing some of your conversation earlier."

"They're just blowing off steam," said Paul.

"I'm not criticizing." Charlie raised a hand. "How many of you think there's a bullying problem in this school?"

Billy's hand shot up. Sheila and Carol raised their hands as well. In a few seconds, nearly every student had a hand up. Paul raised his hand too.

"I'm sorry to hear it," said the principal stiffly, turning for the exit. "Don't forget to stop by after class, Paul."

PAUL PEERED into the dimly lit music store. "Davoud, are you here? Rascal said you were down here." The lights in the display cases were all off. So were the overheads, apart from a security light above the front entrance. Davoud's office door was partially open. The light from the tiny room had the bluish hue of a computer screen.

"In here, Paul." Davoud's deep voice rasped like he'd spent the evening yelling at a party.

Paul picked his way through the darkened display area. "You don't believe in lights?"

"Can't afford them." A chair scraped and Davoud flicked on his desk lamp, the yellow light pooling on stacks of invoices.

"I'm not bothering you?" Paul pushed the office door open and stepped inside. Before he could say anything, Davoud's long arms enveloped him. The tall man leaned down to kiss him. Davoud's hands found their way under Paul's overcoat and jacket to rub his back. "I guess that's a 'no,'" Paul murmured, his lips still brushing Davoud's.

"I was hoping you'd come."

Paul rested his head against Davoud's shoulder, a little surprised that Davoud allowed him the intimacy, but pleased. "How's Jonah?"

"Hard to say. He's with Esmé and Rascal. She got in an hour ago. They're finishing some Chinese Rascal picked up from the place on the corner."

"Thanks for rescuing him."

Davoud exhaled, warm breath tickling Paul's ear. He smelled faintly of garlic and ginger. "I was hoping at least one person wouldn't be angry with me come morning."

Paul pulled back to examine Davoud's face. "What do you mean?"

Davoud shuffled them over to the desk. He let go to take a sheaf of papers from an ink jet printer. "Take a look."

Paul skimmed the sheets. They were property leases for Aida Kazmi, Rasul Avakian, Davoud Avakian, and even one for Esmé Winfield.

"With the additional people, the heating bill for the Music Box could fund a small orchestra."

"I don't understand. Isn't the building owned by your family? How can you charge them rent?"

"In point of fact, the building is owned by Avakian Music LLC, which is owned by the family. As the managing partner, I have a 51 percent share. So yes, I can charge them rent. I had hoped I wouldn't have to, or, fool that I am, that they would offer to help once they'd seen the whole financial picture."

"No one's said anything? Offered to—"

"My mother gave me a check, which helped with the heating bill last month. She's the only one, so far."

"You did warn them."

"The only lease I haven't decided about is Esmé's. If I ask her to pay, do you think she'll drag Jonah to Chicago?"

Paul's heart stuttered. "Please don't…."

Davoud made a soothing sound, a tuneless hum that set off a chain reaction in the nerves from Paul's ears to his toes. "It's okay, baby. We can carry them a little longer. I suspect Rascal might not be entirely happy to see Esmé go either."

"You're kidding. He stares like a deer in the headlights every time I see them together."

Davoud chuckled so softly Paul felt it as a vibration in his chest. "Spell that d-e-a-r."

The elephant in the room stamped and dragged his chains. Paul's thoughts went to the conversation he and Davoud had thus far avoided, despite all the time they had been spending in each other's company.

Davoud's hand resumed its slow migration up Paul's spine. "You're very quiet."

"I haven't caught my breath since October."

"Ever since I saw those boys pushing Jonah around outside my shop."

"Yeah, and you called to tell me what I jerk I was for daring to suggest an instrument to Jonah."

Davoud's hand stopped. Paul wanted to mewl at the loss. "That's not quite accurate. I wanted to understand what prompted you to choose the bari sax. It seemed a reasonable question, given Jonah's ability with the piano."

Paul found his way under Davoud's sweater to explore the delicate knobs of his back. "I forgive you."

Davoud huffed, but his hand resumed its gentle ministrations.

"I'm enjoying this, but maybe we should go upstairs. Have you finished plotting to relieve your relatives of their cash?"

Davoud growled. "I'm not sure I want to go anywhere with you."

"You know I don't mean the stupid things I say, right?"

"I think you have a fetish for feet—particularly your own."

"Do you mind if I ask you something?"

"I'm making no commitments."

Paul tensed, and he felt Davoud begin to laugh silently, his shoulders and chest shaking. "I guess I jumped the gun."

"Who's got his foot in his mouth now?" said Paul.

"The answer is yes."

Paul resumed exploration under Davoud's sweater. "I haven't even decided on the question yet. I mean, there are so many I could go with. Is this thing we're doing serious? Do you want it to be? Should I be packing away my 'fuck me' pants?"

Davoud whispered in Paul's ear between licks that sent shivers down his spine. "That would be yes, yes, and hell no, but if you wear them for anyone else, I'll send Aida after you with gardening shears."

Paul tightened his grip on Davoud. "Upstairs now?" he pleaded.

"In a minute. I've got something to finish." Davoud's mouth moved down to nip at Paul's neck.

"Hey! What will my students think?"

"That you're mine now, Jack."

"If you don't stop, I'll be climbing your bean pole right here."

DAVOUD'S BEDROOM was the long-time haunt of a confirmed bachelor. Above the dark wood of the baseboards, faded wallpaper formed a leafy pattern in mantis green, teal, cream, and power blue. The bed was queen-size, the mattress mounted high on a cherrywood frame. The handmade quilt had an aquatic theme, each square filled with an Escher-like repeating pattern of whales, dolphins, or seals. A large, freestanding wardrobe, which might have inspired C.S. Lewis, took up one corner. An antique dresser, single chair, and floor-to-ceiling bookshelf rounded out the furniture. The room had no mirror or vanity, no walk-in closet, and no rack for the shoes lined up in a neat row beside the wardrobe.

Paul noticed none of this until later. He was too busy exploring the warm interior of Davoud's mouth. When they got into the elevator, and Davoud had closed the cage, he placed his hands on Paul's shoulders and turned him around before he could press a button. Paul opened his mouth to accept Davoud's gentle exploration and reciprocated with his own. Davoud's mouth tasted of ginger and citrus from the herbal tea Paul had seen in his office, a spicy complement to the musk of his aftershave. As they kissed, the warmth and comfort of Davoud's embrace turned harder and more urgent, and he felt the press of Davoud's erection against his hip.

Good. We're on the same page. Paul's own cock was crushed painfully in his jeans. He pawed at Davoud's shirt, pulling the tail free in his quest to reach bare skin. Davoud shivered at the touch and pressed Paul against the wall of the elevator for another kiss. He groaned when Paul turned his head to breathe.

"Press the damn Up button—" Paul panted, "—before I hurt myself."

"Can't have that," Davoud murmured as he pressed the button. He eyed Paul's crotch appreciatively as the elevator jerked into motion. "That how it is?" When they reached the second floor, Davoud dragged Paul out of the box. He fished his keys from his pocket and opened the door to the apartment. "Can I get you anything before...?"

"Get. Into. The. Bedroom."

Davoud raised an eyebrow. "Something you need in there?"

"You." Paul hummed with satisfaction when he saw the big bed and night table strewn with open books and magazines.

"One would think you've been here before," said Davoud.

"Take off your sweater."

Davoud hesitated for the first time since Paul had arrived that evening. "You know, I'm not exactly an athlete like—"

"Please," Paul said, more softly, "I want to see you."

Davoud raised his arms and pulled off his sweater.

Paul pulled him in for another kiss. "You're a beautiful man, Davoud. Never let anyone tell you different." He tugged the rest of Davoud's shirt from his pants. Davoud's skin was hot, as if he'd been lying in the sun. "I want to taste you," Paul said.

Davoud shivered. "My turn," he said, tugging off Paul's overcoat and jacket. He removed Paul's dress shirt and T-shirt and tossed them on the chair by the dresser.

Paul reached for Davoud's shirt. "God, you're hot." He traced a finger from one dark nipple down to bump each rib.

"I'm skinny. Always was, always will be."

"Skinny? I don't like that word. Slender, maybe. Elegant," Paul murmured, fascinated. He leaned forward to suck a nipple and then flick it with his tongue.

Davoud groaned.

"You like that, do you?" Paul tweaked both nipples between his thumb and forefinger.

"This is fun, but I want you on the bed," said Davoud.

Paul allowed himself to fall backward onto the quilt.

"Let me help you with those." Davoud unbuckled Paul's belt and drew down his pants and briefs. Paul helped by lifting his hips from the bed. When his briefs came off, his cock, released from its cramped quarters, sprang to attention, curving up like a scimitar, a bead of precum already forming at the slit. Davoud's eyes darkened. "I want a taste of that."

"Come here, then."

Davoud dropped his trousers and shorts together and stepped out of them quickly, his cock springing up to slap against his belly. Like the rest of him, it was long and elegantly shaped, with a dark engorged head. Were he to press it flat, Paul thought it would extend past Davoud's belly button. He started to make room for Davoud on the bed.

"Wait, I want to look at you."

Paul bunched his biceps in a parody of a body builder. He might not have the muscle of a lifter, but he was lean and toned from running.

"Whew!" Davoud pretended to wipe sweat from his forehead. "Is it hot in here?"

Paul smirked. "I have my way, they'll be accusing us of melting the ice caps."

Davoud climbed onto the bed and caught him up in a skin-to-skin embrace, his mouth finding Paul's as they lay on their sides, hands tracing each other's spines. Serious again, he explored Paul's mouth and lowered a hand to grasp Paul's butt cheek and pull them closer. He ran his fingers down the crease. Paul made a guttural sound deep in his throat. His cock slid against Davoud's, and he moaned with pleasure. Maybe all Davoud had needed was a little encouragement. In any case, he wasn't shy now. Paul wanted to pant like the hound on the bacon-flavored dog food commercial. *Oh boy, oh boy, oh boy.*

PAUL'S SKIN smelled like warm milk and tasted of sea salt. Leaving his mouth for the moment, Davoud pushed Paul onto his back and licked a trail down his body, stopping to taste the clavicles, to tug gently at Paul's nipples, and to lave long strokes across his belly.

Paul pushed his fingers into Davoud's hair, raking and tugging lightly as Davoud worked his way down the light trail of hair to the thicket of tight curls around his cock.

Paul moaned. "Please."

"Please what?" Davoud teased, lifting his head briefly.

"Please…." Paul seemed unable to complete his thought.

Davoud brushed a finger over Paul's scrotum, which was already drawn up tight against the base of his cock. He cupped a ball and squeezed lightly. Paul's body convulsed, and his hips jerked up from the bed. Davoud moved with him and buried his nose in Paul's pubic hair, letting the grit of his unshaven cheeks brush lightly against Paul's cock. Paul made a needy sound in his throat and gripped Davoud's hair more tightly. Davoud moved his hand up and gripped the base of Paul's cock. The muscles of Paul's belly tensed. Davoud licked the slit at the head of Paul's penis with the tip of his tongue. Paul's hips strained upward. Davoud licked around the head of the penis, making little flicks of his tongue against the corona and the loose skin of the frenulum. Paul moaned and tugged Davoud's hair. Davoud slid his mouth over Paul's shaft and took in as much as he could without choking. At the same time, he worked his tongue around the middle part of the shaft. Paul's movements become spastic, and he began to whimper softly.

Davoud used his left hand to balance and began moving his head up and down, sucking Paul's shaft as deep into his throat as he could with each stroke, squeezing the base with his right hand. He could tell Paul was getting close from his uncontrolled movements and increasingly loud sounds. Paul moaned something incoherent and tried to lift Davoud's head from his cock. Davoud ignored him and accelerated his movements. He shifted his right hand to pinch one of Paul's nipples. Paul thrust his hips upward and froze. He let out a loud groan and pumped a hot flood into the back of Davoud's throat.

Davoud let Paul's cock slide out until only the head was in his mouth and swallowed as much as he could, letting the excess dribble down his chin. The bitter salty taste and the rush of Paul's orgasm had brought him close to coming himself. He let go of Paul's shaft and reached for his own. It only took a couple of strokes until he pumped pearly ribbons over Paul's thigh. Finished, he collapsed onto the bed and tucked his head into Paul's armpit. He threw a proprietary arm over Paul's chest. Paul's heart thundered in his ear.

After a moment, Paul's breathing slowed. "Um. Wow." He seemed to have difficulty speaking.

"Relax, fella. I'm fine."

"I didn't mean for you to—"

"You have a delightful taste."

"Don't you want me to—"

"Just relax for a minute. Then, when you're good and ready, you can fuck me."

Davoud heard Paul swallow. "Uh. You wouldn't happen to have a condom and lube? I didn't think to—"

"In my nightstand. Don't worry. I'll drive, if you want."

Paul laughed. "Would that make you a backseat driver?"

"JONAH, I want you to speak to an attorney about what happened at school last week."

His mom's lined face was hard to read. Did she really think he was some kind of criminal who needed a defense attorney, or was she just working his case like any other? She'd been teary and tired when she arrived from the airport in Rascal's car, but her expression had hardened when Jonah offered to carry her luggage up to the apartment with the cool professionalism of a doorman at a fancy New York apartment building. Civil was the best he could manage with her. When Rascal left to wrangle some takeout, she slumped onto the leather couch in the living room, her floral silk scarf still wrapped around her neck. He took her things to the bedroom and returned to offer a cup of her favorite chamomile tea. It wasn't much in the way of a peace offering, but it was all he could muster. They maintained an uneasy silence until after Rascal returned with the food. When his mom started to look like she might say something more substantive than "Pass the egg rolls," Jonah jumped to his feet and began to clear the table.

"You know this is just a precaution, in case Mr. Scarelli insists on filing assault charges."

She'd caught him by surprise, and he continued to clear takeout containers and dirty plates. "Whatever."

"Whatever? Do you want to have a criminal record? Go to juvenile detention?"

"No."

"I can't understand what you were thinking. Your dad and I always taught you not to hit. You had to know it would make things worse."

"Don't talk about him." Jonah was inexplicably angry at the mention of his dad, his heart suddenly banging like a drum, his hands in fists.

Esmé stared at him tiredly. "Jonah, he was my husband. He may be gone, but I can't pretend he never existed. I won't."

"I don't care. I don't want you talking about him."

"The attorney's name is Robert Baxter. He's coming over tomorrow morning."

"I already told Davoud what happened."

"Yes, well, Davoud is not your attorney. Mr. Baxter needs to know exactly what happened in order to help you. He won't tell me anything you say without your permission."

"I know about attorney-client privilege. I also know I'm still a minor. He'll tell you anything you ask. Anyway, I don't know what you think I'm going to say that's going to make any difference."

"You haven't said *why* you attacked Antony. What was different this time?"

"Maybe I was just fucking sick of it. Anyway, I hit him in the parking lot another time."

His mother sighed. "You know, I'm actually a pretty good attorney."

It had never occurred to Jonah to doubt that his mother was a good attorney. He was perfectly capable of imagining her arguing before the Supreme Court, robed justices falling before her logic like frozen crows from a power line.

"He said something to you, didn't he?"

She was too close for comfort. "I have to practice now. There's something I'm working on for Rascal." He knew she liked Rascal.

Esmé smoothed her skirt over her knees. "There's something else I need to speak to you about, Jonah."

"It's really important that I practice, Mom. We're going to perform at the opening."

"What opening? Who's performing?"

"The Rascals and Mr. G—Rascal, Davoud, Paul, and me—we've formed a group, and we're going to perform at the opening of the new coffee bar."

Esmé frowned and shifted on the couch. "The Avakians have been very kind to encourage you with your music, but I'm not sure this group is such a good idea."

Jonah bristled. "Why do you always have to ruin everything?" He felt like the summer when his father told him he couldn't go to music camp. He knew it was because they didn't have the money, but his face had gotten hot, and he'd been so angry he couldn't speak. In desperation, his father had promised that they would have their own music camp at home, with rehearsals and a show. Jonah had been so taken with the idea, he'd run straight to the cabinet where his music books were stored to start picking out songs.

"There's no need to get overwrought. I only meant we're not likely to be in Glen Falls much longer, so I don't—"

"I don't want to move to Chicago." He spaced out the words like she was deaf and a poor lip-reader.

"Jonah, I have to earn a living. With your father gone, there's nothing to—"

"I want to stay at the Music Box."

"I thought, given your problems with Antony, you'd—"

"I don't give a shit about Antony or his stupid fan club. I'm not going. You can't make me."

Esmé's mouth formed a flat line. Jonah noticed her lips were chapped, like she'd forgotten her lipstick or she'd been licking them too often. "You have homework. Did someone bring it over today?"

"Billy."

"I don't know how your father...." She trailed off. Maybe it was because he'd already slammed out of the room.

POUNDING. DAVOUD woke with the weight and sticky heat of Paul's naked arm across his belly. Paul's head was tucked under his arm, a lock of blond hair tickling Davoud's nipple. He didn't want to move. Whoever was pounding would just have to wait.

"Whasamatter?" Paul grumbled, tightening his hold on Davoud's midsection.

"Sorry, baby. I expect they found the lease agreements."

Paul let go of Davoud and stretched languidly. "I knew we should've waited until morning."

"I was afraid I'd chicken out."

"I wouldn't have let you."

The pounding intensified.

"I'm going to strangle my brother."

"Better yet, raise his rent."

Davoud laughed. "You're a keeper. Stay where you are. I'll get rid of him." He extracted himself, but not before Paul brushed a hand over his hipbone and down the inside of his thigh. His body lit to the memory of last night's activity, eager for more. "Hey! Now I've got to find my bathrobe."

"Come back soon."

Davoud found an old terrycloth bathrobe with *Hotel Karton* across the back. In the early '80s Rascal had gotten them embroidered for the family as a joke. Shrugging it on, he belted it over his boxers and unhooked the privacy chain on his front door. He'd barely turned the handle when the door was shoved open. Rascal pushed into the apartment, waving his lease agreement like a signal flag.

"Nice move, Davy. Mother's convinced you're trying to get rid of her."

Davoud followed him into the kitchen. "Good morning to you too, Rasul. By all means, have a cup of coffee."

"Where are your filters?"

"There's a French press in the cabinet by the fridge."

"What's with your hair? You look as if—oh shit."

"I don't suppose you'd come back in an hour—or three?" Davoud watched Rascal's eyes widen, and he spun around. Paul emerged from the bedroom, chest bare, casually buttoning his jeans. The sight of Paul's sharply defined pecs and taut abs had him reflexively checking the closure of his bathrobe.

"Too late," said Paul. "Make a cup for me, Rascal, would you? You know, I think I left my shirt on the couch."

"I'm impressed, brother mine. I think you've hit on the one thing that's sure to distract Aida from your treachery."

"Ah, but who was hitting on whom?" said Paul, as he pried his shirt from the cushions of the velvet monstrosity.

Davoud glared at his unrepentant partner, wishing he'd tone it down in front of his brother. Rascal would be teasing Davoud for the foreseeable future and didn't need any encouragement. "Treachery? That's a bit harsh."

"You've met our mother, right?"

"I'm just trying to be fair—and keep the roof over our heads."

"I wish you'd talked to us first."

"What?" His adenoids were probably on display, but the shameless inequity left Davoud speechless.

"Rascal," said Paul, plucking the coffee cup from Rascal's hand. "I know this thing with Jonah has been a distraction, but while Davy recovers his power of speech, perhaps you and I could review the past month?"

"Okay, I grant you he's mentioned the finances, but it's not like—"

"Let's think back together." Paul put an arm around Rascal's shoulders. "There's the smell in Aida's dining room, which caused you to move Thanksgiving and Christmas to 3B."

"Well, yes, but Aida said—"

"He showed you the bank books, didn't he?"

"Yeah, but I assumed—"

"Did you offer to help pay for the new roof?"

Rascal appeared to notice he had no coffee and frowned, his hands groping the counter for the tin and press like he'd been struck blind. "I was going to, but then Jonah...."

Paul took a sip from the mug in his hand. "Oh, good, that's settled, then. The lease indicates the amount of your monthly contribution right on the first page. See, Davy? You were all worried about nothing."

Davoud closed his mouth and pulled Paul over for a kiss. He didn't mind the mismatched flavors of coffee and toothpaste. After a while, he noticed Rascal was still there. He sighed. "The least you could do is make some more coffee, Rascal, and stop staring like you've never seen people kiss."

JONAH SPRAWLED across his bed, still wearing the sweatpants and T-shirt he'd worn the day before. He rolled over to check the time. Already 9:30. His mother was going to roast his nuts for breakfast if the lawyer showed and he wasn't ready. He didn't know why it should matter, but he was fairly certain she expected him to shower and put on clean clothes. He grabbed a clean pair of boxers from the bureau and headed for the bathroom, shedding his sweatpants and T-shirt as he went.

He'd finished his shower and was brushing when his mother called from outside. "Jonah, are you ready?"

"Be out in a minute," he called, his mouth full of toothpaste. Spitting, he grabbed his dirty clothes, and then threw open the bathroom door. "Shit! Sorry." His mom and a strange man in a pinstriped suit were standing in the hall. Holding sweatpants and T-shirt in front of his underwear, he galloped to his room, where he stuffed his legs into the first pair of jeans he could find. Grabbing a black T-shirt with a treble clef on it from the pile on the top of the bureau, he dragged it over his head and smoothed it into place.

"Jonah!"

"I'm here," he said, trotting into the kitchen.

His mom's expression was bland, but he knew she was mad from the set of her shoulders and the way she kept checking to see if her blouse was properly tucked into her slacks. "This is Robert Baxter. He's the attorney I told you about. BB, this is my son, Jonah."

"Pleased to meet you, Jonah. Call me BB, if you want."

"BB, right." Jonah gripped Baxter's hand, wishing he wasn't still damp from the shower.

"I'll leave you two at it," said his mother. "I'll be in the living room if you need me."

"Thanks, Esmé."

BB pointed to the kitchen table as if they were in a conference room at his law office. "Have a seat. You understand that everything we discuss will stay between you and me unless you tell me otherwise, right?"

"I'm going to make tea. You want some?" said Jonah.

"No, thanks. Your mother tells me that the incident at school last week wasn't the first time you've had a problem with Antony Scarelli."

Jonah filled the teakettle with cold water before answering. "Nope."

"Your mother told me about the saxophone case. Is it true that you're gay?"

"Jesus, fuck! You don't beat around the bush, do you?"

"No, I take my work seriously, and I'm pretty expensive, so I thought your mother would appreciate it if we didn't waste a lot of time."

"Right." Jonah stared at the kettle for a second and then turned it off. "You mind if I get some socks, first? My feet are freezing."

"It's your dime." BB leaned back and crossed his legs.

Jonah ran to his room and snagged a pair of dirty socks from the floor. He ran back and pulled them on while Baxter watched patiently. "I suppose you never oversleep?"

"Not often."

"What did you want to know?"

Baxter took a notebook and disposable pen from a black leather briefcase. "Are you gay?"

"I'll be seventeen in May."

BB looked unimpressed. "Let's try it this way. Your mother says you refused to have the saxophone case cleaned and have been carrying it around with 'Faggot' painted on it."

"I was pissed. I didn't paint the word, I just embraced it."

BB sighed. "You know, there's no point in doing this if you won't take it seriously." He started to rise. "I'll tell your mother you need a new lawyer."

"Wait!" Jonah rubbed his stockinged feet together to warm them. "Why do you need to know if I'm gay?"

BB dropped back into his chair. "I need to know if you've ever behaved in a way they can use against you should this go to court."

"So if I'm gay, I must have done something wrong. Is that what you think?"

"It doesn't matter what I think." Baxter leaned forward and examined Jonah curiously until Jonah dropped his gaze to the black and white kitchen tiles. "But if you are gay, it changes the case. On the hate crimes side, it's probably a good thing. With regard to your behavior, it might not be as helpful."

"If I'm gay, I must be fucking around."

"Have you been?"

"No."

"I make no value judgment, Jonah, but I have to know exactly what has gone on between you and Antony if I'm going to be effective."

"Whatever."

"Has Antony ever seen you engage in sexual activity such as kissing or touching another boy?"

"No."

"Have you ever had sex with Antony or anyone else at your school?"

"He shook his package at me," said Jonah, "but I don't suppose that counts, does it?"

BB made a note. "No, but that's interesting to know."

"He grabbed my balls in the boy's room."

Baxter frowned. "Were you dressed at the time?" At Jonah's shocked nod, he continued. "So he groped you through your clothes."

"He was threatening me. He grabbed my balls to hurt me."

"I see. When did this happen?" When Jonah told him, he pursed his lips. "Did anyone see this?"

"Justin was there."

"Who's Justin?"

"Antony's sidekick. Hangs out with him all the time. He changed schools 'cause he got nabbed for stealing a car."

"You think he would lie to protect Antony?"

Jonah shrugged. "Probably."

Baxter made another note. "I need you to write down his full name and any contact information you have."

"I don't know him that well, but I know he is—he was—on the wrestling team. Billy might know more 'cause he's a jock."

"Who's Billy?"

"Billy Preston. My…." Jonah hesitated. He hoped Billy was still his friend, even if Billy was clueless sometimes. "My friend. He plays trumpet in Jazz Ensemble."

"Really? I played trumpet too," BB murmured as he made another note. "Never any good at it."

By this time Jonah felt kind of dizzy, as if he'd been drinking on an empty stomach.

BB raised his head and gave him a kind look. "Hold on there, partner, we're almost done. Now, I need you to think back to the incident when you attacked Antony. You did attack Antony, right?"

Jonah nodded.

"How exactly?"

"I don't remember very well. I kind of charged into him, and he fell down."

"Did you punch him?" Baxter opened his briefcase and took out some papers. He consulted one. Even upside-down, Jonah recognized the police department logo. "Stay with me, Jonah. You punched him?"

"Yes."

"How many times?"

"I... I don't know. I kind of lost it."

"Were you high?"

"No."

BB flipped to a new page. "What did Antony say before you hit him?"

"I don't remember."

"Sure you do. What did he say to you before you charged him?"

"He called me a fag."

"That's the word he used?"

"Yes."

BB stared for moment, tapping his pen on the notepad. "Okay, I'm going to stop now, but we'll need to talk again soon. Before we do, I want you to write down everything you can remember about what Antony and Justin said to you. Every word, Jonah, even the ugly ones, and how you replied. Can you do that for me?"

"I guess."

"Is there anything else you want to tell me?"

"No."

"What about questions?"

By this time Jonah was floating like he'd had a few tokes. He could hear BB's words, but they seemed distant. "Questions?"

BB replaced the little notebook and pen in the briefcase. "Do you have any questions for me?"

No, Jonah only had two questions. *Why did you kill yourself, Dad? And why didn't you leave a note to tell me why?*

CHAPTER 13

BILLY THREW his pack on the floor and dropped face-first onto Jonah's bed like a felled tree. "So what happens now?"

Jonah leaned back in the swivel chair Rascal had loaned him to go with the desk. "My mom gets home and sues everyone into submission." It came out less like a joke and more like a wish than he intended. Billy didn't seem to notice. His butt stuck up slightly from the bed. He pulled off his knit cap, displaying static-charged hair like antennae. Jonah wanted to run his fingers through the brown spikes.

"Jazz Ensemble sucks without you." Billy addressed the pillow on which his face rested.

"I didn't mean to hit him."

"The bastard deserved it."

"My dad said...." Jonah stopped, pretty sure it wasn't cool to quote your dead dad.

Billy rolled over and looked up, his amber eyes serious, his cheeks flushed from the cold or from being smashed into the pillow. "I don't care. You can talk about him if you want."

Jonah wasn't sure whether he actually wanted to talk about his dad. Most of the time it was better to concentrate on simple things, like the smooth cool of piano keys or maybe the way the waistband of Billy's underwear peeked above his low-cut jeans.

"How come you're not at basketball practice?"

"Coach has the flu. Half the team has it. I'm safer here with a violent criminal." Billy drew up his knees and dug his bare feet into the quilt.

"Don't your feet get cold without socks?"

"Nope, they're impervious."

"My dad would never… shit."

"Just say it, would you? It's really annoying when you start saying stuff and just stop like that."

"Sorry. My dad would never let me out of the house without socks."

"Mine doesn't care about socks, so long as we won last night."

Billy spread his legs and brought a foot up to pick at a callus. Jonah didn't know why picking at a callus should be erotic, because it was really kind of gross, but he felt himself hardening and wished he'd put on something other than sweatpants.

"How's the band? You guys going to play for us sometime, or you just jerking off?"

It was idiotic. You'd think he was one of Pavlov's dogs, but at the mention of masturbation, Jonah's hard-on was counting down to blast off. He spun the chair to put his back to Billy and tried not to think about it. "Amir is coming this weekend to help Davoud and Paul move the sheet music and install the espresso machine. Davoud wants to open the café in February. You can help, if you want."

"That thing got speakers? I wanna show you something." Billy bounced off the bed, attention on Jonah's laptop. Jonah hunched over to rest his arms on his knees. Billy peered over his shoulder at the screen. "Get your bony ass out of the way, would ya?"

Jonah slid off the chair to make room for Billy, landing on his hands and knees, still trying to conceal his erection. Fortunately, Billy was paying more attention to the laptop than to Jonah. Jonah crawled around to the bed and got onto it facedown, smashing his determined prick into the quilt.

Billy dropped his butt onto the swivel chair. Jonah could hear the clicking of the keys. "There. What are you doing? Come take a look. This video is hilarious." When Jonah didn't move, he batted the sole of Jonah's foot. "Hey, Whale Bait, quit rubbing yourself and take a look at this."

Jonah's neck burned. "Fuck off, Bigfoot, I'm tired. Maybe I'll take a nap."

With his face in the pillow, he didn't realize what Billy was going to do until Billy grabbed him by the feet and flipped him over revealing the turgid state of his cock.

"Shit. Sorry." Billy's eyes dilated, and he dropped Jonah's feet like they were on fire, but he continued to stare at Jonah's crotch. Whatever the rest of him was feeling, Jonah's unrepentant dick had his sweatpants stretched like a circus tent.

"Just go, would you?" Jonah snapped.

Billy sprang into motion, but not before Jonah noticed an answering bulge in his jeans. "I'll leave you to… uh, burp the worm."

Jonah waited until he heard the crash of the elevator cage, then resignedly drew off his T-shirt and sweatpants. It only took a few strokes until he pumped hot jets onto his bare chest. The orgasm left him exhausted, with spunk drying on his cheek. Lying on the bed afterward, he started to cry, his tears mixing with the semen until he furiously wiped it off with the rumpled T-shirt.

THAT NIGHT, after practicing on the Steinway until his fingers ached, Jonah texted an apology to Billy, but Billy didn't reply, and his phone remained silent. He went back to his room and flopped on the bed, thinking about the bulge in Billy's jeans and what it had meant. If Billy was turned on by Jonah's boner, did that mean he was gay too? Or bisexual? He'd said he liked girls. Jonah knew Billy went out with the team after basketball games and that he usually sat with a girl at the diner where the team hung out, although none of the girls lasted very long. Most likely his arousal was just a sympathetic reaction—like when you heard someone cough in a movie theater and you had to cough too. He wanted to text or call again, but his stupid fingers wouldn't move.

SATURDAY MORNING, Davoud gathered a motley crew in the back room of Avakian Music to review assignments. The shop was officially closed for the weekend for renovations. Aida was babysitting Zhara, up in 3A. Davoud had talked Paul into wiring the new sound system. Paul was the only one who played an electric instrument, after all. He'd assigned Rascal to install the raised floor to make the corner stage. Who among them had seen more stages? Well, that would have been Aida, but those were big stages. Amir and Dorothy had agreed to move the sheet music collection to its new home in 1A, with muscle from Jonah and Billy.

That is, if Billy showed. "I thought you said you were going to ask Billy," said Davoud.

Jonah looked away. "I mentioned it."

Paul sent Davoud an inquiring look. He shrugged. *Beats me.*

Davoud was stuck with installing the new espresso machine. As the small business owner, it was his fate to deal with plumbing issues. "You know I'll probably have coffee grounds shooting from the milk nozzle. Are you sure you don't know anything about plumbing?" he asked Paul.

Paul laughed. "Just wait until you hear the Muzak from next door on the sound system."

There was a shocked silence from all five Avakians.

"Okay, just kidding, folks. No Muzak."

"We don't speak that word in polite company," said Amir.

"What's wrong with it?" Paul asked innocently.

"Ha, ha," Rascal said. "Keep it up and we'll toilet paper your front lawn."

"I don't have a front lawn."

"No wonder you're living here."

"Neither do you."

"No, but we've got a lobby."

"Some spy you are," said Dorothy, glaring at Rascal before aiming a high-wattage smile at Davoud. "Paul is living here?"

"I'm not."

"He's just here all the time," said Rascal.

"Jesus, haven't you people ever heard of privacy?" said Jonah.

"Nope," said Amir. "You walk in that door and you might as well sign a disclosure agreement."

"I thought those were called nondisclosure agreements," said Paul.

"Not around here, they're not," said Rascal flatly.

"Excuse me, family and friends, but this is not an episode of *The Bickersons.* Can we get started, please?" Davoud pleaded.

"Who are the Bickersons?" Jonah asked Paul.

"Beats me."

"Way to go, little brother," said Rascal. "Wow your friends with your encyclopedic knowledge of 1940s radio comedy. That's sure to get you laid."

Davoud caught Paul's smirk and returned it.

Amir whistled. "Whoa! You *have* been holding out on us, Rascal."

"Or too busy with his own affairs," said Paul, grinning at Rascal. Rascal shrugged, his look clearly stating *I have no earthly clue what you're talking about.*

Jonah's attention whipped back and forth between Paul and Davoud. "Mr. G?"

Paul was clearly uncomfortable disclosing his sex life to his student.

"Someone said something about privacy?" said Davoud.

They were distracted by tapping on the front door. Rascal caught Davoud's attention. "I thought you put out a sign."

Jonah appeared to be looking for a place to hide.

"I did. Would you please get the door, Jonah? I expect that's your friend," Davoud said.

Jonah lurched into motion reluctantly.

Paul leaned over to whisper in his ear as he ducked past. "Buck up, kid. Whatever it was, he's not holding it against you." The back of Jonah's neck turned bright red.

Jonah opened the front door and stepped back. "Everyone, this is Billy. He's a friend of mine from Jazz Ensemble."

"Hi, Billy," said Paul, grinning. "Welcome to the circus."

BILLY DUG his toes into Jonah's quilt. "This is so fucked up."

Billy stretched out on the bed while Jonah sat at the desk. It was the first time they'd been alone together since the tent incident, and Jonah wasn't sure what to expect. Every time Billy visited, Jonah felt like there was an alien baby crawling under his skin. His neck hurt from keeping a tight rein on his emotions. Whenever Billy passed close enough for Jonah to feel the heat from his skin, Jonah found himself checking if Billy still used the same citrus-scented shampoo or if he'd gotten sweaty jogging from school. The brief hiatus in Billy's visits had apparently done nothing to weaken Jonah's attraction.

Billy seemed to want to pretend he'd never seen Jonah's boner, but Jonah's embarrassment lingered, so his conversation suffered. "Mr. G says I can probably make up for the missed term this summer."

"Aren't you pissed off about it?"

Jonah shrugged. "It's better than being hassled every day. You want to play a video game? Rascal set me up."

Billy rolled onto his stomach. "Sure."

Jonah got out the controllers and tossed one to Billy. "You pick." Billy shuffled through Jonah's meager collection and picked a game that involved carjacking and street racing. "You like this shit?" asked Jonah.

"It's this or air guitar."

"Oh, fuck me." Jonah shoved Billy's legs out of the way so he could sit on the bed.

"I thought not."

They played a couple of games, but Jonah could tell Billy wasn't really into it. After a while he tossed his controller onto the desk. "You wanna talk about it?"

"What?"

"You didn't even try to run over that police officer."

Billy rolled his eyes. "Maybe I'm not a violent offender like you."

"That's me, hardened criminal. Soon to be butt boy for some knuckle-dragger in juvie."

"Shit. Don't joke about that."

"You started it."

Billy rallied. "Now you're just being a criminal ass."

"That's my Billy."

Billy's grin faded and he slumped onto Jonah's pillow.

"Jesus, what's with you today?"

"Just moody, I guess."

Jonah had had enough. As usual, his mouth was the first to know. "What's it gonna take, dude? Want me to turn off the lights, so you don't have to look at me while you talk? Should I steal some whiskey from Rascal and get you trashed?"

"I'll never see you," Billy said bitterly. "You'll be stuck in school all summer, and I'll be at basketball camp."

"Come on, you've got better things to do than hang with a runt like me. Last time I went to a game, the girls were lining up for you. Pick one."

"I don't want them."

Something about the way Billy said it had Jonah's chest tightening. "What are you saying?"

"I don't want them."

"The girls at Martin Luther King? All girls?"

"I can't be gay, Jonah. You don't know what my dad's like. He'll disown me."

"You know it doesn't work like that."

"I know it doesn't work *at all.* Not in high school. Not here. Look what happened to you. And most people don't know you, or at least they didn't until you started carrying around that stupid saxophone case like a fucking badge of honor. They know me. They have expectations."

"Fuck you, Billy." Jonah shoved Billy's feet out of the way and jumped up to pace. He heard a faint sound. Billy had drawn up his feet and clasped his arms around his knees. His lashes were wet. Jonah stopped moving, unsure what to do. He wanted to soothe Billy, pat his hair, but he wasn't sure Billy wouldn't just bolt.

"I'm fucked. Don't you get it? I'm not brave like you. I can't be gay. Not and play basketball like my dad did. Not and get a sports scholarship, and how else is an idiot like me going to get into college?"

"Shit." Jonah slumped to the floor with his back to the bed. "Why'd you start walking me to Jazz Ensemble?"

"My friends thought I was doing charity work."

Jonah tasted bile as his stomach tried to climb his throat. "Is that what you thought?"

"No. Maybe a little at first. I mean, Antony and Justin are jerks, and I hated what they were doing to you, so I thought I'd help out, right? But then I got to know you... I mean I already knew you were a billion times better as a musician than I'll ever be, and then I started liking you. Don't you get it? You're the one who's slumming."

Jonah was still pissed at being thought of as charity work, however briefly. "Let's have a pity party, why don't we? I'll start. Let's see, I'm the one whose dad—"

"Don't talk to me about your dad. You've got any number of people around here I'd happily swap for the jerk who knocked up my mom."

The idea that he might have something Billy didn't brought Jonah up short. He turned around. "I never—"

"Forget it."

Jonah returned to what suddenly felt like safer ground. "Let me get this straight: you do actually like me? I mean *like* like?"

Billy raised his head and his mouth twitched. "Now you're fishing."

"Yeah, and I got a longer pole than you do."

Billy smirked. "Not when I'm looking at your ass." Jonah's face heated. "And you're cute when you get all hot and bothered."

Jonah's body was as confused as Billy's messages. He was angry at being treated so cavalierly—and acutely conscious of Billy's body. He watched Billy's long pale toes knead his quilt. Before he knew it, he'd leaned over and planted his lips firmly on Billy's. The kiss was neither soft nor gentle. Billy froze long enough for Jonah to feel the heat of his mouth and to taste a hint of cola-flavored lip balm, and then he jerked away. He scrambled off the bed like he was afraid Jonah would start humping him. "I told you, I can't be gay."

Jonah was unable to look at Billy or keep the bitterness from his voice. "Good luck with that." He went to his desk and started randomly shuffling sheet music. "I have to practice."

Billy grabbed his pack and took out a folder. He tossed it on the bed and hesitated. "Should I keep bringing the assignments?"

"Whatever."

JONAH DIDN'T fully process the events of the next few days until after they'd happened. He was a wide-eyed reporter strapped into a biplane while the pilot performed loops and barrel rolls. It started with a phone call from BB Baxter. Antony's father had filed formal assault charges, and the Scarelli's attorney was petitioning the court to have Jonah charged as an adult.

Before they went to juvenile court, both BB and his mother instructed him not to say anything *whatsoever* unless the judge addressed him directly, in which case he was to stand and address the man as Your Honor—the capital letters plain in their speech. The day before they saw the judge, BB took him shopping to buy a suit, saying the one he'd worn for his dad's service made him look like a lawyer wannabe. Jonah thought that was probably a joke, but he didn't dare ask. They also went to a barber to get his shaggy hair cut to something "more boy next door." Esmé stayed in her room, saying that her strength was in preparing legal arguments, not playing games with judges. Jonah thought she was mad at him and worried about what her colleagues would think. Then he caught Rascal's worried expression and thought something else might be going on, but BB dragged him out the door before he could ask.

The next day, Paul played hooky and Davoud closed the shop so they could support him in the courtroom. In a blue blazer and gray slacks that looked to him like a military-school uniform, Jonah felt like he'd already been convicted and sentenced. The hearing was only to decide where he'd be imprisoned. Not even a series of encouraging texts from Billy could convince Jonah he wasn't marching to his doom.

The actual hearing was nothing like he expected. They waited outside the courtroom for hours. Antony and his parents were squeezed onto a bench across the corridor, but they said nothing—even to each other. Antony had a little plastic brace on his nose and bruises on his cheeks, but he was healthy enough to give Jonah the evil eye. When they finally shuffled into the courtroom like a misdirected funeral procession, they waited again while BB and another guy Jonah figured must be the Scarelli's attorney dealt with some procedural stuff that Jonah didn't really follow. He was too busy watching the judge's hairline bounce up and down, and trying to figure out whether the guy was wearing a wig, or if his scalp was just loose on his skull. Finally, he felt a dig in the ribs and realized the judge had asked him a question. He scrambled to his feet as he'd been coached.

"Do you need me to repeat the question, Jonah? I asked whether you meant to hurt Antony."

Jonah wasn't ready for the question. When he'd thought about the questions he might be asked in court, he'd imagined himself at the center of a detective story in which the prosecutor had to prove first that he'd been in the bathroom. A line-up of forensic experts would then explain who'd done what to whom. By assuming that Jonah had been there and attacked Antony, the judge bypassed everything Jonah thought he knew about legal process.

There was another problem he hadn't anticipated. He didn't know the answer to the question. He looked at BB for help, but BB's face communicated only professional detachment. His mom looked tightly controlled as ever, even if there were twin furrows between her carefully plucked and shaped eyebrows. Maybe it didn't matter what he said. It was ritual, wasn't it, the actual decision having been made in a back office while BB and the other guy gossiped about the judge's hairpiece. In the end, he just told the truth.

"I don't know, your honor. I was pretty mad…."

The judge contemplated Jonah before tapping his temple. "Did you *think* about hurting him, before you moved?"

Jonah relaxed a little when he realized that he did know the answer to this question. He shook his head and then saw the clerk, who had been typing continuously on her laptop, point at her mouth. "No, your honor, I didn't think about anything before I—" Jonah heard a tiny sound like a squeak from BB. "—before I moved."

The judge glared at BB, his lips pursed, and then glanced at Antony before speaking. "Okay. On the one hand, I have evidence of serious injury and a petition from the victim's family that Jonah Winfield be charged as an adult. On the other hand, I have a young man with an excellent record at school and no history of violence or misbehavior of any kind. My concern throughout this process must be to see that both Jonah and Antony receive appropriate help so that *neither* boy ends up in the hospital—or in this court—again." He looked at the papers arrayed before him. "I see no compelling evidence to support a petition for Jonah Winfield to be treated as an adult. That petition is denied. However, the defendant's petition to have the charges dropped is also denied. Despite the suggestion of a pattern of bullying prior to the fight that put Antony in the hospital, I cannot simply ignore the seriousness of Antony's injuries." He paused. "There is more to this story than these documents tell me, and without a full picture, I don't feel prepared to determine what further action is appropriate. Therefore, I'm ordering that both parties and their attorneys return to this court for a full hearing in…." He looked at his clerk. She raised her eyebrows as if to say, *What do you want? I'm not the one who filled up his calendar with more cases than he could hear.* The judge rolled his eyes. "At a time to be determined. Gentlemen, when we address this issue again, I want to know what really went on between these boys. In the meantime, Jonah will remain in the custody of his mother." He tapped his gavel, his focus already shifting to his clerk and the next case.

"That could have gone a lot worse," said BB to Jonah's mom.

"Yeah, this way you're still employed," said Jonah, some of his tension translating into snark.

BB laughed unexpectedly. "You think I don't have any other clients?"

The capper to the whole fucked-up week came when Paul called to tell them that Mr. Wong had suspended Jonah from school indefinitely, pending the outcome of his hearing. Worse, Jonah had already missed so many days he was probably going to have to repeat the term. Billy was more upset than Jonah. The trumpet player texted Jonah to say that he and some friends were going to TP Wong's house. It took Jonah fifteen minutes of furious texting to persuade Billy that he shouldn't get anyone else into trouble.

I want 2 do smthg, Billy texted.

Hang w me, Jonah responded.

BB SCANNED the oak-paneled conference room, his gaze stopping at each face in turn: Arturo and Ellen Scarelli, Antony, their lawyer—Mr. Falcone, whose first name Paul hadn't caught—Davoud, and Jonah. He ended at Esmé with a nod. "The purpose of this meeting is to collect information as requested by Judge Beaufort for the Juvenile Court hearing scheduled for March 7. I would remind you that, although this is an informal meeting, everything you say here is being recorded. Your statements may be submitted as evidence at the hearing. Any inaccuracy or discrepancy between what you say here and what you say there will be noted."

"Listen to the big, scary, lawyer."

Mr. Falcone caught Ellen Scarelli's gaze. "Arturo," she said, glaring at her husband.

"I don't see why we even need to be here."

"We went over that with Mr. Falcone."

BB cleared his throat. "Most of my questions will be for Antony. Mr. Falcone will also have the opportunity to ask any questions of Jonah. Either Mr. Falcone or I may stop the deposition at any time if we feel it to be unproductive or not in the best interests of our client. Is everyone clear on the ground rules?"

Falcone looked at Arturo and Ellen. "Yes."

BB looked at Esmé. She nodded once, briefly. "Yes."

"Antony, I want to ask you about what happened on October 2 of last year."

"I got no idea what happened on October 2. It's not like I keep a calendar."

"Fair enough. Perhaps I can jog your memory. This was the day, last fall, when you and Justin followed Jonah from school and caught up with him in front of Avakian Music on Main Street."

Antony shrugged. "Justin and me spent lots of quality time with Jonah." Falcone leaned over as though he were whispering in Antony's ear, although Paul couldn't see his lips moving. Antony rolled his eyes. "Yeah, okay." Antony hadn't mastered the art of ventriloquism like his lawyer.

"What did you say to Jonah on that occasion?"

"Fuck if I know."

"I have a signed statement from Mr. Avakian indicating that you placed your hand on your crotch and shook your genitals. Perhaps you recall what you said to him at the time?"

Antony smirked at his father. "I bet the little faggot remembered that." There was a faint sound from Ellen Scarelli. Antony's gaze slid to his mother for a moment before returning to BB.

Falcone leaned over to whisper again. Antony jerked away. "Whatever, man. Get away from me."

So it went. BB took them through each incident, some Paul had known of and others of which he'd been completely ignorant. It was painful to listen, so Paul concentrated on the expressions on the Scarellis' faces as they learned about their son's behavior. Ellen Scarelli seemed to veer between distaste for her son's behavior and anger at her husband. By the time BB reached the second incident in a restroom at Martin Luther King High, she leaned from Arturo like a tree in a storm. Antony reserved the most egregious of his remarks for his father, whether for the purpose of spreading accelerant or gaining his approval, it was impossible to say. Either way, by the time they reached the final incident, Paul wasn't sure which parent's aspect was scarier, Arturo Scarelli's crusted scab over swollen magma or Ellen's frozen distaste.

"What did you say to Jonah before he attacked you, Antony?"

When Antony didn't answer immediately, Ellen Scarelli's dry voice cut through the room like a knife. "What did you say to him, Antony?"

"I don't remem—"

"What did you say?"

"Ellen, who's side you on?" said Arturo.

"Shut up, Arturo, I've had about enough of both of you," she said, ice to his fire. "What did you say, Antony?"

Paul noticed Davoud watching Jonah intently with something more than support in his expression. *What did I miss?*

For the first time, Antony looked uncomfortable. "I told him his dad probably killed himself because he couldn't stand that he had a fag—a gay son."

Rage passed through Paul's body like an electric current. Without realizing how he got there, he was standing with BB's heavy hand on his shoulder. "Sit down, Mr. Gaston." BB actually smiled at Antony, a predator showing his teeth. Ellen's face stiffened and her gaze went to Esmé's, as though dragged. Esmé did not acknowledge her. Jonah's eyes closed, his face appearing shrink-wrapped around his skull. Davoud took his hand under the table.

Arturo jumped to his feet, his face red. "So what? He probably did. I know I'd—"

Ellen didn't move. "If you say another word, Arturo Scarelli, I swear on the Virgin Mary it will be the last you ever say to me." Arturo glared, but he deflated like a punctured tire. Ellen turned her head. "Mr. Falcone? A word, please?"

Falcone nodded and ushered her from the conference room. Paul could see her speaking to Falcone through the glass door, her lips barely moving. Falcone nodded and opened the door. "Mr. Baxter?"

When BB returned, he shut off the tape recorder.

Arturo's eyes narrowed. "What are you doing?"

"We're done."

"What do you mean, we're done? We haven't even heard what that kid did to my son."

"I think you'd better consult with your attorney, Mr. Scarelli."

"Come on, Antony." Scarelli dragged his son from the room.

"What happened?" Jonah asked tiredly.

"It's finished. They'll drop the charges."

"Mr. Scarelli didn't sound like he was ready to—"

"It seems *Mr.* Scarelli was not paying their attorney."

CHARLIE WAVED at Paul through the open door of his office. He held up his phone and motioned to Paul to stay where he was. He listened, speaking little, and then put down the instrument and disappeared behind the door, reappearing an instant later with his coat and hat. The hat, which was an English trilby, was the source of much snickering around the school. Paul believed that Wong knew this and wore it anyway as a means of softening his naturally dour appearance. It was political theater on a small scale.

"Thank you for agreeing to see me, Charlie."

"Have you got your coat? Good. I want to get out of the office. How about a walk along the river?" Paul's surprise must have shown on his face. "Come on, Paul. I need to get out of here. I'll explain in a minute."

"I suppose I can put my briefcase in the car."

"Yes, yes, come on."

Once they were outside the building, Charlie's animation fell away. "Thank you for indulging me. I don't want to receive any—wait, I had better do this too." He lifted a battered courier bag and extracted his phone with two figures like a magician showing off his sleight of hand. He switched the phone to vibrate and dropped it back into the bag. "There."

Paul led the way across the parking lot to his car. Any other day, he would have marveled at the behavior of his normally dignified and grave boss. "What's going on?"

"I don't want to receive any calls."

"I gathered."

"In my office, I was on the phone? That was Sergeant Haskel, from the police department. Do you know him? Nice man. His son was in my social studies class a few years ago…." He laughed out loud. "I couldn't say the sky was blue without the kid arguing. I was following up with Haskel to document the resolution of Jonah's case. Anyway, he told me that Scarelli wants a piece of me because I allowed Jonah to return to school, and I don't want to talk to him until he's cooled down a bit."

"You're not going to let Antony come back, are you?"

"Yes, I am."

"I can't believe you'd do that after what he did to Jonah."

"I have a responsibility to all our students, Paul, especially the troubled ones. Antony has been dropped from the football team. He will continue to attend counseling sessions. If there are any further incidents—with any student—he will be expelled. The sanctions may serve to get his attention, which can't hurt. Listen, I know punishment rarely solves these problems, but I'm hopeful about the counseling."

That was as good an opening as Paul was likely to get. "Charlie, I'd really like to discuss something with you before I have to get over to the Music Box. We're rehearsing this afternoon." Paul unlocked his car and tossed his briefcase into the passenger seat.

"You have a little time, I think." Charlie led them to the park, the green feather in the band of his trilby hat vibrating in the wind. "I saw Jonah go into the café with Billy Preston."

They reached the entrance to the river park. Charlie trotted between the retractable concrete posts designed to keep people from driving their vehicles onto the gravel paths. Paul followed, the wind whipping his hair into his eyes and mouth. He hunched over and wished he'd brought a hat. "I haven't told you my decision regarding my course load for next fall."

"I don't think there's anything further to discuss. You know your options."

"I like to think I'm a good enough teacher to be worth trying to keep."

"Come on, Paul. You know the constraints I'm working under. What do you expect me to do?"

"I have an idea I'd like to run past you, before I tell you my decision."

Charlie must have heard the seriousness of Paul's tone. "I hope you have a plan B besides quitting."

"You heard the kids in my classroom the other day. Jonah isn't the only person being bullied at Martin Luther King. We've got a culture that encourages, or at least enables, bullying. It's going to take a systematic approach to change. Treating each case individually doesn't work. The other day I went online to see if there were any program materials or lesson plans related to bullying. There are. There's good research too. With a little time I think I could—"

"Paul, there's no money in the budget for—"

"I know. Just hear me out. I found more than lesson plans. There's private grant money that could be applied to this, and I think I could find more. I want to explore ways to incorporate problem resolution and interpersonal skills into everything we do, from how we address violence to how we teach sex education. It would be a lot of work, but we could make a real impact, not just here but at the other schools in the district."

"Slow down a second, would you? You're a good teacher, Paul. On a good day, one of my best. I've already given you a lot of leeway in order to keep you in the classroom." Charlie all but trotted down the path as he marshaled his thoughts.

On a good day? Paul bristled at the idea that he had bad days in the classroom, even though he knew it was true. It had been particularly true lately. He speed walked after Charlie, the wind off the river cutting his face like grains of sand on a beach.

"I admit this bullying issue has been intractable," said Charlie. "But I'm not sure you're the person to address it."

Paul was cold and tired and losing patience. "Why not?"

"First off, there's Julie." Julie was the school's guidance counselor. "Bullying really ought to be her bailiwick."

Paul wanted to stamp in frustration. "Antony has been seeing Julie every week since we learned he was the ringleader. What good has it done? Even I know Julie is marking time until retirement. I'm not saying she's a bad guidance counselor, but she's clearly not had great success with this issue. She hasn't even gotten that assembly you were talking about off the ground. I think we need to do something radical. We need to involve all the students and staff, not just the ones who have disciplinary problems. We need to get people talking—like you saw in my class the other day. We need to tell each other our stories." He stopped suddenly, forcing Charlie to backtrack a few steps in order to hear him. "I attended a party recently, and I mentioned I was dealing with a bullying issue at school. Everyone in the room had a story. *Everyone.*"

"Paul, it's colder out here than I thought. Do you mind if we go back?" Charlie turned toward the gate.

Paul rushed after him. "Besides Julie, why else shouldn't I be the one to help with the bullying issue?"

Charlie shot him a glance from under his hat brim. "You're gay, but not openly so, which gives some people the idea that you've got something to hide. At a minimum you'd have to be more upfront. Then, at least, you could present your personal experience as an asset. But having an openly gay teacher heading the project could make the program a target for controversy. People like Scarelli—"

"Jesus, Charlie. I can't win, can I? If I keep my sexual orientation to myself, I'm hiding something. If I'm open about it, I'm a target for controversy."

"This is exactly what I worry about, Paul. You've got a hair trigger. You need some detachment, even when people say things you don't like or don't agree with." They were back at the park entrance. Charlie strode through and aimed for the school parking lot. "You can't always react."

Paul shivered. His ears felt as though someone was holding a match to them. "Will you at least think about it?" He took Charlie's arm and turned him so they were facing. "Please, Charlie. I can be your point man, if you let me. I know what it's like for kids like Jonah. Won't you let me help?"

Charlie stared, eyes searching Paul's face. "I'll have to get approval from the district—even if you find the money."

At least it wasn't a no.

JONAH THREW his pack into the locker and eyed the clutter of old food wrappers and overdue assignments. He prodded the duffel bag of gym clothes he'd left behind when he was suspended. He was kind of afraid to open it for fear of what might be growing in there.

"Pretty rank, dude. I think it's officially ripe."

He flinched and slammed the door shut. "I'll take them home later."

"You should consider a funeral pyre."

Jonah turned around and looked at Billy. "I thought you weren't talking to me."

"I'm pretty sure it was the other way around."

"You're full of it, you know that."

"Hey, it's your word against mine. I figure that's pretty good odds."

Before Jonah could figure how to continue the ridiculous conversation, the bell rang, indicating the start of next period. "Shit. We're late."

Billy grabbed his arm and started to run. "Come on."

They stopped to grab Faggot from Paul's office. Jonah wasn't sure who'd first started calling his sax Faggot, but he figured it was better than calling him Faggot, so he tolerated it. They sneaked into the band room just as Mr. G was tapping a music stand with his conducting baton.

"Look who's decided to join us. It's Jail Bait and Billy the Kid," said Sheila, the fat girl who'd recently discovered her tongue and hadn't shut up since.

Paul glared, but Jonah could see he was trying to keep from smirking. He jerked a thumb at their places. "Sheila, do we need to have a conversation about name-calling?"

"Not unless you need me to explain my cultural references," said Sheila, smiling like a Southern debutante.

Paul rolled his eyes. "I'm getting too old for this. That reminds me, I have an announcement to make. This Friday evening, on the new stage at Avakian Music, I'm proud to announce the debut of a new music group…." He coughed. "The, ah, Rascals and Mr. G, featuring, of course, our very own Jonah Winfield. There are announcements by the door, if you'd like more information. Share them with your friends." He waited for the lethargic smattering of applause to peter out. "I can see we're assured a huge success. Thank you for your support. Now, please direct your attention to bar forty-two, where the horns come in. Guys, your entrance is ragged. Actually, ragged might give someone the impression you've actually been coming in at approximately the same time. Now I know it's all most of you can do to count to forty-two, but I promise that if you condescend to glance in my direction now and then, I'll signal when it's your turn."

"Wow, who spiked his coffee?" Sheila muttered loud enough for the whole room to hear.

"JONAH, IT'S time for dinner."

It was typical of his mom to dispense with greetings on the phone. Two could play at that game. He said okay and disconnected.

Jonah set his phone on the piano bench next to him. Flexing his fingers to loosen them up, he went through the new piece in his head before putting his fingers to the keys. There was something missing compared to what he'd heard on the radio, something he hadn't quite picked up. He'd ask Davoud to listen. Davoud would know what it was. Chances were he'd be able to name the composer as well.

His phone rang again. The display showed it was his mom. He tapped Ignore and reluctantly gathered his sheet music before heading upstairs.

He dumped the stuff in his room and girded himself for another fun-filled hour in the torture chamber.

"It's about time. The flank steak's going to be cold."

Jonah looked at the platter of meat that held place of honor at the center of the table. "You know I don't eat meat anymore."

"Really? That's news to me. Please try it. It's good, a recipe I learned from one of my friends in Washington."

When had the lines on either side of his mom's mouth gotten so deep? Maybe she wasn't using so much makeup these days. He guessed there was nobody to impress now she was mostly telecommuting.

Jonah stabbed a piece of meat and arranged it on his plate. He wasn't about to admit it, but the smell was making his mouth water.

"Some vegetables too, please."

Did she realize how much she sounded like his dad when she said that? It was weird, but he was reminded that he really did like vegetables. He took big helpings of broccoli and glazed baby carrots without comment. She'd gone all out, which probably meant she wanted to talk to him about something. *Please, not Chicago!*

Esmé seemed to relax a little. She sat down across from him. "How was practice?"

"Good. The Steinway is way better than the crappy piano they have at school."

"Mr. Wong said you've missed too many days to get credit for the term, but you can probably test out pretty quickly this summer, since you've kept up with the assignments." She speared a head of broccoli and chewed it thoroughly.

Jonah wanted to kick himself for opening the door to another topic he didn't really want to discuss. School meant Billy, and he and Billy were still dancing around each other. He went with the previous topic. "I'm working on a new piece, another one I heard on the radio, but I don't think I've got it quite right yet. I'm going to ask Davoud to help me with it."

"You like Davoud a lot, don't you?"

This was an odd question to come from his mom, and he didn't know how to respond to it. He was pretty sure she wasn't asking if he liked him *that* way, but it was hard to tell with her. "He doesn't judge me."

She took a sip of water and sized him up like he was trying out for first chair. Where was the glass of wine she usually had with dinner? Jonah had the uncomfortable feeling that something was happening, and he was clueless what it was.

"Rascal's helped you with your music too, hasn't he?"

It was the first time Jonah heard his mother use Rascal's nickname, even though everyone else in Davoud's family rarely called him anything else.

Jonah speared the slice of flank steak, let go, and watched his fork slowly tip over. He caught it just before it clattered on the side of the plate. "Yeah. You know, Mom, the dinner's really sick, but I don't think I'm gonna be able to eat until you get whatever it is off your chest, so can you like… spill?"

Esmé set her fork down beside her plate. "Okay, Brainiac, I should have known I couldn't slip one past you."

"You haven't called me that in a long time."

"You and I haven't had the right kind of conversation for a while now, bud."

There was a brittle edge to her tone that hadn't been present until now. Jonah surprised himself with the strength of his desire to make it go away. "I'm sorry."

"So am I."

"No, I mean I'm sorry that I haven't been... that I've been kind of hard to get along with since...." He was terrified to see tears in his mom's eyes. "Shit, Mom, I didn't mean to make you—"

"Jonah, I love you more than anything else in the world. You know that, right?"

Did he know that she loved him? It was something forgotten and remembered, like finding a favorite toy from his childhood.

"I guess I do."

"Good." She dabbed at the corner of one eye and then the other. "You were right. There's something I want to ask you."

His chest tightened in anticipation. *Fucking Chicago, here we come.*

"You know that Rascal and I have been spending a lot of time together."

It was like putting a nickel in a parking meter and getting four hours.

"Rascal has asked...." She patted down her skirt. "He's asked if he might take me out to dinner, and I wanted to make sure that you wouldn't feel... I want to know if it's okay with you."

Dinner? She wanted to ask him if it was okay to go to dinner? She smiled at him, and he saw a softness he hadn't seen for a very long time. He saw the mother he remembered from before they'd moved to Glen Falls, before his dad lost his job, maybe even before she'd returned to law school to get her degree. *Oh.* "You mean like on a date?" All at once, his anger washed over him like an acid bath. "Jesus, Mom, he's only been dead a few weeks and you want to fuck somebody else!"

She retreated to her usual precision and cold logic, her face hardening. "He died three months ago, Jonah. You know things weren't right between us for a long time before that. Our marriage was already dead."

"Yeah, and who killed it? You killed it with your fucking cases and all your travel and never being home. You killed him!" Jonah strained to get air into his lungs.

His mother froze. "I'm not the one who stopped talking to him," she hissed.

She might have punched him in the stomach. He doubled over, his whole body cramping. For a while he was only aware of his own fight to breathe between the sobs that wracked him. Then he became aware that his mother was rubbing his back through his T-shirt and repeating "Please forgive me, please forgive me," over and over like a mantra. A part of him wanted to pull away, but he couldn't bring himself to do it. Instead he leaned into the heat of her hand.

"I didn't mean for him to die," he gasped.

"I know, honey. I didn't either. Neither of us did."

Jonah thought about telling her that it was okay if she went out with Rascal, because the truth was that he didn't care, but he was afraid to open his mouth because he wasn't sure what would come out. *Give me time*, he pleaded silently, looking into her red-rimmed eyes, *give me time*.

JONAH SETTLED his pack on his back and balanced Faggot on his shoulder like a one-man funeral procession. Billy fell into step beside him. "You want help with that?"

Jonah raised his eyebrows and glared at Billy like his friend had just offered to tie his shoes for him. "I can manage. I don't need an escort everywhere I go. Christ, you'd think I was Obama at a KKK rally."

"I always wanted to be a secret service agent."

Jonah marched out the front entrance of Martin Luther King High and started across the parking lot toward Main Street. When Billy showed no sign of peeling off toward the line of yellow school buses idling on 5th Avenue, Jonah picked a dry spot where the salt had reduced the last snow to white residue. He put down Faggot and sat.

"Okay, Billy. What's up?"

"Couldn't it wait until we get inside? It's cold as a witch's tit out here."

Jonah waited.

"Jesus, Jonah. You sure don't make it easy for a guy."

"Do you even know what you want?" Billy managed to look hurt, but he still seemed unable to spit out whatever it was he wanted to say. Jonah relented. "Fuck this. I'm freezing." He hopped up and hoisted Faggot. "Let's get some hot chocolate from the café."

He was rewarded with one of Billy's achingly bright grins. "I knew you couldn't resist me."

"I don't have very long. We're gonna rehearse this afternoon for Friday's gig." Jonah relished using the word gig. It made him feel like a professional.

When they were seated with steaming mugs of hot chocolate covered with floating islands of whipped cream, Jonah once again fell silent, tired of maintaining the aura of indifference he'd cultured since returning to school. Billy fidgeted with his mug, sliding it around in circles on the table and blowing dents in the whipped cream. Finally, Jonah couldn't stand it anymore. "Billy."

"Don't. Just let me get this out." Billy looked around the room. Apparently satisfied no one was listening, he leaned forward. "I liked kissing you the other day. I think—"

"I kissed you."

"Jesus, will you let me finish?"

Jonah put a hand over his mouth and raised his eyebrows. In that moment he felt a kind of power he'd never experienced before. He knew it was probably wrong, but he enjoyed Billy's discomfort.

"I think I might be bi or something." Jonah removed his hand from his mouth, but Billy replaced it with his own. "Wait. Mr. G's been trying to get you to apply for early admission to a music school, right? I'm graduating soon. I was kind of hoping we could like, coordinate. You know, see if we could end up somewhere close. I mean, high school won't last forever, right?"

If Billy wanted an answer, he was going to have to stop holding his hand over Jonah's mouth. Jonah opened wide and licked Billy's palm. It tasted salty and faintly metallic, like Jonah's horn.

Billy jerked his hand away. "Gross!"

Jonah smacked his lips.

He knew he'd gone too far when Billy's eyes got shiny. "Please, Jonah...."

Jonah sipped his hot chocolate, if only to buy them both some time. The chocolate was thin like it had been made with water instead of milk—something else that wasn't quite what it was supposed to be. He looked down at the stained surface of the table. "I can't promise anything... I mean, I don't even know if I'm gonna get accepted."

"That's okay," Billy said, leaning forward. "I know it's a long shot. I just... I don't want to be alone. When I'm playing basketball, I'd like to know one person who's watching really knows me."

"Fuck, Billy. There will be others."

"I don't want them." Billy's shining eyes found Jonah's. "I want you to be the one watching me."

"YOU KNEW, didn't you?" Paul said.

Davoud's arm tightened across Paul's shoulders. Paul squirmed. They were lounging in the embrace of the velvet monstrosity.

"Knew what?"

"Jonah told you what Antony said to him, didn't he?"

"Yes. He told me in confidence when I picked him up at the police station."

Paul supposed it was to Davoud's credit that he didn't attempt to deny it. Paul's hurt was probably inappropriate and self-centered, but he still felt betrayed.

Davoud examined him seriously. "He trusts you, Paul. That's not why he didn't tell you, or why I didn't. He knew his father was vulnerable. He blames himself for his dad's death."

"I know that. I'm not an idiot. What does that have to do with anything?"

"It has everything to do with how he feels about you. Jonah sees you and his father as alike."

"I'm nothing like John Winfield. I would never—"

"Hush. Let me finish, Paul. John wore his heart on his sleeve, just like you do. That isn't a bad thing, but it scares Jonah, because it reminds him of his dad and what his dad did when things got too intense."

"How am I supposed to…." Paul stopped when Davoud brushed a finger along his lips.

"The second thing you share is how Jonah feels about you. He wants to protect you."

"I'm not gonna go crazy and kill myself because I get upset about something."

"I know that. But Jonah is still recovering from a trauma. In time he'll figure out you're not his dad."

Paul thought about it for a while, his mind replaying the events of the past months and his reactions. "I do get emotional at times."

Davoud touched Paul's face. "Yes, you do, and it's one of the things I love about you."

Paul stiffened involuntarily.

Davoud's eyes widened in mock alarm. "Darn, I seem to have used the L word. Are you going to have a conniption now?"

Davoud's complacency was somehow reassuring. Paul walked his fingers down Davoud's thigh. "A conniption? Where did you learn a word like that? You people are Persian. Persians don't have conniptions."

"Leaving aside the fact that I was born and raised in Glen Falls, let me point out that you've never seen Aida when the dressing room is too cold, when there's lavender, or when someone wears perfume into the—"

"What the heck is wrong with lavender?"

"She's allergic to it."

"I'm still angry with you."

"Uh-huh."

"Just because Jonah was too scared to tell me doesn't mean you couldn't have."

"Jonah told me in confidence."

Paul leaned back to look at Davoud. "Aren't couples supposed to tell each other everything?"

"You hadn't given me the ring then."

"What ring? I haven't given you a ring."

Davoud examined his hand. "I could have sworn...."

"I'm serious."

Davoud lost his smile. "I hear you. I'm sorry. Will you forgive me?"

"You may have to work for it."

"Oh, good. I like it when you get demanding."

"IS ANYONE out there?" Paul asked, nodding at the curtain.

Davoud pushed the curtain aside and peeked into the newly opened-up space at the front of Avakian Music. Six people were scattered among the twenty folding chairs they'd optimistically arranged before the tiny stage. One of them was Esmé, looking elegant in a wool suit and silk blouse. "At least they outnumber us now."

"Oh, that's encouraging," said Paul. "Are they buying drinks?"

Davoud craned his neck to see the counter where Aida was seated on a tall stool next to Marta. There was a conspicuous absence of activity in the vicinity. He scanned the crowd. "One has... nope, that cup's from the café."

Paul bristled. "What? I'm going out there and tell them they—"

"You are doing no such thing," said Rascal languidly from the back of the room where he'd been tuning his violin. "We are trying to attract an audience, not scare it away." Rascal ran through a couple of arpeggios and scales. "You're looking glum, Jonah. You know it takes time to build a following."

Jonah stacked and restacked his music on top of the piano. "I know. Just nervous, I guess."

Paul looked a question at Davoud. Davoud shrugged. If Jonah was nervous, it wasn't because they were about to play a set for six strangers off the street. Something else must be bothering him. Davoud checked the wall clock. "It's almost time to start."

Paul grimaced. "Maybe we should give it a few more minutes."

"Nope," said Rascal, "we treat the audience that's here with respect, and we start on time."

Davoud scanned the audience and sighed. Their plan to revitalize the Music Box wasn't looking like a success. It wouldn't gain him support from his family if he had to raise rents again in six months. "Okay, here we—" The front door swung open, and he stopped to watch a group of teenagers, two male and one female, make a beeline for the espresso machine. "Looks like we've got a few stragglers, and they're going for drinks."

Jonah jumped up to peer through the gap in the curtain. "Let me see."

Davoud moved out of Jonah's way. "Anyone you know?"

"Some students from the high school." Davoud heard the doorbell jingle again. "Hey, I know them," said Jonah. "They're in Pep Band."

Rascal grinned and started to hum Gershwin's "Somebody Loves Me."

The door jingled again, and Jonah stiffened. Davoud leaned over to look through the opening, his head above Jonah's. Billy Preston had come in leading a group of students like he was the Pied Piper. By the time the door stopped jingling, all the folding chairs had been claimed and people stood in the back. More waited for drinks at the counter.

Davoud turned to address the band. "Ladies and gentlemen. I'm delighted to report that we have a full house. I hope the fire marshal isn't out there. Jonah, will you help me get some chairs from the practice rooms?"

"Who are you calling a lady?" said Paul, his eyes dancing.

Jonah let the curtain fall into place. "Everyone I know is out there."

Rascal picked up his violin. "Quit yakking and get moving. We've got a show to put on."

JONAH FELT his body relax as though he'd just teleported home from a planet with higher gravity. He'd not realized how important it was for Billy to be there until he saw him leading his friends like the drum major at a parade. He'd thought he was waiting for a bigger audience, when apparently he'd been waiting for an audience of one. It hit him then what Billy had been saying about having someone watch him play basketball. The thing was, when Jonah was a kid, his dad had always been the one watching him. Some priest might tell him he still was, but Jonah couldn't bring himself to believe it. Maybe it was time to find someone he could touch.

"You coming?" Paul paused at the curtain, guitar in hand.

Davoud waited behind, a hand on Paul's shoulder. "You need a moment?" he asked Jonah.

"No, I'm ready."

FAMILY HISTORY

KAZMI AND AVAKIAN FAMILY MEMBERS

Arash Kazmi (1865-1931)

Leila Kazmi née Turani (1868-1940)

Reza Kazmi (1885-61) Son of Arash and Leila.

Stephan Avakian (1887-1958) Married Yasmin Kazmi in 1927. First violin Chicago Symphony. Founder of Avakian Music.

Yasmin Kazmi (1890-1962) Daughter of Arash and Leila. Married Stephan Avakian in 1927. Trained at La Sorbonne. Singer at the Paris Opera.

Karim Parsi (1891-1967) Married Suri Kazmi 1920.

Suri Parsi nee Kazmi (1895-1981) Daughter of Arash and Leila. Married Karim Parsi 1920.

Samir Parsi (1921-2001) Son of Karim and Suri.

Zhara Parsi (1923-) Daughter of Karim and Suri. Concert pianist.

Nathan Avakian (1927-1998) Son of Stephan and Yasmin. Married Agnes Portner in 1945, before leaving to fight in World War II.

Agnes Avakian née Portner (1927-2005) Married Nathan Avakian in 1945. Music snob.

Farhad Avakian (1946-2007) Met and fell in love with Aida Campari in 1967, while accompanying Zarah Parsi on concert tour in Italy. Died of heart attack.

Aida Avakian, née Campari (1942-) Married Farhad Avakian in 1967. Took stage name of Aida Kazmi in tribute to Yasmin Kazmi, Farhad's grandmother.

Amir Avakian (1967-) Son of Farhad and Aida. Cellist in Chicago Symphony.

Rasul Avakian (1969-) Son of Farhad and Aida. Violin in the Falling Water Quartet.

Davoud Avakian (1970-) Son of Farhad and Aida. Managing partner of Avakian Music.

Dorothy Avakian née Carpenter (1971-) Married Amir in 1995.

Zhara Avakian (2004-) Daughter of Amir and Dorothy.

JOHN C. HOUSER'S father, step-mother, and mother were all psychotherapists. When old enough, he escaped to Grinnell College, which was exactly halfway between his mother's and father's homes— and half a continent away from each. After graduation, he taught English for a year in Greece, attended graduate school, and eventually began a career of creating computer systems for libraries. Now he works in a strange old building that boasts a historic collection of mantelpieces—but no fireplaces.

Also from DREAMSPINNER PRESS

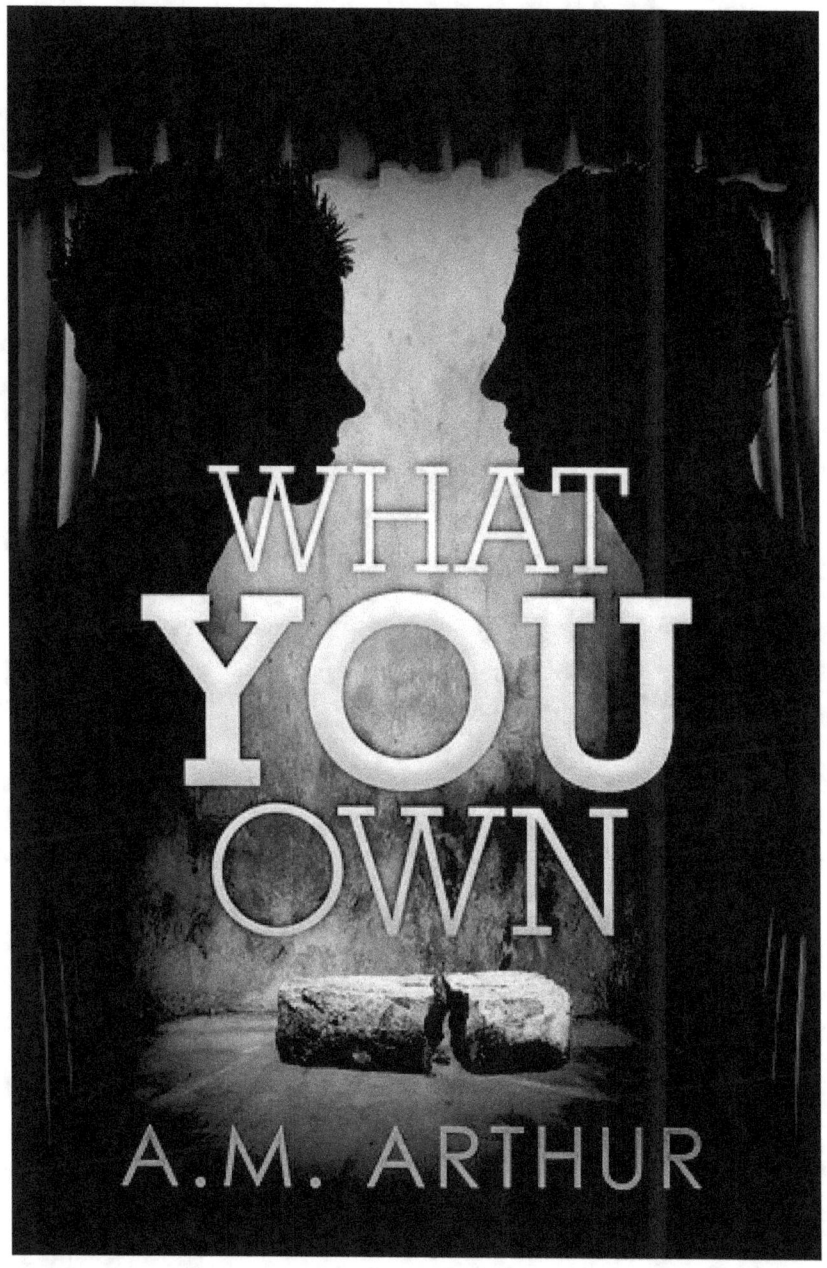

http://www.dreamspinnerpress.com

www.ingramcontent.com/pod-product-compliance
Lightning Source LLC
Chambersburg PA
CBHW070104260626
47160CB00004B/1312